THE PENANCE OF VALENTINE CASH

REBECCA ROOK

For my mother.

I'm so proud to be your daughter. The best parts of me come from you. I miss you every day.

THE PENANCE OF VALENTINE CASH:
SOUNDTRACK

The Penance of Valentine Cash Playlist is available on **Spotify**.

1. "If I Die Young" by The Band Perry.

2. "Runnin' Down a Dream" by Tom Petty & The Heartbreakers.

3. "Hurt" by Johnny Cash.

4. "Lean on Me" by Avi Kaplan.

5. "Far From Any Road" by The Handsome Family.

6. "Crazy" by Patsy Cline.

7. "Born Alone Die Alone" by Madalen Duke.

8. "Midnight in Montgomery" by Alan Jackson.

9. "Ghost Riders in the Sky" by Johnny Cash.

10. "Baby Outlaw" by Elle King.

11. "Elvis Presley Blues" by Gillian Welch.

12. "Summertime Sadness" by Lana Del Rey.

13. "Aberdeen" by Avi Kaplan.

14. "Devil Went Down to Georgia" by Charlie Daniels.

15. "Jimmy" by L. E. J.

16. "Route 66" by Chuck Berry.

17. "Turn the Page" by Bob Seger & The Silver Bullet Band.

18. "River" by Leon Bridges.

19. "All is Well" by Avi Kaplan and Joy Williams.

Contents

CHAPTER ONE

"This is it, kid," Loretta said. The manager sat back in her chair and sipped on a Lariatini. "This is the start of something *big*."

After Valentine's album deal had been signed at Defiance Studios earlier that afternoon, Loretta had insisted on treating Valentine at their favorite bar, a gaudy pink refuge called the Hoity Toity. The rundown honky tonk was festooned with velveteen damask patterned wallpaper and bordello lamp shades draped in heavy fringe that rested upon worn wooden tables, and served Western-themed cocktails: Lariatini. Barrel Race. Saddlesore. Valentine knew that Loretta couldn't get enough of the fancy concoctions, and if they sat in the minors' section, with the tourists and their loud children, the barkeep didn't bat an eye in their direction. Valentine always got the YeeHaw Tots – tater tots smothered in cheesy bacon heaven.

It had been a good day.

One of the best days of her life, actually.

Valentine looked up from the YeeHaw Tots after Loretta finished speaking. She swallowed hard, searching for the right words. Talking about the real things, the stuff that mattered, had always been hard for her. "Thank you, Loretta. For everything. I really... I mean it."

Loretta waved away her gratitude, chuckling. "Save the thanks until after the first tour. You may curse me instead. Tours are brutal."

"What were your tours like?" Valentine asked.

"Awful." Loretta took a healthy swallow of her cocktail. "Of course, I traveled with my alcoholic ex-husband on a derelict bus across the country, so that may have been why."

"Did you enjoy any of it?" Valentine ate another tot.

A child at a nearby table squealed as he dropped his toy on the floor. The parents sniped at each other, arguing over something Valentine couldn't quite hear.

Loretta thought for a moment, her gaze unfocused as memories crowded in. "Yes. When the fans shared how much a particular song meant to them, or that they'd used one of my songs for a wedding or a funeral – I loved those moments. I felt like I had contributed something...decent to the world instead of just fighting with my husband at the time." Loretta shook her head. "You'll see. This road, it changes you."

Valentine nodded, more to herself than in response to Loretta. She understood that compulsion, the want to give something to the world, something decent and brave and honest. She thought of all the work that had led up to this evening.

Loretta looked up from her salad. "So, what are you going to do with the money?"

Valentine paused, a tater tot in mid-air. Cheese dripped onto the plate. "I hadn't thought that far ahead."

"Do me a favor?" The older woman sipped from a new cocktail, the Rhinestone Cowboy, with a pearlescent rim around the top.

"What?"

"Don't spend it on women and drugs."

Valentine gave a crack of laughter, then shook her head. She avoided looking at Cara, a pretty brunette waitress with a gap in her teeth and the widest, most welcoming smile, working across the dark room. Cara was the best thing about the Hoity Toity, as far as Valentine was concerned. Even better than the YeeHaw Tots.

"No, I'm not gonna do that." Valentine winced. She wasn't exactly at ease with the ladies. She'd never even made eye contact with Cara, let alone flirted with her. "I need someone to spend my money on first."

Loretta snorted; her lips twisted. "Don't worry. Once they know you've got money, they'll come crawling out of the woodwork. Not everyone is a user but..." Loretta finished her drink in one long swallow. "But it's better to be wary."

Valentine ate another tot. "It's kind of silly but...I want to buy one of those little shotgun houses. You know, one or two bedrooms. Simple. It doesn't have to be big." She shrugged, trying not to reveal the depth of her feelings. "I want my own home."

A brief silence. Then, "I get that, kid."

Valentine sneaked a glance over at Loretta. The older woman watched her with a tender look, equal parts of pity and understanding. Her throat closed, and Valentine looked away. She went back to working on the mess of tots in front of her.

Valentine said her farewells to Loretta inside the bar.

"Congratulations again, Valentine." Loretta's voice was somber, hushed. "You've worked hard for this. I know you'll make the most of it."

Valentine shuffled on her feet as a flush of warmth stole through her. "Thanks," she said, her voice gruff. She wasn't used to hearing praise from others. At least, the ones that meant something to her. "Goodnight, Loretta."

"Goodnight, kid."

Out in the parking lot, Valentine approached the worn-down lime green economy car she had purchased from a co-worker. The vehicle was on its last legs, or wheels maybe, and she had kept the little car alive through thoughts and prayers but mostly curses. *Now I can afford to replace it.* She smiled, pleased by that thought, as she unlocked the driver's side and jimmied open the half-broken door. Valentine could name a dozen songs about these feelings but hadn't felt them often in the last few years: Pride. Happiness.

Relief.

The roads were thick with cars, and rain had started up just as Valentine drove out of the parking lot adjacent to the Hoity Toity. Leaning forward, she peered through the sheet of water barely held back by the creaking windshield wipers.

Her phone buzzed in her shoulder pack on the passenger seat.

Valentine ignored it. *This rain is something else.*

The phone buzzed again.

And continued to buzz.

Without taking her eyes off the road, Valentine reached over to grab the phone. She glanced at the screen and almost dropped it. Shock, then trepidation coated her stomach.

Her parents were calling.

She hadn't heard from them in two years. *Why now?*

Bright lights sliced through the edge of her vision. Valentine whipped her head to peer through the obscured windshield.

Somehow, she had wandered across the double yellow lines, into oncoming traffic. A dark blue sedan approached her, its horn blaring a siren of danger.

The sound jarred her out of her shock, and Valentine wrenched the steering wheel to the right, hoping to get into the correct lane.

But it was too late.

Valentine heard the impact before she felt it.

Metal grated on metal, an accordion screech that hurt her ears. The headlights popped, and the lights went out. The windows shattered –

Valentine threw up her hands to protect her face. Then, the impact came.

Valentine felt the stinging cuts of the glass, the slam of her body first against the seatbelt, then to the driver's side door. Her left arm broke on the second slam. She heard the snap and looked down. Bone and blood rose from the serrated flesh.

She heard the screams from the other vehicle.

I'm sorry. Oh shit, I'm sorry, I'm so sorry.

Black crept across her vision. The cold and the pain that draped across her body grew dimmer and fainter, then ceased altogether.

Chapter Two

Valentine woke up in a casino.

She poured into her body like the slow seep of a sunrise, her presence a creeping sensation from her torso to her limbs to her fingers and toes. She had the distinct feeling of being a passenger in a vehicle that wasn't quite hers. Her head felt right – kind of. She took a deep inhale, tried to fill her lungs, but started to cough. Her eyes teared up, and Valentine braced herself against the bar. She gulped air, noisy and desperate, until finally she could breathe again.

Her pale hands rested on a polished copper bar top that gleamed in the golden light of the room, stretching from either side of Valentine and encircling a raised dais of polished black marble inlaid with gemstones. Turquoise, amber, and emerald motifs disrupted the unrelenting dark in a repeated pattern across a floor that didn't seem to have edges. Within the dais, Valentine saw a cut crystal case that held every whiskey, liqueur, and tequila she knew of, and many more besides. Behind the crystal case, an ornate and heavy mirror rose from floor to ceiling. The glass held imperfections, blemishes that twinkled, faded, and then brightened in irregular patterns. Almost like starlight.

Valentine saw herself in the mirror and did a double take.

Instead of her usual uniform of jeans and a shirt, Valentine wore an outfit that she, Loretta, and a stylist had selected for most of her gigs and performances: a black cowboy hat with sterling silver accents and a single blue feather atop a face as pale as bone bleached by a desert sun; black jeans sinking into black cowboy boots with blue floral stitching; and a black camisole under a thin white button-down blouse with an anatomical heart stitched in black and blue threads across the left side of her chest. Her stick-straight blonde hair hung down either side of her face, well past her shoulders and down her back. Her eyes were black, not blue or green like most blondes. Fierce red lips broke the monotony of the white, blue, and black color scheme.

Something shifted at the back of Valentine's mind. Why was she wearing these clothes in this place? How did she get here? Did she have a gig? Where were her instruments? The questions flooded her mind – and no answers followed. Valentine tried to remember how she had come to the casino. But her memories of the evening felt like vapor in a windstorm. Valentine turned away from the mirror.

Down the copper bar, a barkeep – a slender woman with high cheekbones, brown skin, and corkscrew curls – talked with a patron who had glittering green scales on his cheeks and gills on the side of his neck. The beginnings of a head fin peeked from beneath the black velvet fedora he wore.

Valentine tried a discreet stare out of the corner of her eye. She failed and after a moment, openly stared.

What the hell?

The barkeep looked over at Valentine and frowned.

Unease rippled through her. Valentine swallowed hard, then looked away from the woman and the patron with scales to the rest of the casino. *What is going on? This is...weird.*

Beyond the bar and the dais upon which it rested, the black marble floor revealed inlaid gold motifs, rune-like symbols Valentine didn't recognize. Lush carpets with art nouveau designs graced the walkways. Rows of slot machines with polished glass, old-fashioned font, and delicate filigree gleamed in the golden light that filmed the entire room. Crystal and gemstone chandeliers twinkled from the ceilings while lighted sconces lined the walls, casting shadows that flickered and shuddered against a backdrop of ornate wallpaper. Several tables with green velvet tops were surrounded by players, gambling in fine fabrics and jovial spirits. Loud laughter and a keening noise unlike anything she had ever heard echoed through the room.

Valentine cast surreptitious glances at the casino patrons. She usually tried not to judge anyone – goodness knew *normal* didn't exist – but the customers here were...unusual. A violet-skinned woman dressed in feathers and nothing else sang the blues at the edge of the room, her husky voice evoking the taste of whiskey and salt in Valentine's mouth. A man with the head of a panther, dressed in the tailored yet loose fashions of the 1940s, sauntered by and gave Valentine a wink and a purr when he caught her staring. A pair of women draped in beaded flapper dresses and adorned in bandeaus with feathers and gems openly stared at Valentine as they walked by.

"Is that a human?" one murmured to the other, their heads nestled together.

"No. Specter, I think."

They both giggled and hurried forward. Valentine saw gossamer wings, like those of a dragonfly, stretch up from the women's backs and extend out. The wings bounced and rippled as they moved away.

"Do you want a drink?"

Valentine turned away from the casino floor and found the barkeep staring down at her.

She ignored the offer of a drink. She was underage, but something told her that didn't matter in this place – whatever it was. "Where am I?"

A faint look of pity crossed the woman's face. "You'll find out soon enough. You may as well have a drink while you wait."

Valentine shook her head. "I'd like to keep a clear head, thanks."

The woman shrugged. "Suit yourself." She moved on to serve a tall man with six arms, the palest blue eyes, and night-black hair.

"Valentine Cash?"

A short woman dressed in the casino livery, metallic accents against hunter green, stood before her. A pair of small gray antlers perched at her temples peeked through her red hair.

"Yes?"

"They are ready for you now," the horned woman replied. "This way, please."

Who is ready? What is happening? Valentine stood and almost stumbled. She felt a pull behind the sternum of her chest, like an anchor being reeled into a boat. The horned woman led her on a circuitous path throughout the casino, weaving around patrons and service staff with ease. Valentine had to duck a few times; she also tripped twice.

Finally, the horned woman paused before golden double doors that formed an ornate arched entry into another room. She knocked once, then reached forward to push open one of the doors. She gestured to Valentine, her hand a sweeping motion. "After you, please."

Valentine stepped into the room. Blush pink velvet couches lined the room, with a large, low wood table in a herringbone pattern in the middle. Luxe patterned wallpaper with a gingko leaf motif swept the walls. A large chandelier draped from the center. Large urns with pampas leaves, palm sheaves, and enormous feathers rested in each corner. The light was brighter in this room than the rest of the casino, and more silver than gold. Valentine heard the door close behind her.

Three people waited for her.

A white woman in a blue satin dress with elegant beading and a perfect coiffed bun smiled at Valentine, her ruby lips revealing white teeth. She seemed a tall woman, even sitting – long legs stretched out from where she sat on the pink velvet couch, an acoustic guitar resting against the cushions next to her. The guitar bore strings of silver and copper against a golden body along with an abalone backing and frets. It was beautiful. Valentine had seen a great many guitars, but never anything quite like this.

Then Valentine saw the lumberjack. A tall white man, thick with muscle and almost two feet taller than Valentine, dressed in old denim, thick boots, and a flannel button down rolled up to expose his forearms. Tattoos decorated the backs of his large hands. The left had a double-sided ax, the right a bright blue ox with a flared tail. His hands bore the scars, nicks, and calluses of a blue-collar man, ones like the men Valentine grew up around in her hometown. A scar cut through his right eyebrow, white against the black line. The rest of his face twisted into a grimace. Valentine almost stepped back when she caught sight of his glare. She looked away, uncomfortable with the anger.

A third man emerged from behind the lumberjack. Slender but muscled, the Black man had a strong nose and amber eyes crowned by loose curls that fell away from his face. He wore a tailored burgundy button-down shirt had an asymmetrical drape that slashed down from one hip to the opposite calf. Black snakeskin pants encased his legs, and his shoes were gold and black Oxfords.

Valentine blinked, then squinted. She swore she had seen a crown upon his head, a thin circlet of hammered gold. But every time she tried to focus on it, the certainty danced away.

"Welcome, Valentine." The woman spoke, and Valentine heard traces of the American South in her voice. "Please, do sit down."

Valentine settled herself on the edge of a pink couch opposite of the older woman. She looked between the three. "H-have we met before?" Her voice shook. Nerves tapped along her spine like fingers along the fret of a fiddle.

The woman smiled. "No."

That didn't clear anything up. "Um, where am I?"

"The Truckstop between life and death." This time, the lumberjack spoke. He glanced over Valentine and gave a derisive snort, his lip curled.

"Paulie," the woman scolded. "Be nice."

"Why?" He jerked his head to Valentine, then shook it. "A young, silly human, practically a child, who killed others through carelessness and stupidity? Hardly original. She's not worth our time."

A hot smear of shame washed through Valentine, chased by cold fear. *Who are these people?*

"You know the rules." The woman stared at him with a steel gaze. "She gets a choice."

The Black man stepped closer, and Valentine almost saw his crown again. "Paul, calm yourself. Let's get the formalities over with." His tenor voice contained echoes of an unfamiliar rhythm Valentine couldn't quite place, like an irregular heartbeat.

The three turned to focus on Valentine. She gave a hard swallow. She couldn't feel her heartbeat in her chest. Shouldn't she have a heartbeat? This couldn't be good.

The woman spoke. "Valentine Cash, you are dead."

Somehow, she had known that, deep down. The casino, the gamblers, these three – none of them were normal. Still, shock arced through her body. Grief seeped in, slow at first and then all at once. Finally, she *remembered*.

Valentine heard screams. She felt the impact of the seatbelt and the car door slam into her body again, jerking her back into the pink velvet couch. Air sawed in and out of her lungs. Her limbs trembled and shook. Tears streamed down her face. She could feel the others wait while she tried to get herself under control. Valentine thought of her parents, of Loretta, even of Cara and the stupid YeeHaw Tots.

Was this it?

Was this the end?

Valentine wiped her face and looked up. "If I'm dead, is this h-heaven or the afterlife?" Valentine struggled to find the right words. *Oh, God, is this hell?* Her old church said people like her went there.

The Black man looked amused. "A casino – an elegant casino, I grant you, but a casino nonetheless – is your idea of heaven?"

"High John, don't tease." The woman shook her head. "She's a fish out of water, this one. She's only trying to make sense of what she's seeing."

The lumberjack stopped pacing. "Let's get on with this."

"Paulie, you've absolutely no patience for an eternal creature." The woman heaved a deep sigh, then sat up straight with a proud tilt to her head and a broad smile on her face. "Valentine Cash, let's have some introductions. I'm Dale. This impatient one is Paul –" she gestured at the lumberjack – "and he is High John." The woman waved at the Black man.

Valentine studied Dale. The name combined with the face, the 1950s fashion, and the voice prompted recognition. "Dale? Dale...Wright? *The* Dale Wright?"

Paul rolled his eyes. "Another fangirl."

Dale smiled. "Yes."

Valentine shook her head. "I don't understand." She looked at Paul and High John. Paul Bunyan, she realized. "Paulie" was Paul Bunyan, the legendary lumberman of American tall tales. She looked at High John, who stared back with a challenge in his gaze and a slight smirk twisted on his lips. Valentine could see the hammered gold circlet on his head clearly this time. High John, High John, High... She didn't know what prompted it, but Valentine remembered a single lyric from an old Muddy Waters song she heard sung in a bar a long time ago.

Recognition flashed through her mind like lightning, and she refocused on the man. "John de Conquer Blue?"

The man's face was impassive. "Most often, I am known as High John the Conqueror. But yes, that's another name."

Dale chuckled. Paul – *Paulie*, Valentine thought in half hysterics – snorted.

Valentine looked at the three legends before her. Her grip on reality felt tenuous, loose. Panic set in, grasping at the edges of her vision. "If I'm dead, then why am I here?"

"Valentine Cash, you are one of the lucky ones." Dale leaned forward. "You get a choice."

"O-okay." Valentine still didn't understand.

"Do you remember how you died?" High John asked.

Valentine flinched. "Car crash."

He nodded. "Yes."

"And you took two others with you," Paul added. Contempt coated each word like honey on a comb. "Because you were careless."

Nausea swirled up Valentine's chest and into her throat. She heard the screams, then remembered dying while her phone buzzed in the distance.

Valentine looked up. "There was a couple. In the blue, uh, blue car? They died, too?" Her voice broke on the last word.

Dale nodded. "Yes. They both passed."

Ice congealed in Valentine's chest. She bent her head. She didn't pray; she wasn't religious, not after leaving behind a Southern Baptist church who had made their opinion of homosexuality quite clear. She just cried. The silent tears filmed her vision before they dripped down her face and onto her clothes.

"I'm s-so sorry," she choked out. Valentine didn't know who she offered the apology to, the two people who had died or the three legends before her.

"Dry your eyes, girl." Paul's harsh command drew her gaze up. "You've got a choice to make."

Valentine looked between the three. "I don't understand."

"Valentine Cash, your careless action cost those two their lives." Dale leveled the crime against her with no judgment or censure. "You have the choice to do penance, to amend for the loss that you caused. If you complete the tasks we set before you – and trust me, there will be many, and they will be difficult – you may win back your life. As it was. Record deal and all."

"She doesn't *deserve* this," Paul muttered.

"Paulie, we agreed." Dale didn't look away from Valentine. "She gets the choice, and she will succeed or fail. It's that simple."

"I could have my life back?" Valentine didn't know what to think. Would it be possible? "I could live again?"

"*If* you succeed at completing each task," High John answered. He didn't seem confident about her chances.

"So, I complete these tasks, and I will be alive again?" Valentine thought of Loretta. The manager who had become a friend and a mentor would be so disappointed with her death. They had only just signed the record deal earlier that day. Her parents, who called earlier after a silence that spanned two years. Another thought intruded, black ice coating her insides. "What about the couple? The ones who d-died?"

High John stared at her, a faint frown across his face. "They don't concern you."

Valentine flinched. She looked at Dale. "What do I have to do?"

"First, answer this. Do you accept this offer?"

The room fell silent. The legends went still, watching Valentine with sharp, watchful eyes. She felt the weight of their gaze like anvils on her chest, and it was too much. She had to look away. Glancing down at her hands, she saw the calluses on her fingertips and the knobby joints of her fingers, any softness worn away by years of playing instruments and making music and working shit jobs to pay for her meager existence. Valentine remembered the thrill and the sense of relief when she and Loretta had signed the record deal. Finally, she could focus on the music. Finally, she wouldn't have to work two jobs just to live. She wanted that future, the one of potential and success and acceptance, back.

She wanted possibilities again. To feel hopeful once more.

Valentine looked up. "Yes, I accept."

Dale smiled, her ruby lips and white teeth gleaming in the silver light of the room. "We recognize your choice." The words were formal, almost an incantation of sorts. Paul gave an irritated sigh. High John looked bored. Dale continued, "The penance begins."

Fire encircled Valentine's wrists, and she cried out in pain. Looking down, she saw black designs of ash traced into her skin like wood scarred by electricity. She blew hasty breaths on her wrists, trying to alleviate the burn. The pain faded as the lines darkened. A residual ache gave a slow pulse as Valentine studied the design: lines from a musical sheet wrapped around her wrists with twelve notations.

"What the hell?" Valentine scowled at the three.

Paul smirked. "Already upset? That ain't a great start for you, brat."

High John rolled his eyes at the other man.

"These are the symbols of your acceptance." Dale sipped from a cocktail that Valentine would have sworn wasn't there a minute ago. "Your penance requires you to complete several tasks. As you complete each one, those notes" – Dale nodded at Valentine's hands – "will track your progress." Dale took another sip. "They will also tell you when you are running out of time."

Valentine shook her head, her thoughts like mud at the bottom of a dark pond. "Out of time? What does that mean?"

High John spoke. "The penance must be completed within an allotted period. You don't get forever to make amends." He stared into the distance, and Valentine had a feeling that he saw something no one else in the room could see. "Mortal time and our time are difficult to reconcile; they are too different. You have, perhaps, two months?"

Nausea swirled through Valentine. "I-is that enough time?"

Paul sneered. "Guess you'll find out."

Valentine stared at the legend, and a familiar resentment flared up. She had been heckled and yelled at by old men with broken dreams and long-deserted gumption too many times over the last two years. Thanks to performing gigs in every venue that would have her, Valentine knew what angry, dismissive men sounded like.

I'll show you, you bastard.

She ignored him and turned to look at Dale. The woman – ghost? Creature? – had finished her cocktail.

Dale continued as if High John and Paul hadn't spoken. "You have until the marks fade to complete the penance. Once the ash is gone, so is your chance at renewed life."

Valentine swallowed hard. Suddenly the pain in her wrists felt comforting somehow. It meant she was still alive.

"We acknowledge that you are new to the liminal lands that lie between your reality and the others. To navigate this wilderness alone would be akin to sending a babe into the woods without food or shelter. So, to even the odds, we offer you a gift: a guide to assist you along your journey. You will find them at the bar." Dale paused. "Do not fail any of your tasks."

Valentine took a deep breath. The room was redolent with ozone and amber and the unfamiliar scents further unsettled her. "What exactly am I supposed to do?"

"At the bar, Valentine Cash," Dale scolded lightly. "Find your guide. They will have instructions for you." The other woman shook her head. "You had best get started. Your penance will take time – and you don't have much of it."

Chapter Three

Valentine didn't quite remember how she left the room occupied by Dale, High John, and Paul Bunyan. She simply found herself back at the bar in the center of the casino, the copper top gleaming under the gold light and elegant chandeliers. The noise from the slot machines and the low rumble of conversation at the green tables rushed forward, and Valentine realized just how quiet the room behind the double golden doors had been.

She glanced around. The blues singer from before had been replaced by a traditional country western musician who wore a blindfold beneath a white Stetson with a fringed white jacket and jeweled lapels. An acoustic guitar wailing a mournful ballad about lost love echoed through the casino.

"Do you need a drink *now*?"

Valentine looked back at the bar. The barkeep with corkscrew curls stared back, sympathy and perhaps dry amusement in her eyes. "Yes." Her wrists gave a painful pulse, as if in agreement.

The barkeep nodded, then poured a shot of a blue liquid that resembled a tide pool at the edges of an ocean. "Drink up."

Valentine tossed the drink back, then gasped. The drink burned all the way down, leaving a trail of heat that cracked through her body like a whip. Tears welled in her eyes, and black spots danced across her vision. She coughed hard.

The barkeep chuckled. "Careful. The drinks here are for gods and legends. They can be tough on humans. Even dead ones."

Valentine blinked through the tears. "Gods and legends?"

The barkeep's brow furrowed, and she paused, her hands on the countertop. "Of course." The frown deepened. "What else could they be?"

"Of course." Valentine didn't know what else to say. She sagged against the bar. Exhaustion, grief, and no small amount of fear weighed on her like chains wrapped around the bones of her very being.

The barkeep leaned forward. "Here, have another drink. By the way, I'm Amaretto Sour." She gave Valentine an expectant look.

"Like the drink?" Valentine asked.

The woman gave a wry smile, as if she had answered this question many times. "Yes."

"Oh." Valentine sipped her drink this time. "I'm Valentine Cash."

Amaretto's brows flew up. "Oh."

Valentine cut a sharp look at the woman. "What?"

Amaretto shrugged. "Word gets around. The gods took an interest in you. That's unusual – and it makes for great gossip." The woman grinned, and her canines were crooked. Valentine found them endearing.

"Which gods?" Valentine asked.

Amaretto nodded to the back of the casino, where Valentine had been. "Dale, High John the Conqueror, and Paul Bunyan. There are others, of course. Those three aren't the only gods or legends, obviously."

"Obviously." Valentine wondered if this was what drowning felt like. She was out of her depth, overwhelmed. The invisible chains wrapped around her bones felt heavier, threatening to drag her down to murky depths.

Amaretto eyed Valentine. "You'll be here a while. You'll get used to it, I promise."

Valentine sipped her drink again rather than answer. She wasn't so sure about that.

"Amaretto, darling, could I trouble you for my usual?"

Valentine looked up at the new voice.

A tall white man stood next to her at the bar. Tall, tanned, and handsome, with bright blue eyes and wavy black hair gelled away from his face. He wore a tailored three piece, a neutral navy suit over a patterned vest and white button-down shirt. The shirt was open at the collar, exposing a slender neck that led up to a sharp jaw.

"Sure thing, Six." Amaretto looked over at the bar. "Anything for Church?"

Valentine followed the other woman's gaze, then blinked a couple times. An enormous black dog with ghost white eyes sat next to the man. His size reminded Valentine of Irish wolfhounds, but his fur was slick and short, with only extra tufts of hair on his ears and tail. His tail gave a gentle thump at Amaretto's attention.

The man glanced down. "No, nothing for this odious beast." Affection warmed the otherwise cool words.

Amaretto smiled. "Coming up."

As the woman stepped away, the man turned to study Valentine Cash. His eyes seemed to have multiple shades of blue at once: the blue of the deepest cavern in an ocean. The teal of a glacier-fed river. The ice blue of a tundra. They shifted from one color to the next, and Valentine shook her head, trying to clear her muddled thoughts.

"Valentine Cash, I believe?" The man's voice was resonant and warm.

"Who are you?"

"I'm Six." The man nodded down to the dog that sat beside him. "This is Church."

"Six?" Valentine echoed.

Faint irritation crossed the man's face, then cleared. "I have other names, of course. In this place, we all do. But for you, Six will serve."

Valentine didn't know what to do with that. "So, who are you?"

"I don't follow." The irritation deepened on the man's face, deepening the grooves between his eyes. "What exactly are you asking?"

"Who are you?" Valentine repeated. She nodded at the casino floor. "Or maybe, what are you? Everyone here is *something*, right?"

Six scoffed, then shook his head. "We're going to need to work on etiquette, I see. You can't simply wander around and ask these people what they are. Aside from being rude, it's often...dangerous to do so. Yes, I'm a legend. The three sent me to you. I am to guide you through your penance."

Valentine stared at Six. Tears threatened but she swallowed them back. "I don't understand any of this."

Six shrugged. "You'll figure it out along the way. I only hope you take this chance seriously. Mortals don't get these choices very often. You should not waste it."

"He's right." Amaretto was back. She slid a martini with two olives across the copper bar top to Six.

"Okay." Valentine would figure out what that meant later. "So you're a guide? What do guides do?"

"Advice and wayfinding." Six shared a smile with Amaretto. "I'm quite good at navigation." The woman chuckled. Clearly, it was a private joke between them.

"What do I need to do now?"

"You need to wait until I finish this drink." Six winked at Amaretto. "I cannot leave one of her creations unfinished. It would be an injustice."

The dog let out a rumble, then slumped to the floor.

Six grimaced down at him. "No, we will not be here all night, Church. Don't be so dramatic."

Valentine blinked, then turned back to her drink. Reality seemed distorted, a funhouse mirror version of her known world.

She shivered. *I hope I survive this.*

Six led Valentine and Church out of the casino through a side door. Instead of a hallway or staircase, the door opened to a waffle house. The noise of cutlery against plateware and loud voices assaulted her ears. The coffee smelled burnt. Valentine stuttered questions and tripped over the door that led into the busy restaurant, but Six simply pulled her upright and ushered her outside, the dog on her heels, into the blistering and dry sunlight. He strolled up to a light blue American 1950s Chevrolet coupe parked at the edge of the lot, an older make and model that Valentine hadn't often seen outside classic car shows.

"I'll drive," he announced and slid into the driver's seat.

Valentine didn't argue. With the accident, she was in no hurry to get behind the wheel of a car anytime soon. "Where are we?"

"North Texas." Six peered through the driver's window and scowled. "Church, get in already."

"And where are we going?"

The car rocked as Church appeared in the backseat.

"West." At Valentine's puzzled look, Six shrugged. "That's as much as I know. I assume Dale will send further instructions."

Valentine thought of how they had stepped from the casino and into the waffle house, the immediate transfer disconcerting but convenient. "Why can't we simply step through another doorway and just...be there? Wherever we need to go, I mean? Like we did with the waffle house?"

Church rumbled from the backseat. Valentine turned to look at him and found the black dog staring at her, his white eyes milky and solid.

"Quite right, Church." Six's words drew Valentine's gaze back to the man driving beside her. "I know you're new to this, but there are rules, rules you have to observe and obey. Otherwise, the penance is void and you die a final death."

Valentine swallowed. "The final death sounds bad."

"That's not the desired outcome, no," Six agreed. Valentine watched him drive the short distance down the main street of the small town they were in. Beyond the narrow strip of grocery stores, pharmacies, and other businesses, Valentine saw flat land painted in shades of dull greens and faded browns stretch out as far as she could see.

"So we have to travel the old-fashioned way?" The car's leather bench seat chilled her backside. The dog kicked the back of her seat, startling her. Valentine tried to make sense of what she had seen, what meager bits of information she had.

Six flicked on the turn indicator, then merged onto a ramp that led onto a highway. "We do. Or rather, you do. I'm just your guide, along for the ride."

"Okay..."

Six sighed. "Listen, a penance is an act of sacrifice, yes? Contrition and sacrifice to pay for a transgression." *He sounds like he's quoting a manual.* She wished there *was* a manual or a rulebook she could read, but she doubted any of this, whatever it was, would be that easy. "If any of what's to come is easy or straightforward or *convenient*, it wouldn't be a sacrifice on your part."

Valentine thought for a moment. "You mean everything must be done the hard way?"

Six waffled his head from side to side, a thoughtful expression on his face. "Eh, yes and no. But mostly? Yes."

"Do you know what I'm supposed to do? Or how many tasks I need to complete?"

Six chuckled, and in the backseat, Church gave a sharp bark that sounded like laughter. "No clue," Six admitted. "The ambiguity is all part of the contrition and sacrifice, I'm afraid. I can promise you that you're in for the long haul. Gods and legends aren't satisfied with simple quests."

Despite the light tone, Valentine heard a dark current in Six's words. She stared out the window, uneasy. Her fingers twitched in her lap, missing an instrument. *Can I do this? Can I do this before I run out of time?* She glanced down at her wrists, where the music bars and black notes were hidden behind the cuffs of her button down. She swallowed hard.

After a few miles of the empty and desolate highway, Six broke the silence. "Tell me about yourself, Valentine Cash. What brought you to the attention of those three?"

Valentine looked over at Six. He seemed earnest, as if he were truly interested. She turned to stare out the window again. "I don't know why I'm interesting to them, or if I really am. Interesting, that is. But I'm a musician and a songwriter."

"Ah. That's why Dale is involved." Six gave a half smile. "She's the unofficial patron saint of American musicians. She loves a good lost cause." When Valentine didn't say anything else, he prompted her again. "What else? What do you play?"

"Mandolin, guitar, and piano but only sometimes." Valentine cast a quick glance at him, preparing herself for some judgement. Music was such a personal thing for so many people, and lots of folks had opinions about her genre. "I write and perform alternate country music."

She watched the man brighten like a sunbeam. "Like Hank Williams?"

Valentine choked on her sudden laughter. "Uh, no. More like Neko Case? Steve Earle?"

Six stared into the distance, his lips pursed. "Who?"

Valentine shook her head. Her lips stretched into a smile, and the expression felt odd, unpracticed. "Never mind. I'll play something for you sometime, if I can find an instrument."

"All right." Six nodded. "Leave anybody behind? A family or a girlfriend? Or a boyfriend?"

"Uh, no. No family and uh, none of that..." Valentine stuttered to a stop. Embarrassment heated her cheeks, and she stared straight ahead. She felt pathetic and lonely. *Do I have anyone?* "My manager. Loretta." She felt relieved that she could name someone, anyone.

Six frowned. "You don't have any family?"

Valentine thought about the phone call just before her death. Why had her parents called, after years of silence? And what had prompted her to look at the phone while driving? *Stupid, so stupid.* And that couple had been the ones to pay for her brief moment of carelessness. Then she thought of Loretta, the woman who gave her unexpected acceptance and love.

Valentine had lied about her age and worked under the table at a series of restaurants as soon as she arrived in Nashville. She had rented a barely-furnished studio in a boarding house, paid her bills in a motley assortment of tips, coupons, and chores, and lived off bagels and ramen and leftovers at the restaurants for the subsequent year. Between shifts, Valentine had played at every open mic she could, tweaking the lyrics and the melody of each song until they were the best possible version of themselves.

Valentine had met Loretta at an open mic night, just another Wednesday. She had been in a rundown bar that had a thin frayed rope that sectioned off the minors from the rest of the crowd. Valentine still remembered the thrill she felt when Loretta strode up to her in the dim bar, her artful blonde and silver tresses arranged in a cascade around her tan skin and bright pink lips. The woman had worn a tailored pink pantsuit with rhinestone trim, winged eyeliner, and a no-nonsense demeanor. She braked in front of Valentine like a speeding locomotive, too fast and with some recoil.

"Do you have representation?" the woman had demanded.

"N-no," Valentine had stammered out. She held her mandolin like a shield. Her heart hammered inside her chest.

Loretta had pulled out a business card from her billfold. "You do now."

Valentine pushed the memories aside to answer Six.

"My parents and I don't speak. And I've been working a lot lately." *For years.* "My manager, Loretta, and I had just signed a record deal with a studio in Nashville before...all of this." Valentine waved at the car and the land around them.

Six seemed to think over Valentine's words before responding. "No family to speak of, no loved ones. What did you *do*?"

Valentine bristled at his words. "I worked. Awful jobs to keep myself afloat with the music to keep me sane. I didn't have time for anything else." She glared out the window.

Church growled from the backseat.

"Yes, I know. Thank you for stating the obvious, Church." Irritation filmed over Six's retort. His voice softened as he continued speaking. "Valentine Cash, I apologize. I wasn't trying to belittle your life, only understand what brought you here."

Valentine looked over her shoulder at the big black dog sprawled across the narrow backseat, then to Six. "You understand him?"

"Of course." Six cast a quick look at Valentine. "If you learn to listen, you will hear him, too."

Valentine turned in her seat to study Church. The black dog stared back, his pupil-less milky eyes somewhat unnerving. He panted, the air conditioning in the old coupe insufficient to protect them from the sweltering heat outside.

Valentine felt a bead of sweat roll down her spine. "How can I learn?"

Church grinned, mouth open and tongue out.

After a moment, Valentine spoke. "I'm not hearing anything."

Six looked in the rearview mirror at the dog. He chuckled and Church rumbled. "You won't hear it with your ears. Give it time."

Valentine turned back to the front. She glanced over at Six. "So, what's your story? Have you always been a guide?"

Six stared out the front window, his posture relaxed. "In some ways, yes, I have always been a guide."

It was Valentine's turn to prod. "And?"

Six leaned forward to turn up the air conditioning and the bench seat squeaked in protest. "For me to make sense, you need to understand how gods and legends work. Gods and legends are...beings, I guess, or entities, imbued with enough belief and lore to elevate them to something *more*."

"More than what?"

"Just...*more*." Six seemed to struggle to find the right words. "More than mortal trappings, with magic and potential and power. Gods and legends manifest because the lore around them grow beyond mere stories and into the power of what *could be*, rather than being limited by mundane reality."

Valentine shook her head. "What does that even mean?"

"Simply put, gods and legends are formed by belief and powered by potential and hope," Six answered. "Mortals *hope* for something beyond their daily toils and troubles, something meaningful and heroic and even majestic. Something that transcends the daily nonsense of mundane living. They tell themselves stories about those hopes – and from those stories, the gods and the legends manifest."

"So...you're a hope, or a wish, that came true?" Valentine offered. She didn't quite understand.

Six laughed outright. "If only it were that simple. I'm the story – or rather, the stories – of empire building, of capitalist expansion into a brave new world where everything is easy and available to any who seek, and nothing hurts." A bleakness had settled over Six, and Valentine shivered despite the heat.

After a moment, Valentine asked the obvious question. "Then who are you? Are you a god?"

Six gave a grin with bared teeth, and *power* rolled off the creature beside her like a minor sun had flared to life in the front of the coupe. She remembered, abruptly, that whatever sat next to her was *not* human. Valentine leaned back in her seat, wary.

"I am Route 66. The Mother Road of America."

Valentine frowned. "But you're...man-shaped, at least. Male. How can you be a...an interstate highway?"

Six laughed, and a few black curls fell into his forehead. "Don't be so literal. I'm not a man. I'm not human. I have no gender. I am, most correctly, a legend. An assortment of stories that humans told themselves, stitched together like a quilt, to resemble this entity." Six gestured at himself with an elegant sweep of his hand. "I came into power in the 1930s, though technically I manifested as soon as the road had been built in 1926."

His voice deepened with his next words. Valentine heard fondness and nostalgia and power etched into the words like an intaglio carved into a gemstone. His tanned skin was luminescent, and the myriad blue shades of his eyes swirled like a whirlpool, one hue chasing another. "I traced through Chicago and across the country to California, weaving through this land like veins and capillaries within a mortal. Every mile, every rest stop, and every town has a story about what could be – or what was lost. What it cost to create me."

The leather bench seat beneath Valentine began to vibrate at a different frequency than the smooth glide of the wheels on the highway. Apprehension rippled throughout her body. Church gave a growl from the backseat, and Valentine flinched. She clutched the leather seat beneath her legs with both hands, seeking something solid. Real.

"Eh?" Six looked like he woke from a dream. He stared into the rearview mirror at the black dog. "I'm scaring her? Nonsense." He looked over at Valentine. "Am I scaring you?"

Hell yes. Valentine glanced from Church to Six. "This is new to me." She tried to keep her response non-committal, neutral.

Six sighed. "Yep. I scared the hell out of you."

Chapter Four

Six pulled off the highway somewhere in New Mexico and into the parking lot of a diner in the early evening.

"You're somewhere between dead and alive, but you still need to eat," he informed Valentine. "If you don't eat enough, the lack of sustenance speeds up your clock and reduces your ability to complete your tasks." Six nodded towards her wrists.

Valentine wrapped one hand around the other wrist and swallowed hard. "Uh, okay."

"Good." Six smiled. "I love mortal food. Humans are so creative with it."

Valentine hesitated, then asked, "What do you usually eat?" She was a little worried about the answer. Her mythology was scarce, not that her high school in northwest Tennessee that she had dropped out of would have provided much of a classical education. But Valentine assumed gods and legends didn't need the usual sources of sustenance.

"Oh, I don't need to eat at all." Six held open the door for her. "I just like to. It makes me feel closer to humans, like we have something in common."

Valentine gave an absent nod. *Yep, that was a normal answer.* She rubbed a hand over her tired eyes and almost dislodged her hat. The frequent juxtaposition of the normal and the supernatural, the familiar and the alien, kept wearing on her like a blister on her foot from ill-fitting shoes.

They settled into a booth and ordered dinner. Church had accompanied them inside and lay under the table. No one in the diner had batted an eye at the enormous black dog in their midst. Valentine watched their eyes skate over Church with a faint frown that faded as soon as they looked at something else. She removed her hat and set it beside her, studying the menu on the wall.

A waitress came by. "What can I get you folks?"

Six gave a warm smile. "I will have a ribeye steak with cornbread. A glass of cola with ice. Two slices of pie, one peach and one lemon meringue. And a side of sweet potato fries."

Valentine side-eyed Six.

He stared back, then shrugged. "What? I'm an empire builder. I have an appetite."

Valentine directed her gaze at the waitress, who was tapping her pencil on the notepad. "I'll have a hamburger. No onions."

"Sounds good." The waitress nodded and walked off.

Valentine saw Six studying the parking lot, and she followed his gaze. "What are you looking for?"

"A message." Six turned back to Valentine. "We need to know where we're going and what you're supposed to do, after all."

Valentine glanced through the parking lot. It was full, with mostly pickup trucks and minivans. "How will we get the message?"

Six shrugged. "We'll know it when we see it. They're unmistakable." He gave a chuckle.

Valentine wasn't comforted.

During dinner, Valentine watched in astonishment as Six put away enough food for three people. *Or three humans,* Valentine amended. As he had polished off the peach pie, Valentine watched his head jerk up and swivel to peer out the window. Valentine followed his gaze.

An enormous black bird sat on the hood of the coupe.

"Time to go," Six muttered. He hailed the waitress. "We'd like our check, please."

They walked out of the restaurant after one last purchase – "Hard candies for the road," Six explained as he gave her a handful. The cool breeze from the evening swirled around Valentine. The brilliant sunset encompassed the western half of the sky, oranges and reds fading into purple. When they arrived at the midcentury coupe, Valentine stopped as Six greeted the creature.

"Welcome, friend. What brings you here this evening?"

The black bird was not a raven or a crow. It had a copper beak and matching claws, with a white feather ruff that looked like an elaborate lace collar. *Too large – even bigger than an eagle*, Valentine thought. *More like an albatross.* She wondered how the hood of the coupe hadn't buckled under the weight.

Then it spoke.

"Dale asked me to carry a message to you."

"We thank you for your service," Six said. His words were oddly formal, as if he observed a ritual of some sort, and when he cast a sidelong glance at Valentine, she realized he wanted her to say something.

Valentine pushed her hat down her head, studying the ground beneath her. She felt awkward, out of her depth. Sneaking a look, she saw the bird stare at her before swiveling its head back to Six. Valentine had the sense that it – she? he? they? – was unimpressed.

"The message, then." The bird's voice changed. "You are to go into the Four Corners to capture a cactus cat. You will bring the creature back to Dale Wright, High John de Conqueror, and Paul Bunyan within three days." The bird shifted to look at Valentine. "If you fail, the penance is void, and you will die a final death."

Valentine swallowed, then nodded.

"Is that everything you have for us, friend?" Six asked.

The bird glanced back at Six. "Yes."

Six withdrew a small, elegant bottle with a filigree stopper from within his suit jacket and approached the coupe. "Then we thank you for your trouble and wish you well on your journeys."

The bird ruffled its feathers. "You give nice gifts. I hope we meet again." Valentine thought she heard a ripple of humor in the bird's voice. In a delicate motion, the bird accepted the bottle with its copper beak. Spreading its wings, the bird launched from the car and into the sunset sky.

Six turned back to Valentine and Church.

"We only have three days. Let's get on the road."

Six declined Valentine's offer to drive.

She tried not to take it personally.

Six turned the coupe north, turning on the radio to keep them company as they drove through the dark desert night. The stations were different from those Valentine had heard in Nashville. One talk show debated the merits and effects of free will versus fate among the different species, the species being gods, legends, humans, and creatures.

Another station emitted an unholy, painful noise that had Valentine covering her ears with clenched fists.

Six had hastily changed the station, then apologized. "Banshees," he told her. "They sound terrible to human ears. Or so I'm told."

He finally settled on a station that played Appalachian folk music but...something was different. Off. *Dangerous.* Valentine could hear the notes, the melody, and each of the individual instruments within the music, but she also *felt* them. The song vibrated her bones in a faint hum.

"What is this?" she asked.

"Hmm?" Six looked away from the road. Church snored in the back seat. "Oh, the music? Appalachian legends, I think."

"What instruments are they using?"

Six shrugged. "I'm afraid I don't know. The usual ones, I guess, though not quite the same as the ones you would use. Legends often have instruments made from different materials."

Valentine frowned out the passenger window. "Like what?"

Six cast a wry glance at Valentine. "Like bones, teeth, and hair. Gems and precious materials. The composition of the instrument largely depends on the purpose of the instrument."

Valentine stared at Six. "Bones? Hair?" A belated thought occurred to her. "Do those even hold up to playing?" She tried to imagine stringing her guitar with her own hair. Or using a fingertip bone as a pick.

"Valentine Cash, the sooner you realize you're no longer in the human world and thus no longer subject to its constraints, the easier a time you're going to have with all of this."

"So, anything is possible?" Valentine said.

"Not anything, no," Six admitted. "There are constraints upon our worlds and those who reside within them. Rituals, obligations, and etiquette we must observe. Speaking of etiquette, we need to discuss your manners."

"What about my manners?"

"Precisely." Six looked over at Valentine with a stern glance. "Nothing is free in this existence. When someone, or something, provides you a service or a gift, you must thank them and offer a small tribute in return. You needn't be effusive or over the top, but you must be sincere."

Valentine sighed, then rubbed her forehead. She could feel the start of a headache coming on. "So, there's cotillion even in purgatory?"

Six barked a burst of laughter. He looked over at Valentine with approval and humor etched into his face. "You're funny. They didn't tell me that." The humor faded from his face. "The manners matter, I'm afraid. Some interactions have...consequences for those who don't abide by the etiquette."

Cold washed over Valentine and she shivered. "Aren't I already dead? What more could happen?"

Six gave her a pitying glance. "My dear, there are worse things than death."

They reached the Four Corners region by dawn the following day.

Valentine had managed to nap for brief periods but woke up more fatigued than before. Church continued to snore in the backseat, but Six didn't seem tired, despite the hours of driving. He pulled into an observation point alongside the two-lane highway, and Valentine stepped out of the coupe, grateful for a break. She pulled the bench seat forward inside the car, making space for Church to get out. The black dog rubbed his head along her forearm before trotting off into the scrubby brush and red stone.

Valentine stretched and stamped her boots, trying to wake her body up. She looked over at Six, who had strolled to the observation deck, a stone half-circle that allowed a panoramic view of the canyon below. Though it was only dawn, the sun already felt too warm.

"Where do we go from here?" she called out.

"Shh." Six beckoned her forward. "Come here."

Valentine walked over.

"Now listen," Six said. He stared over the canyon before them.

Valentine listened. She heard the distant rumble of a vehicle on the road further down the canyon. The dry wind whistled between the red rocks and the withered pinyon pines. A pheasant chased through the underbrush nearby. Church padded over to sit next to Six.

Valentine tilted her head. "I don't hear anything," she admitted after a moment.

"You won't hear it with your ears," Six murmured. After a moment, he straightened. "We'll need to go west, into the desert proper."

Valentine followed Six and Church back to the coupe. "The bird said we're looking for a cactus cat? What is that, exactly?"

Six slid into the vehicle, his answer muffled.

Valentine waited to let Church into the car, then slid in herself. "I didn't get that."

"A cactus cat is a creature of legend, one humans only encounter on solstices or other astronomical events of note. They often look like a bobcat and a cactus had children, with spines all over their bodies." Six grunted, an inelegant sound that caught Valentine by surprise. "They also have the personalities of violent, drunken buffoons."

Dread draped over Valentine like a shroud. "And we're supposed to catch one?"

"*You* are to capture one," Six corrected. "Church and I can provide wayfinding and limited advice, but you have to do the work."

Dread blossomed into full alarm. She choked on the breath that rushed through her. "I don't know the first thing about trapping an animal."

Six chuckled. "I know."

Valentine glared at him. "This isn't funny."

Six sobered and slanted a glance at Valentine. "It's not funny to you, no, but it is interesting to *them*. They didn't have to offer you a penance, you know. Dale and the others could condemn you to a final death without a second thought. But this" – Six waved a hand around – "*this* is interesting to them. They want to see what you're made of and what you can do, when pushed beyond your limits."

Valentine sighed, irritated. "So, I'm entertainment?"

"Honestly, aren't we all?" Six sounded almost cheerful as he turned the car down a street.

Valentine stared out the window and didn't bother to respond. She had never felt so lonely in her life.

Six drove them down into the canyon, following the winding two-lane road further west until they reached the edges of the sand dunes that stretched into the horizon. It was at the start of the yellow sands when Valentine felt it: a pressure behind her sternum, an invisible line of energy that stretched forth towards the horizon. It *pulled*, like a hand had wrapped itself around the front of her ribcage and eased her forward. It didn't hurt, precisely, but it wasn't comfortable, either.

Valentine rubbed at her chest, trying to alleviate the disturbing sensation.

Six noticed. "You are feeling the pull, then? Good."

"What is it?" Valentine asked. "This feeling?"

"An indicator that you're moving in the right direction." Six offered a smile. "You're closer to your quarry. It's a good sign for you. It will help you on the other tasks, too."

"Hmm." Her chest ached with a slow beat that seemed to push against her sternum. Valentine wished there was some other kind of signaling system.

The further west they traveled, the tighter the invisible grip on her sternum. At last, Valentine gasped aloud. The grip gave a painful squeeze, causing her heart to skip a beat, then redouble in panic. "Stop. Stop *here*."

Six pulled over without comment. He killed the ignition, then looked over to Valentine. "Where to from here?"

Valentine looked to her right. Sand dunes in every shade of yellows and beiges arched up into the bright blue sky. Rare patches of dull green grasses broke the monotony. "There. We need to walk out there."

The heat was unbearable, the wind nonexistent. Valentine had begun sweating as soon as she'd stepped out of the car and was grateful for her hat.

The grip around her sternum squeezed again, and Valentine blinked. Perhaps it was a mirage, but she thought she saw a wisp of light that stretched forward from her chest and around the bend of a dune. She followed the vapor-thin trail, her heart rate accelerated.

On and on and on they walked into the desert, Six and Church besides her. The man seemed unperturbed by the heat, his tailored clothes undisturbed. He didn't even sweat. Church also seemed unaffected. Valentine envied them.

They continued into the desert for hours. In a distant corner of her mind, Valentine knew she should have keeled over from heat exhaustion some time ago. *One of the advantages of death?* she wondered as she stopped to wipe her brow with her forearm. *I probably can't die again.*

It was twilight by the time she reached the forest. She stopped and stared, worried it was an illusion. But she squinted and looked again, and it was still there: a forest of cacti, with different shapes and sizes and textures, that stretched across the twilit horizon. A few stars in the east had appeared. Among the forest, Valentine recognized saguaro, nopales, aloe vera, and a few others, but everything else was a mystery to her. Simply a sea of pachyderm green flesh with small and large spines.

"This is it," Valentine said.

Six and Church stopped besides her. "Here?" Six asked.

"Here," Valentine confirmed.

"Go forth and good luck." Six stood to the side.

"Wait, you're not coming?"

"Rules are rules, Valentine Cash. I can only provide limited advice and wayfinding."

"You can't provide advice over there?" Valentine gestured at the cacti forest.

Church flopped onto the ground. Had the beast rolled his eyes at her?

Six huffed a low laugh. "No. Remember, you need to capture a cactus cat alive and bring it back to the legends."

"Anything else I should know?" Valentine grumbled.

"Use the materials available to you." Six nodded at the forest.

"Excellent. Great advice. Thanks so much." Valentine twisted around, then stalked forward to the forest. Irritation lined her insides. What on earth was she doing? She didn't know anything about magical creatures, let alone how to trap one.

The edge of the forest seemed to spring out of nowhere, the saguaro cacti a vanguard that protected against the dunes. Valentine slowed as she approached, pausing to listen. She heard chitters and chirps, the sounds of birds and insects.

The wind had stilled. Valentine crept into the cacti forest, taking care where she placed her boots. She continued forward for several minutes before she stilled.

Iridescent eyes peered out in the faint moonlight.

She found one.

Chapter Five

The creature was half her height and stood on its hind legs. Like Six had warned, the furry creature looked like a bobcat: spotted fur of medium length, wide paws, and long whiskers.

But the similarity ended there.

Valentine shivered in fear. The night seemed colder.

Enormous spines extended from the top of the head and down the back of the creature. The spines were thick at the base, where the bone met flesh, and glistened with a fluid of some sort in the weak moonlight. Shorter spikes littered its arms and legs. The eyes, intelligent and calculating, stared from behind a cactus at Valentine.

He looks like a stuffed animal out of a nightmare. But how am I to catch one of these creatures?

She started forward, a single hand outstretched.

The creature disappeared in a flash of fur and sand. She heard the footsteps skitter away.

Valentine sighed. *That worked well.*

Something slammed into her right side, and Valentine folded, doubled over in pain. She gasped out a breath. *What was that?* She looked up and froze.

The cactus cat leapt away, then crouched on its hind legs. It sprung forward, and Valentine only had enough time to throw her hands up in front of her face before the cat bowled her over and onto her back. She squeezed her eyes shut and wrapped her arms around her head, trying to protect her face. Valentine felt the spines and claws of the cat cut into her stomach, thighs, and arms, leaving behind lacerations that burned and bubbled. Valentine gasped and half-sobbed from the pain.

Then teeth sank into her arm. Valentine screamed from the shock and the pain. The goddamned cactus cat *bit* her.

Anger swelled up through Valentine. *Enough. This is bullshit.* She rolled to her side, drew up her feet, and kicked the cat. Surprised or pained, the cactus cat let go and tried to scramble away.

Valentine threw herself forward and grabbed the creature by a hind leg. She managed to stop his progress but earned a kick to the face.

A burning sensation swept across her nose and cheek. She shook her head to clear the blood from her eyes but held on. *You're not getting away.*

The cactus cat kicked and scrabbled and hissed and howled and lunged away and even threw sand at Valentine's face. She hung on like a limpet, her arm and body growing sore from being tossed like a dishrag across the desert floor. The creature flung her to and fro, and Valentine slammed into one cactus, then another. She welcomed those spines and sharp pricks. They didn't bubble and burn into her flesh like the fluid on the spines of the cat.

Valentine slammed against another cactus and saw something out of the corner of her eye: a length of a hollow rind, the withered and desiccated remains of an old cactus. As long as her legs, the tough flesh had a small opening on one end. Without thought, Valentine grabbed the edge of the rind and to her surprise, it came loose from its mooring in the sand.

When the cat whipped her into another cactus, Valentine somehow managed to get her feet under. She pushed against the loose sand and lunged forward, surprising the beast with her sudden move. She grabbed the creature by the scruff of the neck, ignoring the cuts and the burns, and yanked the creature toward the hollow length of the cactus.

The cat hissed and wailed and resisted, bracing its feet against the edges of the tough rind. Valentine shoved and leaned and pushed with her hands, holding the rind between her knees and forcing the creature inside.

The desiccated flesh expanded and rippled from the struggles within but didn't break. Valentine heaved a sigh of relief while the creature hissed, spat, and growled, and its iridescent gaze glared a promise of retribution. She knew the cactus rind would only hold up to so much abuse. She looked around for something, anything, that would keep the cactus cat trapped.

Her eyes lit on an aloe vera plant. She staggered upright, then dragged the cactus rind over. Breaking off the leaves, Valentine scraped and squeezed the thick ooze of the aloe into the desert sand. She made a paste of sorts and smeared the ends of the cactus rind with the mixture, sealing the cat within the impromptu cage as best she could. Valentine heard the squalls and hisses inside and tried to dodge the swipes from within the rind.

She swallowed hard against sympathy for the trapped, angry creature. She remembered all those years in her small town; she hated feeling trapped herself. But she couldn't feel bad for the creature. Dale and the others had demanded this task.

Valentine had to do this if she wanted her life back.

After she had finished sealing the ends, Valentine sat for a minute. Her shoulders sagged. She took deep breaths and tried to calm down. Night had truly fallen, and the desert chill seeped into her bones. Valentine could feel sweat slip down her face and spine; she hissed when the salt water grazed her lacerations. She placed her head in her hands, bowed by the bizarre nature of what she had just done. The rind continued to rattle and to shake, interspersed with fierce growls.

After a moment, Valentine pulled herself up. She sighed against the pain, then bent over to grasp the cactus rind with both hands, lifting to cradle the odd bundle in her arms. More pain lanced through her. Valentine whimpered, and a few more tears slipped down her face.

She staggered a few steps forward, then straightened as she began her slow progress back to her unlikely companions, where they waited for her at the edge of the cacti forest. When they finally reached the car, Valentine almost fell over when Six removed the yowling cactus rind from her arms. Six put the captive cactus cat in the trunk of the coupe. Church appeared and braced her with his large body until she steadied.

Get into the car.

Valentine looked down at Church. "Is that you?"

Church panted a grin. Beneath the loose folds of his lips, the black dog's teeth were long, sharp, and many, Valentine realized.

After a moment, she climbed, or rather slumped, into the coupe, exhausted. Six slid into the driver's side while Church simply appeared in the backseat. "We should get back to the casino well before the deadline. You should get some rest while you can, Valentine Cash."

Six drove through the night and into the new dawn. He retraced their path down the two-lane highway up the canyon and then past the Four Corners region into hill country.

Valentine napped most of the drive, trying to find a comfortable position on the bench seat. Her clothes had glued themselves to her abraded skin with blood, sweat, and aloe. They tugged at the open skin and rubbed sand into her wounds. Her hat was a lost cause, bent and misshapen, and her hair was filthy, matted by blood and sand.

She hoped the casino offered showers. And a bed.

To her surprise, Six drove them to the same North Texas waffle house they had arrived in two days ago. *Was it only two days?* Valentine wondered. *It feels like a century.* Her cuts and lacerations had turned warm, either from the sun or from infection. She felt lightheaded as she unfolded from the car.

Six stepped out from behind the trunk, carrying the cactus cat. "You'll have to carry it inside, I'm afraid. Those are—"

"The rules. I get it." Valentine took the cactus rind with a grimace. It rattled within her hold with a hissed protest from the cactus cat. The smell of aloe vera and blood wafted up every time the beast moved. Her arms were sore, and her back ached something fierce.

Valentine followed Six and Church into the waffle house. Despite the odd appearance of their party – a bloody girl holding a cactus, a polished man dressed in 1940s fashion, and a large black dog – no one looked up from conversations over breakfast, nestled in the booths and against the long tables. Cutlery still rattled, coffee was poured, and everyone ignored them. Valentine gave a mental shrug. It wasn't the weirdest thing she had encountered that day.

Six swept open a swinging door that led to the kitchen for Valentine, and she stepped through. Her vision blurred, and her hearing went mute. Pinpricks scattered over her body, the cold tingles rippling over her skin. The sensations cleared – and Valentine blinked in surprise.

They were back in the casino.

The elegant environs hadn't changed. Faint golden light gleamed against the black marble floors with inlaid gemstone motifs as patrons played games, drank, and paid no attention to the trio of women with pale white skin, red eyes, and long black hair performing on the stage in the corner of the room. Valentine did a double take. The women, likely sisters by the resemblance, played instruments she'd never before seen. Valentine twisted to get a better view and tried to listen to the music over the noise but could only catch a few strains.

"Valentine."

She looked at Six.

He seemed to hide a smile. "We have to deliver your gift to the legends."

Valentine looked at the bundle in her arms, then back at Six. "This is a gift?"

"Your trophy, then. We're almost there."

He led the way across the casino floor and down the discreet hallway to the double golden doors, then knocked.

"Enter."

Six opened the doors. Valentine followed him, Church close on her heels.

Inside, the three legends awaited her. Dale sat on the pink velvet couch while High John de Conqueror stood at the edge of the room, his eyes thoughtful. Paul Bunyan paced the room, his irritation and impatience obvious. At her approach, Paul looked up at a clock on the wall, one Valentine hadn't noticed before. Shaped like an hourglass with a material that fluoresced in the intermittent light and with several hands of differing lengths that extended from the center, Valentine watched a small dribble of black sand drip from the top half into the bottom.

"Cutting it close, aren't you?" Paul glared at Valentine.

"Paulie, you need to learn to relax." Dale smiled at Valentine. "Welcome back, Valentine Cash. What do you offer us?"

Valentine stepped forward, then tripped.

High John sighed. Paul Bunyan snickered.

Valentine could feel her shoulders tense at the sound.

Asshole.

Valentine straightened, then advanced. "I have a cactus cat." She lifted the cactus rind with aching arms. It rattled, and the creature within growled. "It's alive, like you asked," Valentine added.

Satisfaction gleamed within Dale's eyes. She looked at High John, then Paul Bunyan. "Have the conditions of the task been fulfilled?"

High John shrugged. "It's sufficient."

"Sure." Paul clearly wasn't impressed.

Dale turned back to Valentine. "We accept your offering."

The cactus rind disappeared from Valentine's arms. She flinched in surprise, then stilled. Her wounds, her hair, her clothes – all were clean and healed, as though she had never wrestled with the awful creature in the nighttime desert.

Pain rippled across her wrists like water disturbed by a pebble, and Valentine gasped. She pulled back the linen cuff to examine her arm for a wound and found none. Instead, one of the music notes glinted gold up at her.

Valentine looked at Six, then Dale. "W-what happened?"

Paul answered before the other two could speak. "With each successful" — he smirked the word — "task you complete, your marks will turn gold. The remaining marks will continue to fade as you run out of time on this quest." He smiled, a beatific expression that chilled Valentine to her core.

She swallowed hard. She'd rather fight the cactus cat again than face Paul in such a mood.

Dale grinned at Valentine's astonishment. "I've always wanted a cactus cat. I hear they make terrible pets," she confided. The older woman looked past Valentine to Church and Six. "How were your travels?"

Pet? Shock arced through her, and Valentine forced herself to glare at the floor. *All of that for a pet? A magical goldendoodle? I'm fighting for my life here.* Valentine gritted her teeth against the protests that crowded behind them.

Six stepped forward. "Delightful as always," he murmured.

Cramped. Church's disgruntled response echoed in Valentine's mind.

Six rolled his eyes.

Dale turned back to Valentine. "No rest for the wicked, I'm afraid. We now give you the next task: you will travel to West Texas and destroy an errant Bloody Bones."

Six gasped. "A Bloody Bones? You cannot be serious."

Paul Bunyan cast a withering glance at Six. "What's your complaint, Mother Road?"

"They are dangerous. And gross," he added. Valentine didn't know which quality offended him more.

High John chuckled.

"It's a penance, Mother Road," Paul snapped. "It's meant to be difficult. It's going to get worse before it gets better, and you know it."

Valentine raised her hand, feeling foolish. "What exactly is a Bloody Bones?"

Dale waved her hand. "Oh, Six and Church will explain it to you on the road. Have a whiskey before you go, but don't tarry. You have three days to complete this task." The older woman glanced at the hourglass on the wall with the many hands. "Don't waste time, Valentine Cash."

Chapter Six

Six deposited Valentine at the bar. "Wait here," he told her. "I need to make some inquiries." Both Six and Church had disappeared before she could protest. Valentine sighed.

Amaretto slid down the bar to stand before Valentine. "A drink?"

Valentine opened her mouth to refuse but stopped. "Uh, sure."

"Coming up."

Valentine ignored the twinkling mirror behind the bar top and turned to look at the patrons at the casino. The sisters still played on the stage, and her gaze sharpened, caught on the stringed instruments they held. A white fiddle with blood-red strings. A guitar with a round body, black as night. A slender cello that resembled starlight across a navy sky. The sisters played with their eyes closed, expressions of bliss and concentration on their faces. Valentine almost smiled. She was certain the sisters weren't human – humans didn't seem to be the norm in this place – but recognized that look, had felt it on her best nights on stage. When the music came easy and smooth and right, and everything in the world made sense for those few moments.

"Here you go."

The arrival of her drink, a deep purple concoction that glittered with gold and lavender notes, turned Valentine around. "Thank you."

Amaretto nodded. "Welcome back. How long are you here this time?"

Valentine shrugged. "I don't know." She sipped the cocktail. In the mirror, she saw lightning spark over her head. Cool tendrils trickled through her chest, and she gave a sharp exhale. "Oof."

Amaretto grinned, as if expecting that reaction. "On to the next task, then. What is it?"

"A Bloody Bones?" Valentine offered. "I'm not sure what it is."

A faint grimace crossed the other woman's face. "They aren't...pleasant."

"That's what Six said." Valentine took a deep swallow of the cocktail, focusing on the coolness and the lightning. She wanted to feel anything but the anxiety that chafed at her insides. *What have I done? Am I crazy to do this?* Valentine drank another sip.

Amaretto wiped down the bar, nodding towards the sisters on the stage. "You like their music?"

"I like music. Period."

"A musician, then." Amaretto smiled.

"Yes."

"You'll have to play for us sometime."

Valentine cast a doubtful look at the sisters. "I'm not sure I'm the right fit for this place."

Amaretto let out a laugh. "Oh, I doubt that."

Valentine opened her mouth to ask a question, but Six appeared. "We should leave now. Amaretto Sour, lovely to see you as always. Valentine, finish your drink."

Valentine tossed back the rest of her cocktail. "I'm ready."

I hope.

Six ushered Valentine and Church out of the casino, through a discreet door in a hallway. This door led to the frozen aisle of a convenience store, the familiar logo and colors prompting recognition within Valentine. The clerk didn't bother to look up as they passed the withered hot dogs rolling limply in the brightly lit deli case. Outside, the daylight was bright but chilly. Valentine shivered as Six marched them to a new mid-century sedan, this one black with a cream stripe that lined the length of the car. The leather bench seat and the interiors echoed the cream touches.

Valentine settled inside and fastened her seatbelt, feeling a little foolish for doing so. *I'm already dead, after all.* She waited for Six to get in before asking, "Where are we?"

"Southern Oklahoma."

Valentine nodded. "And where are we going?"

"El Paso."

She nodded again. "Okay, so what is a Bloody Bones?"

Six started the car and backed out of the convenience store parking lot. "Nasty business, that's what."

"And?" Valentine prompted when he didn't continue.

They are the lost souls of murderers.

Church's voice in her head had Valentine twist around to look at him in the backseat. He had simply appeared back there. "Lost souls?"

No one becomes a Bloody Bones without extreme violence towards others. A faint distaste coated Church's words. *To become such a creature, you must kill, often and with great cruelty. After death, they are doomed to a twisted existence.*

Valentine swallowed, and a frisson of fear skittered down her spine. "D-do they look like humans? Or something else? How do you recognize them?"

Six snorted, drawing her attention. "Oh, they're easy enough to recognize. Covered in blood, with no skin, and sharp teeth. Shadows everywhere host and shelter them."

"You've encountered one before?"

"I am a highway, Valentine Cash, that crosses half a country. I have many creatures, Bloody Bones and otherwise, littered alongside my lanes to salt and season human suffering." Six's brows furrowed deeper and deeper with each grim word he spoke. "But the Bloody Bones? They *feast* on violence. They are trash, the bottom dwellers of the afterlife." He practically spat out the words, his breathing erratic.

Valentine waited, unsure of how to ask her next question. "Why did Dale and the others send me after this one?"

Six shook his head, and his frown lightened somewhat. "I'm not sure."

There is likely something unique about this one. Church sounded...eager? *We may have to hunt it down.*

Valentine twisted to look at Church again. "So how do you kill one?"

They are already dead.

"The more correct question is, how do you contain or destroy them? And we can't tell you that, unfortunately." Six cast a rueful glance at Valentine. "Rules, you know."

Valentine sighed. "Oh, yes. Rules."

As Six drove through the day, the scenery outside the sedan didn't change. Flat, dry grasslands and broken sod stretched for miles into the empty horizons, interspersed with an infrequent bush or tree. Six had found a different radio station, this one a recital of a murder ballad Valentine recognized from the bluegrass hoedowns in her Tennessee hometown. Church snored in the back, oblivious.

The bright sun blazed against Valentine through the windows, and she shifted on the bench seat, uncomfortable. It had warmed up throughout the day and this heat was so different from back home. In Tennessee, both in her hometown and in Nashville, the high heat came with the thick humidity, a marriage of temperature and texture that was unmistakably the American South. But here in west Texas, the heat felt like an oven without baked goods or dinner: dry, desiccated, and pointless.

Valentine thought of the phone call she received that rainy night she had died. Had someone passed away? What news would prompted her parents to break the silence of five years? They certainly hadn't called when she had left town with no note, nor had they called to check on her during the two hard years she had supported herself with shitty jobs and studio apartments in rundown boarding houses. Valentine shook her head. No, it must be a death in the family. But who? To her shame, she didn't know who she would miss most – her mother or her father.

They had been absent long before she had left home.

Guilt left a sour taste in her mouth. Was she a terrible daughter? A bad person for thinking that? Maybe she was.

Thinking of the phone call made her think of the couple in the crash. An echo of screams, the glass shattering, the metallic screech chased through Valentine's mind, and she shuddered. She stared out the window, hoping that Six and Church wouldn't notice her discomfort.

I killed them, Valentine thought. She hadn't meant to, clearly. But she had killed that family through her thoughtlessness and poor timing on the rainy evening that had delivered the best news in a very long time: Valentine Cash would be a star. A musician.

Valentine couldn't remember seeing the other two in detail but somehow, she knew them. The man was a baker, and the woman was an engineer.

Valentine squeezed her eyes shut.

How can I forgive myself?

Valentine knew the answer. *I can't. I might do this penance and avoid going to whatever version of hell exists for people like me, and I might get my life back. But I won't get forgiveness.*

Sometimes the costs of a transgression were too high.

Not even gods and legends could change that.

CHAPTER SEVEN

They rolled into El Paso late that evening.

Six parked in front of a rundown bar on a busy street. It seemed at odds with its gentrified surroundings: dirty windows with neon signs advertising American beers and cigars. A spin cycle studio rested against one side, a chain coffee shop on the other, both storefronts sporting polished windows and sleek signage with modern fonts. Valentine watched the thick crowds shuffle and flow from one shop to another, carefree with family and loved ones.

Sadness trickled through her. God, she envied them.

Six held the door open for Church and Valentine, then followed them in. Inside, the bar was unremarkable, predictable. Familiar. She felt her shoulders settle. Valentine had performed in bars and joints identical to this one: a wooden bar top that lined the back of the large room, held up by drunks of varying levels of intoxication and a wall of alcohol in pretty bottles behind the scarred length. Booths and tables were scattered across the room, atop a dirty floor that didn't bear close scrutiny. Even the people were the same – quiet desperation or loud, forced merriment, they all sought escape and abstraction from whatever awaited them outside.

Six led them straight to the bar in the back. He slipped a bill with a large denomination over the scarred surface towards the bartender. "I'm looking for Bill."

The barkeep, a mountain of a man with biceps as wide as a river, nodded as he took the money. "Bill's in the back. C'mon."

They walked through a dark hallway to a room. The mountainous man knocked three times, then opened the door before he left.

Six glided in. "Bill, it's been a while," Valentine heard him say.

She stepped inside the room and glanced around. They were in a windowless storeroom, the shelves against each wall lined with alcohol, food, and cleaning supplies. Four men gathered around a small table in the center of the room, poker cards in hand and a pile of golden watches and jewelry, money, and gambling chips in the middle.

A blond man with a thick mustache that draped down either side of his mouth leaned back in his chair. The short sleeves of his white T-shirt didn't contain the scrawled artwork of coyotes on one arm and a black horse on the other. His eyes flicked from Six to Church to Valentine in rapid succession, then back to Six.

"I'm busy, Mother Road. Fuck off."

Valentine tensed at the rude words. They clearly weren't welcome.

Six only chuckled. "Busy? Busy losing at poker, you mean?"

One of the other men at the table guffawed.

The blond man, Bill, glared at Six. "I don't have time for you, or your project." Bill cast a scornful glance at Valentine, and she felt an answering sneer creep up on her face.

Oh, great. Another Paulie.

Six held up his hands in a conciliatory motion. "Look, finish losing this game. Then come find us in the bar. We won't take much of your time."

Six turned on his heel and left the room, brushing by Valentine. She followed.

They settled into an empty booth.

"Now what?" Valentine asked.

"We wait." Six waved down a waiter. "Three whiskeys and a plate of fries, please."

The wooden booth bench had deep scratches; Valentine could feel the ridges against her thighs as she settled in. The smell of peanuts and fried oil wafted up from the stained tabletop. "That was Bill? He's not very friendly, is he?"

"That was Bill," Six confirmed. "He's a legend, especially around these parts. The perennial cowboy, wrought to life by persistent lore. He's...contrary. The attitude comes with all of that rugged individualism, I believe."

The three whiskeys arrived, the bar man spilling a bit as he laid them on the table.

Valentine stared at the drinks before glancing at Six. "Thirsty?"

Six looked askance at her, hands in midair above the table. "What do you mean?"

"Are you drinking that third whiskey?"

Six's face cleared. "Ah, no. That's for Church."

Valentine frowned. "The dog drinks?"

Six stared at Valentine. "Church is not a dog." His voice had a hushed, serious quality to it. "That form is simply convenient."

Her flesh prickled with goosebumps.

She wondered if she would ever get used to the weirdness of the afterlife.

They waited. And waited. And waited some more.

Well past midnight and definitely past the end of Valentine's patience, Bill finally strolled out of the back room. He smirked when he saw Six and Valentine in the booth, empty glasses and plates scattered before them. Valentine watched the man stop by the bar and converse with the barkeep before continuing over to the booth where they sat. To her dismay, he slid into the bench seat next to her.

"It's been a while, Mother Road." Bill gave Valentine a confident grin. "Who's the little lady?"

"Valentine Cash, this is Bill," Six said. "He's commonly known as Pecos Bill, the legend who lassoed the moon. And other things."

"Oh, don't start up with the legend nonsense." Bill rolled his eyes. "Y'all take yourselves far too seriously." He leaned closer to Valentine, and she could smell chicory and ozone, like the earth after lightning had struck. "How's the afterlife treating you, Valentine Cash?"

Valentine leaned away. "Too soon to tell."

Bill laughed and looked at Six. "She thinks she's subtle, Mother Road. But the oddness of this life gets to her. I see it."

"It's a lot for any human, I think you'll agree."

Bill shrugged. "I wouldn't know." He reached over and took one of Church's whiskies, slamming the remainder down. "What brings y'all out here? What holy quest is she fulfilling?" Bill jerked his head at Valentine, an irreverent grin on his face.

"We're looking for a Bloody Bones."

Bill stilled, then shot a startled look at Valentine. "Who'd the hell you piss off?"

Valentine stared back at him, not knowing what to say. How could she begin to explain? How to describe the penance?

Bill seemed to read the answer in her eyes. "That's unfortunate, little lady." He glanced at Six. "And you think I know something."

"This *is* your home turf, Bill," Six pointed out. "You would know if something were amiss."

Bill shook his head. "I haven't heard of a Bloody Bones in the area or else I'd take care of it myself. Goddamn filth," he muttered to himself. He thought for a moment. "I have... I've heard of some activity, but I thought it was more human nonsense. They're very good at killin' each other."

Six frowned. "What kind of activity?"

Bill gave a mirthless grin. "The murderin' kind, Mother Road."

Six waited, impatience clear upon his face.

Bill tugged on his mustache before continuing. "There've been a string of rough murders in El Paso over the last several months. Maybe a serial killer. If a Bloody Bones is in town, it's likely attached itself to that one."

Six nodded. "You know where to find this killer?"

Bill snorted. "I haven't looked. Mortals aren't worth the trouble." He slid a glance at Valentine. "No offense."

"We're not asking you to get involved, Bill." Six raised his hands in a placating gesture. "Just point us in the right direction."

Bill stared at Six. "I might be able to do that," he drawled. "What do you have for me?"

Six grimaced. "What do you want?"

Bill looked from Six to Valentine. "I haven't danced with a woman in a while, not since Sue. Maybe this one could favor me with a slow dance from the jukebox?"

Valentine stared Bill down. She thought about every nasty old man who shouted at her from the audience or on the streets, and felt tired.

"No." The word was ice.

Bill laughed. "It's just a dance, darlin'." His gaze was dark with the banked promise of a windstorm.

Six intervened, his brow furrowed. "I don't think that's wise."

Valentine looked Bill over. She remembered the stories in the old ballads, the ones of dancing with the devil only to never come home. Bill didn't seem like a devil, but he clearly wasn't an angel, either. She didn't trust him. What did she know of cowboys, particularly a legend like Pecos Bill? What did he want? What could she give without too high a price? A memory, a faint song remnant tickled the back of her skull, then poured out of her mouth.

"Your lariat," Valentine said. "The snake. Or the one you used to rope the moon. You still use it?"

Bill leaned back, his eyes watchful. "Funny that you ask. It's worn down some. I'm hardly able to use it much these days."

"I could take a look," Valentine offered. "See if I can fix it."

"You?" Bill scoffed. "What do you know about lariats? Despite your get-up, you're not a cowhand or a rancher."

Valentine leaned forward. Somehow, she knew she was on the right track. The same intuition that guided her in writing a great song nudged her further down this line of questioning. "It won't cost you anything to let me look at it. If I fail to fix your lariat, we'll leave you alone and find the Bloody Bones ourselves. But if I succeed, you will tell us where and when to find the killer. Or the Bloody Bones." Valentine tried to be specific. She remembered the folk tales and legends she grew up on all had stories about bargains built on imprecise language or wordplay that ended badly for the mortals.

She couldn't afford for this to end badly. She had to find the Bloody Bones. It was the only way to get her life back.

Bill narrowed his eyes at Valentine for a long moment. Finally, he nodded.

"I accept your terms."

Bill led them upstairs to a humble studio above the bar. Valentine was startled by the appearance of the simple abode; she had stayed in many, many places like this. She had assumed a legend would reside in a worthier home, someplace like the elegant casino where she had met Dale Wright, High John, and Paul Bunyan. Valentine didn't say anything, though. She didn't want to hurt Pecos Bill's feelings. She already felt that she was on treacherous ground with him.

Bill left them standing in the doorway and walked over to the closet. He pulled down a saddlebag made of tanned, worn leather and reached in to pull out a lariat. Walking over to Valentine, he placed it in her hands.

"Here she is." Valentine heard a faint note of pride, and worry. "The lariat I used to harness tornados, to pull Sue down from the moon after the Widow-Maker had tossed her." Bill gave an affectionate smile.

"How is Sue these days, Bill?" Valentine heard Six ask from behind her.

The smile vanished. "Gone."

Bill didn't elaborate.

Valentine turned the lariat over in her hands. The rope was frayed from use, with threads slipped loose from the main coil. The material felt heavier, denser than the rope she had handled on her parents' hobby farm. Silver and copper strands wove through the fabric, with a few faint gold threads, the only other hint of something supernatural about this workaday tool. Valentine bent closer to examine the silver and copper, and her own long, gold hair fell forward, resting against her hand where it held the rope.

She had an idea. "Six, do you have a knife?"

"A knife?" Six shifted his weight on his feet. One hand ruffled through his hair.

"Yes."

"Uh, no."

Bill reached into the saddlebag. "Will this do?"

Valentine looked up to see that Bill held a sheathed, single-sided blade the length of her forearm. "Yes."

Setting the rope aside on a nearby chair, Valentine took the knife from Bill and pulled the blade from the sheath. She swept off her hat, the silver accents twinkling in the faint light of the studio. Valentine gathered her long hair into roughly two chunks, on either side of her face. Using the knife, she sawed off one handful of the golden length, then the other.

She heard Six gasp in surprise. A deep rumble came from Church.

In less than a minute, she had an armful of golden hair.

Valentine handed the blade back to Bill, who took it without comment but with a keen gaze. She picked up the lariat and sorted through the coils until she found one end. She examined the braided coil, holding it at arm's length and then up close. After a moment, she knew what she needed to do.

Valentine placed the lariat on the worn Formica table, on top of a clutter of magazines and old newspapers and dirty dishes. She then reached for her own shorn locks and began to braid thin strips of her hair, one after the other. Silence hung over the room as the legends watched her, and Valentine began to sing, under her breath, an old song about a maid seeking her heart's desire, a bluegrass tune she had first played when learning the mandolin. She sang in a low voice and continued to braid the shorn gold until there remained no more strands.

Valentine picked up the lariat, and starting from one end, she wove the braided gold into the twisted rope. As she wrapped and tucked and twisted the golden strands into the fabric, the silver and copper strands flared and brightened, as if coming back to life. The gold threads glowed in response. Valentine worked her way down the length of the rope. She was relieved that she had just enough hair to repair the lariat. All the while, she sang the old tune. When she ran out of verses, she simply started the song anew.

Finally, the lariat was done.

Valentine finished the last verse of the song. The lariat shone despite the terrible lighting of the studio apartment, the mineral colors deep and rich and true against the beige burlap coil. Everything around the rope – the Formica table, the chair, the clutter, the apartment itself – seemed faded, a ghostly grey version of itself.

Valentine met the impassive stare of Pecos Bill. "I have restored your lariat."

She handed the newly coiled length to the legend, who accepted it with a look of astonishment. He ran his hands over the coils, and a real smile bloomed across his face. He looked up at Valentine, then gave a nod.

Six stepped forward. "Valentine Cash, you have completed your end of the bargain. Pecos Bill, will you meet your obligation?"

Bill nodded. "I will. The killer works on the north end of the city and strikes on the full moon. Likely some ritual that only makes sense to that crazy bastard. I'm betting that if you find the killer, you'll find the Bloody Bones." Bill peered out the window and into the night. "Lucky for you, the full moon is tomorrow."

Six nodded. "The bargain is complete and now final." The formal words rang through the studio apartment like a bell. Valentine felt a shift in the air.

Bill grinned. "I feel like celebrating. Let's get a drink."

Valentine drank more than was wise that night.

Pecos Bill remained in a grand mood all through the evening. He treated every patron in the rundown bar to several rounds, then plied Six, Valentine, and Church with his best stuff. He had wrapped the restored lariat around his body, from shoulder to opposite hip, and would caress the rope every so often. A small, hopeful smile never left his face.

Valentine didn't remember much after the third whiskey. She *thought* Pecos Bill had corralled her into standing atop a table and belting out the tune she had sung to repair the lariat, with the patrons thronged beneath her like a school of fish in a sea. When they had roared and demanded for more, she obliged. She sung the sad songs first, then murder ballads and lost love and grief unending. Then she switched to the light-hearted fare, of first and lasting loves, of battles fought and won.

Of triumph over despair and grief.

Honestly, she couldn't be sure it happened. She supposed it all could have been a drunken dream.

But it felt *real* and true and grand.

She felt like a legend.

CHAPTER EIGHT

Valentine awoke in a midrange chain hotel room, with last night's clothes and boots still on, with her hat tossed onto a chair. She clutched a small bottle of whiskey to her chest; the edges of the bottle left grooves and lines on the palms of her hands. She had no idea where it had come from.

Valentine didn't even remember leaving the bar.

"Good morning."

The cheerful greeting split her head like a hammer.

"Quiet," she moaned. Her hands left the bottle to cradle her head, which ached more with each passing second.

"You should take a shower, then we'll get something to eat." Six sounded amused.

"Stop laughing." Valentine's voice was scratchy, and her throat ached.

Six chuckled. "I'll wait outside."

It took much longer than usual, but finally Valentine was cleaned, dressed in fresh clothes, and upright. Without a word, she followed Six and Church into a nearby diner. After settling into a booth in the back – away from the bright Texas sunlight – Six had promptly ordered Valentine a full breakfast.

As they worked through the food, Six scanned Valentine. "How do you feel?"

Valentine drained the last of the coffee. "Like dog shit."

Church growled.

Valentine held up her hands. "I'm sorry. I feel like shit," she amended.

Six swallowed the grin that crept on his face. "You did very well last night. I was impressed."

Valentine nudged at a pancake with her knife. "You mean with the lariat?"

Six laughed. "And the drinking."

Valentine winced. Loud sounds still hurt.

"But the lariat was inspired, truly." Six examined Valentine. "How did you know to weave your own hair into the rope?"

Valentine studied Six for a minute. "I'm not sure," she said, her words slow. "Growing up in Tennessee, I heard a lot of tall tales about golden lassos and cowboy gear made of unusual stuff." Valentine shrugged. "It just seemed right."

Six grinned, his white gleaming in the sunshine. "Well, you've made Pecos Bill a happy one. He couldn't stop singing your praises last night. That bottle of whiskey he left you? He told me to tell you that you should save it for a special occasion."

Valentine nodded, then thought for a moment. "He told us how to find the Bloody Bones, right? Did I remember that correctly?"

"Yes." Six glanced at an ornate wristwatch Valentine hadn't seen before. "We have eighteen hours to complete this task."

A trickle of fear slithered down the nape of Valentine's neck. "Only eighteen hours? That's not a lot of time." Valentine felt foolish, frustrated that she had spent so much time mending a fancy length of rope for a mystical cowboy. She ran her fingers through the ragged edges of her shorn hair.

"According to Bill, the creature strikes at the full moon – which is tonight. If we kill the creature tonight, you will complete the task in time."

Valentine shook her head. "Where did he say the killer was? And are we sure the Bloody Bones is attached to the killer?"

"Nothing is certain. It's possible that Bloody Bones is operating independently of this human killer." Six held up a quick hand to forestall her protest. "But I highly doubt it. A Bloody Bones needs some kind of connection to this world. They don't appear by themselves. Someone or something must attract them. This killer is our best bet."

"And Bill said they're in the north end of the city?"

"Yes."

Valentine scoffed. "El Paso is kind of a big place, Six."

"Do you remember how you found the cactus cat?"

Valentine frowned. "What do you mean?"

"That feeling." Six leaned forward. "In your chest, that feeling that made you know when and where to stop the car on the highway, that led you through the desert to the cacti forest."

Valentine felt an icy echo of the otherworldly grip around her sternum. She shuddered, then took a deep breath. "Yeah, I remember."

"Pay attention to that feeling. That's how you'll find the killer – and the Bloody Bones."

After breakfast and checking out of the hotel, Six drove them north. The buildings wavered and shimmered in the waves of oppressive heat, the streets crowded with thick veins of cars and trucks. The AC in the mid-century sedan barely kept the interior to a tolerable temperature. Pulling to the side of a main thoroughfare, Six parked before pulling out a map from the glove box. He unfolded the rectangular piece of colored and dotted paper, and Valentine couldn't remember the last time she had seen a paper map.

Six studied the map. "Here are the main arteries of the city. I propose we drive through them until you get a sense of where we should go."

Valentine frowned at him. "That's it? That's the plan?"

Six pursed his lips. looked up. "Do you have a better one?"

Valentine sighed. "No."

"Then we proceed my way."

They drove through the north end of the city all day.

As the hours passed and twilight threatened, Valentine felt the knot between her shoulders intensify and harden. Her stomach soured with fear and worry as they traversed neighborhood after neighborhood, city block after city block, with no signal or start of recognition. No invisible hand gripped her sternum, no internal barometer pleaded with her to pause and examine their surroundings. As the hours ticked by, little incidents – a car horn, a truck backfiring – caused Valentine to jump, her insides twisted.

Valentine clenched her fists in lap. "I don't think we're going to find him this way."

Six shook his head. "Let's take a break."

Six pulled over alongside a busy street. Valentine stepped out of the car, grateful to stand upright. A cacophony of smells greeted her: roasted meat from the food trucks down the way. Gasoline and smoke from the traffic. Piss from the nearby alleys. Valentine wandered down to the row of food trucks, Six and Church on her heels. She placed an order for a bevy of tacos and shared her bounty with Church. Six wasn't hungry. Instead, he smoked three slender cigarettes in rapid succession, a frown carved onto his face.

While Valentine and Church ate, Six stared at the map. "All of the murders have occurred in a five-mile radius. We have visited the locations of each prior murder—"

"Wait, what?" Valentine interrupted. "We just visited each murder scene?" Alarm and disgust seeped through her words.

Six glanced up. "Hmm? Yes, we drove by each location. The nearest one is merely a few blocks away."

Valentine swallowed hard, the food stodgy and leaden in her mouth. "Do you think it would help if I walked through it?" *Please say no.*

Six seemed surprised, then thoughtful. "Actually, that's a great idea."

Valentine sighed.

"You might get a sense of something, pick up a feeling to follow." He folded up the map. "At the very least, we have to try something different."

Valentine gave the rest of her tacos to Church, her appetite gone. She followed Six down the street, dodging the human traffic that clogged the sidewalks. Night had fallen, and the volume of people increased as the intense heat of the day faded. Bright signs lined the shopfronts, and the glow lit the passersby, anointing them in neon. Finally, Six stopped before an alley nestled between a convenience store and an Asian import grocery store.

"This is where the last one occurred." Six glanced up and down the alley, then up. A light shiver shook the man and Valentine wondered what kind of atrocity it took for a legend to feel uneasy.

She peered into the alley – and felt a familiar icy grip on her sternum. Her breath stuttered out of her, and she placed a hand to her chest, her heart beating a rapid drum against her ribcage.

"Do you feel something?" she heard Six ask. Church leaned up against her, as if to offer comfort.

"Y-yes." Valentine straightened. "That feeling – the one I had in the desert – It's back."

Six nodded. "Can you feel anything else? Besides the cold?"

Valentine shook her head, trying to clear her thoughts. "Not sure yet." She peered through the alley, nudging aside trash and debris with her foot. She searched for clues, any trace of the murderer or the Bloody Bones. "I don't know what I'm looking for, to be honest."

"The feeling in your chest?" Six scattered a trash bag with a foot. "It's a trail or a summons – it leads you to, well, wherever you need to go. It's an advantage to those on a quest. Otherwise, this entire endeavor would hardly be sporting – the odds are stacked too high against a mere mortal."

Church growled, and Valentine lifted her head. The black dog stared at the ground a few feet ahead of her, then scratched at it.

He rumbled again. *Valentine, come here.*

Walking over to Church, Valentine looked for what caught his attention. "What is it?"

Listen.

Valentine tilted her head. "I'm not hearing anything unusual."

No, listen. *Close your eyes if it helps you concentrate.* Valentine could hear the frustration in the black dog's voice.

Valentine closed her eyes. At first, she only heard the city sounds in the nighttime: traffic, human and vehicular, amidst the shops, bars, concerts, and myriad activities that surrounded the alley. But underneath it all, like a faint metallic heartbeat, Valentine heard something different, something *more*.

It sounds like a metronome, Valentine thought. *But something's wrong with it.*

She leaned into the sound, trying to sort out and reduce the noise from the nearby street. The steady clicks sped up, faster and faster. The cold grip on her sternum squeezed, then yanked her forward. She gasped –

And was somewhere else.

Valentine opened her eyes, and wished she hadn't.

A man crouched over a body, another man, younger, barely more than a kid, with a knife in one hand and a slice of flesh in the other. Blood stained the ground beneath them.

Beyond the man, a creature stood in the shadows. A skull of something not quite human, freed from flesh, rested atop a long body clad in alternate patches of scales and fur. Empty sockets peered up at Valentine's arrival, and the jaw unhinged to hiss at Valentine, revealing jagged rows of teeth.

Oh, shit. Valentine looked around for Six and Church but couldn't see them. They hadn't – or couldn't – follow her. *Shit, shit, shit.*

The killer had finally noticed Valentine. The man rose, his face twisted by shock and anger at her intrusion, dropping the trophy of flesh. He switched the knife from one hand to the other and started forward. His intent was clear: he was going to kill her. Behind him, the Bloody Bones let out a garbled cry, as if spurring him on.

Oh, god, I'm going to die. This is how I die. Again.

Valentine scrambled for a weapon of some kind. She was at a construction site, the dark skeleton of the future building rising to block out the moon. Her eyes alit on a piece of rebar, and Valentine lunged forward to grasp it with both hands.

The killer was almost upon her.

Her heartbeat hammered in her ears, and she could feel her breath stutter in her chest. Holding the metal length up high, she swung at the killer.

He leapt back, then closed in, the knife flashing in the moonlight. Valentine swung again and again, to hold him at bay. She jabbed at him, aiming for his chest – and the killer caught the rebar in one hand, then yanked.

The metal flew free of Valentine's grasp, and she fell forward, almost onto his knife. She flung herself backwards, but the killer advanced, his bright blue eyes the only color she saw on his face. *This is it. I'm done. I'm so screwed.*

A deep growl rumbled through the night.

Church!

I'm here. The black dog raced past Valentine and leapt onto the killer, his large jaws clamping down on the killer's neck. *I'll take care of this one. Kill the Bloody Bones.*

"Valentine!" Hands grabbed her from behind, and Valentine flinched, slapping at them in reflex. "It's me."

She finally heard Six's voice. She took a deep breath. *I'm okay, I'm okay.*

She heard a garbled screech, rage and frustration twining through the roar. She looked away from Church and the killer to see the Bloody Bones rush forward, arms outstretched.

Oh, shit. Not okay. I'm not okay.

"Valentine, you have to destroy the Bloody Bones." She heard Six's voice in her ears, his hands on her shoulders. "You can do this."

The Bloody Bones came closer and closer, until the skeletal head and empty sockets were all that Valentine could see. *How am I going to kill this thing? What will destroy it?*

Valentine felt an object in her back pocket, the hard edges pulling at her clothes. The shock of the sensation jolted her out of her fear, and she reached around to pull out a small bottle.

The whiskey, she realized. The whiskey that Pecos Bill gave her.

Valentine knew what she needed to do.

"Six, I need your lighter."

She heard him fumble with his clothing, then press the small metal lighter into her hands. He stepped several paces back, his gaze cautious and worried.

Valentine twisted the cap off the bottle with her teeth, then spit it aside. She had no time to do anything else. The Bloody Bones was on her.

She screamed as it reached for her neck, as its talons cut into the tender flesh. Pain lanced through her, and a bone-deep cold chased its trail. She managed to lift her arm up, to douse the liquid gold given to her by a legend over the creature. The motion distracted the Bloody Bones for a moment, then it snarled and snapped forward, its jaws just missing her face as she ducked.

Once the bottle was empty, Valentine flicked the lighter with her other hand.

Nothing.

Despair cut into her. *No. NO.*

She flicked it again.

The flame caught.

Valentine held the flame to the creature, and for a moment nothing happened. She started to cry. She needed this to work. She heard a snap and realized the sound was her collarbone.

At last, the flame took.

Fire raced across the creature, chasing the tendrils of whiskey that soaked its frame. The Bloody Bones roared in pain and alarm and then rage, stumbling back. It turned Valentine loose, scrabbling at the flames that engulfed it. She could smell rotted flesh, now burning, and almost vomited.

She saw the rebar on the ground and snatched it up. Valentine faced the Bloody Bones once again. She leapt forward with the metal length and stabbed the creature in the chest.

A throaty roar died mid-snarl.

The creature fell to its knees, then forward onto the ground.

The flames continued to burn.

CHAPTER NINE

They buried the killer and the creature together in a shallow grave at the junction of a nearby crossroads. Six had helped her roll the bodies onto a tarp Valentine had found, then drive them to the crossroads. "The creature will remain trapped at a crossroads," Six had explained. "It's a powerful kind of magic." His tailored, polished clothes were stained in mud and blood, his hair disheveled.

Using a shovel she had purloined from the construction site, Valentine had managed to dig the shallow hole. She cried silent tears every time she jostled her broken collarbone.

Finally, the killer and the creature were buried.

Six led them down the dark highway for a short time, his gaze sweeping the road for something. Valentine staggered after him, Church at her side to keep her upright. The enormous black dog was covered in blood, his teeth stained black in the moonlight. Valentine gripped his ruff and steadied herself.

"Here it is."

Valentine looked up at Six's words and the move caused her to stagger sideways. Relief filtered through her fatigue like light rain. A gleaming muscle car, American made and red as the flames that engulfed the Bloody Bones, rested on the side of the road.

Six opened the passenger door and held it wide. He gave her a gentle smile, with worry in his gaze. "Get in, Valentine Cash."

The drive back to the convenience store was uneventful. The shop was the same, though a different clerk ignored them as a man in elegant 1940s fashion, a bloodstained girl with a broken collarbone, and a black dog limped through the frozen aisles and through the secret door into the casino. As Valentine took her first step into the golden light of the elegant room, she again gasped and folded over in pain. Her collarbone snapped back into place. Her skin tingled and sparked as cuts and bruises rapidly faded. After a moment, as the pain subsided, Valentine straightened. She reached up to touch her hair, wondering.

The shorn locks remained short, ragged.

It seemed the casino couldn't heal everything.

Valentine followed Church and Six to the ornate golden double doors at the back of the large room. The doors seemed smaller somehow. Still elegant, with filigree and figures etched into the edges. But narrow maybe, or shorter. Valentine couldn't quite tell.

Six knocked three times.

The door swung open.

Inside, the legends awaited them. Valentine paused in surprise. The cactus cat was curled up on the pink velvet couch, next to Dale. *I guess it really is a pet.* It hissed at her, and she glared back. An echo of its claws as it raked her flesh washed through her and she shivered despite the room's warmth. She would never like that beast.

"Welcome back, Valentine Cash." Dale beamed at her. "You had quite an adventure. Pecos Bill loves you, by the way."

Paul Bunyan snorted.

High John shook his head. "Dale, let's not get too far ahead of ourselves. Paul made an excellent point."

Dale cast her eyes skyward and shook her head.

Valentine frowned.

Six stiffened next to her. "Wait. You're not saying that she failed the task?" Anger and disbelief threaded his voice.

"What?" Valentine heard herself ask as though she stood outside her body. *Oh, no. No, no, no.* Fatigue swamped her in a sudden wave. Sadness followed. The gravity of her hopelessness pulled at her shoulders. Was this it? Was this the end?

Paul stood up from the couch. "Valentine Cash was tasked with destroying the Bloody Bones —"

"—which she did," Six argued.

"By herself." Paul glared at Six. "You and that creature—" he pointed at Church "—interfered."

Six gaped at the legend. "Nonsense. Utter horseshit. I can't—"

"Six." Valentine's soft, insistent words cut through the tension like a knife. The highway and the other legends paused in surprise, then looked at Valentine. "I'll handle this."

Six met Valentine's gaze, then nodded. He took a step back.

Valentine turned to face the legends. "I killed the Bloody Bones with whiskey given to me by Pecos Bill, a lighter given to me by Route 66, and a piece of metal I found at the construction site. Church killed the human killer, not the creature." Valentine took a deep breath. "I believe I have fulfilled your task." Her voice shook, betraying her words.

A silence greeted her words.

Valentine didn't look away. *Please agree with me,* she begged in silence.

Dale spoke to the others, her words sharp as cut crystal. "She *earned* the whiskey the right way, by giving a boon to Pecos Bill and restoring the lariat. Yes, the Mother Road gave her a lighter but only after she had solved the challenge. She then finished the task." Dale gave Paul a withering glance. "You just like to split hairs."

"The Grim got involved." Paul was adamant.

The Grim? Valentine cast a puzzled look at Six, who shook his head.

Church growled, then shook himself. *I disposed of the human trash. The world is better off without that one. I didn't interfere with the* task. A snarl underscored his words.

Dale looked at High John de Conqueror. "Brother, you are our tie breaker. Which vote do you cast?"

High John studied Valentine with a bored air. Sweat trickled down her spine. *Please.*

After a moment, High John looked at Dale. "She fulfilled the task."

Paul Bunyan cursed and the air around his body turned a bright blue. Valentine almost took a step back. She noticed Six swallow a gleeful smile.

Dale clapped her hands. "It's finished. Valentine Cash has completed the second task."

Valentine heaved a sigh of relief. She swallowed hard, and blinked away relieved tears. She wouldn't cry in front of the legends. "Thank you," she said, her voice subdued.

Dale gave a benign smile. "Don't thank us yet. We have another task for you." Behind the country music legend and the now purring cactus cat, Valentine saw Paul Bunyan grin wide. His teeth gleamed and he looked... happy? Valentine swallowed. Trepidation filled her like grains of sand rushing through an hourglass.

"What is it?" she forced herself to ask.

High John de Conqueror stepped forward, and Valentine gasped. The tall man held a large crown, a royal object unlike anything Valentine had ever seen. Composed of antlers, bones, and precious gems and metals, the large circlet emitted a faint glow that pulsed like a heartbeat. High John approached Valentine, the crown lifted high. Just when she thought he would place it upon her head, he muttered a few words in a dialect she couldn't understand — and the crown vanished.

A moment later, Valentine screamed.

Her skin stung and bubbled and twisted as the crown etched itself into the surface of her body, encircling her upper back, shoulders, and chest. The pain caused her to stumble forward and Six caught her, braced her upright; otherwise, she would have fallen. The pain wasn't the worst part, though. Grief and rage enveloped her, the intrusive and alien feelings a tsunami from which she wasn't sure she could recover. Those feelings weren't hers, she knew. They belonged to someone — *something* — else. She took several deep breaths. When she felt somewhat normal, she looked up.

High John de Conqueror stared back at her, his deep eyes like the night sky. "Valentine Cash, you must return this crown to a legend known as the Flathead Lake Creature."

Valentine nodded. "O-okay." She tried not to vomit.

She hoped she could, at least.

High John turned away and focused on Six. "Mother Road, be careful. You are a guide, not a champion. If you forget that, if you get involved..." The tall man shook his head. "You will forfeit your own bargain."

The dream came like a wave, all at once and sudden.

A girl and a boy grew up in different cities as though watching two films on separate projectors. The angle of the film made it so she watched them from the side or from behind; she could never quite get a good look at their faces.

The young woman loved to build anything. She started with simple forts in the living room as a young girl, then graduated into tree houses in the suburbs, complete with elaborate awnings cobbled together with leftover materials and a bucket for snack delivery using a pulley system she had fashioned. Her mother and her aunties indulged her and used the system to deliver tiffin tins filled with samosas and sealed cups of mango lassi. The neighbor kids were astonished and envious at this bounty. Valentine watched her grow up, a fast forward montage of highlights and clips that captured joy, temper tantrums, grief, and ordinary adventures. She excelled in almost all areas in school save one: the girl was terrible at sports.

In a parallel reel of film, Valentine watched the boy grow up in a different city. He was quiet, the oldest of three siblings, and a decent student. He simply wasn't interested in most of the subjects, Valentine saw. He read fantasy and science fiction like it was a religion, his family often teasing him for this unusual love. But more than anything, he loved to bake. He started with cookies, eyes alight with his own personal joy at the almost alchemical transformation that occurred when raw ingredients turned into a gift, a treat. He moved onto muffins, cakes, skillet bakes, scones, and much more. He was soon made responsible for baking birthday cakes and dessert for family reunions, holidays, and other gatherings. His two younger siblings loved him, and he spoiled them with extra cookies that he hid from their parents, who pretended to turn a blind eye.

As the two grew older, Valentine saw that the separate reels of film aligned closer and closer – until they spliced together at a specific moment in time.

The girl and the boy enrolled in the same college. Valentine saw that the boy hadn't wanted to go (he'd much rather go to culinary school) but his parents had insisted on a college degree. The girl hadn't needed any convincing. She was going to be an engineer.

They met a party, a loud and obnoxious affair that they each had been dragged to by well-meaning and determined friends. Both held up an opposite wall of the co-op house, a watered-down drink in hand. Somehow, through the ebb and the flow of humanity in this small, cramped building, the girl found herself next to the boy. She eavesdropped on his description of a scone recipe he had written, a combination of mango and lychee and poppyseeds.

"That sounds delicious," she muttered to herself.

Somehow the boy heard her over the din of the room. He turned and stared. The girl flushed at being caught eavesdropping, then at his open admiration. "I'll make them for you," he offered.

She blinked. "Seriously?"

The boy smiled. "Seriously. Let's go."

They left the party without a backwards glance and stopped by the grocery store to pick up what the boy needed to make the scones. At the dorms, the boy used the limited counter space and the dodgy oven in the worn community kitchenette to produce the best scones the girl had ever eaten. Through it all, and well into the night, they talked. They compared family histories, sibling stories, and what it was like to grow up in their respective cities. On the surface, it seemed that they were as opposite as could be — different origin stories, different cultures, different cities.

But they couldn't stop talking.

Valentine could see that they shared an affinity, an understanding, for one another. Though the two had just met, she recognized the spark of something more. *She moved closer. She hadn't been able to get a good look this whole time. She walked around the worn couch in the kitchenette and stood in front of them.*

She froze. She knew those faces.

Valentine had last seen them on the night she — and they — had died.

Valentine had killed the boy and the girl.

Valentine jerked awake, gasping. She struggled to sit upright, to take a deep breath, and banged her knee on the glovebox on the car for her troubles. She welcomed the brief flare of pain, focusing on the sensation in her knee to distract her from the memories. Tears streamed down her face, and she reached up to wipe them away with her shirtsleeve.

John and Emma. Now she had names for the people she had killed.

Valentine? The voice interrupted her grief and shame. She looked over her shoulder.

"What is it, Church?"

The black dog stared at her from the backseat, his milky white eyes pale in the nighttime. *Are you okay?*

Valentine shook her head. "No, not really," she admitted.

Bad dreams?

"Yes. The people —" Valentine stopped. She didn't know how to continue.

The line between life and death is much thinner here than in your world. It's not surprising that you dreamt. You will likely have more dreams.

"Yes." Valentine's voice was small. "I saw them. The couple, I mean. As they grew up, how they met. Jesus, Church, I *killed* them." More tears slipped down her face and she blotted them again. Valentine cast a quick glance at Six. If he heard any part of the conversation he pretended not to, staring straight ahead at the road that stretched before them.

Church crept forward, closer. *You did kill them.*

Valentine hiccupped in surprise. Anger raced through her, pricking her limbs. She felt her face heat. "Thanks, Church. I definitely needed that right now."

She almost heard him roll his eyes. *But you are trying to make amends. That is why you are here, with us. You've undertaken the penance.*

"Church, how is wrestling a feral desert beast and killing a Bloody Bones helping that couple? How is that a penance for what I took from them?" Valentine shook her head. "They are still *dead*. They deserved so much more than what happened to them, what I did to them."

You must trust in the gods and the legends. Church sounded firm in her head, causing her to look back at him. *You're only mortal. You don't get to see the magic and the meaning of it all.*

Valentine looked out the passenger window. As they drove by, a lamp above the highway gave her a glimpse of her own reflection in the glass: Dark circles bagged her eyes, her cheekbones stood like sentinels against the rest of her face, and her skin was pale. She looked as though she were becoming what she was — a ghost. At last, she responded to Church.

"I don't know that I ever had faith, Church, in gods or anyone else. And I think magic is best reserved for someone who deserves it."

Chapter Ten

Montana was beautiful. Despite the lingering low mood she had felt since the dream, Valentine couldn't deny that. The mountains reached up to the sky like an embrace, higher than any of the hills she had seen back in Tennessee. The thick forest painted the land in dark greens and blues and browns, with the slate gray splashes of boulders and cliffs sprinkled throughout.

Six drove them along a narrow highway, two lanes carved into the precarious edge of the mountain. Everyone seemed to drive fast out here, Valentine noted, as yet another truck roared around them and then sped into the distance. Or maybe the old-fashioned, cherry red sedan with black accents Six now drove simply didn't drive well above fifty miles an hour. She glanced at Six and something like affection warmed within her. He loved coupes, sedans, and convertibles from the mid twentieth century. The highway had yet to choose a more modern vehicle.

He seemed to feel her gaze upon him and glanced over. "We'll be at Flathead Lake by early this evening. But we should stop for dinner soon. You haven't eaten much."

Valentine shrugged. She wasn't hungry. "Sounds good."

Six frowned but didn't respond. A few towns over, he stopped at a diner with a full parking lot crammed with minivans and enormous trucks, and eased the car into the lot. He parked in the furthest spot available, well away from the other cars.

Valentine smirked at him. "Are you worried about your baby?"

Six huffed at her. "Yes." He ran a hand over the dashboard. "You're from cowboy country. You'd take care of your horse, right? For companionship and travel. It's the same principle."

"Except this is a car."

Six gave Valentine a blank look. "So?"

"It's inanimate? Not living?" Valentine offered.

Six shook his head. "Heathen," she heard him mutter.

The parking lot delivered on its promise: The diner was crowded, and loud. Six and Valentine managed to find a booth in the back, away from most of the din. Six then proceeded to order a dinner that would feed four men. Valentine ordered a sandwich and soup combo, then added a large order of fries to share with Church, who rested under the table. After a few moments of eating in silence, Six leaned back in his seat.

"What do you know about what the humans call the Flathead Lake Creature?"

Valentine swallowed a hasty bite. "Almost nothing. Except I need to return this—" she waved to her chest "—back to the being. I'm not sure how to do that, though. Get a tattoo off my skin. How do I do that? I know, I know – you can't tell me."

"You'll figure it out," Six said. He had finished one burger and started another. "It's a fairly straightforward task, honestly. You just need to return a lost item."

"Lost?" Valentine studied Six. She remembered the grief and rage that had subsumed her as the crown had etched itself across her body. "Or stolen?"

Six waffled his hand back and forth. "Depends on which legend you believe. Either way, High John de Conqueror wants the crown returned."

Valentine rubbed her shoulder, where the skin still healed from the recent tattoo. "We're going out to the lake tomorrow?"

Church rumbled from under the table.

Valentine peered underneath. "What was that?"

You should tell us what to do.

"That's a great plan, Church, except I have no idea what I'm doing." Valentine ate another French fry, then winced. Too salty.

"He's got a point." Six had somehow finished another burger. "You should listen to what feels right, guide us."

"I thought you were here for limited advice and wayfinding?"

"I thought you were here to complete a penance?" Six shot back. "This is your gig, Valentine Cash. You decide where we go." He sighed. "If I appear to help too much, your penance could be endangered. I would never forgive myself if Church or I jeopardized your efforts."

Valentine gave a stiff nod and finished her sandwich in silence. She still snuck her fries to Church, though.

At Valentine's uncertain direction, they drove around the perimeter of Flathead Lake the next day. The skies were clear and blue, the sun bright and hot. The road twisted and turned, dipped and rose, and Valentine studied the edges of the lake, looking for a sign of the Flathead Lake Creature. Or a sign of anything unusual, really. They pulled over at observation points and docks, and even walked a few trails that led to the lakeside. Families and couples thronged at the campsites, paddled in the water, and picnicked on the beaches. The scenery was majestic, an ancient, raw beauty she had never seen.

But she couldn't enjoy it.

Valentine knew she only had until tomorrow night to complete this task. She could feel the time constraint eat away at her like termites in wood. By the time they had finished the loop, it was late afternoon. Valentine's hands trembled from anxiety and frustration. *How would she find this creature?* She clenched them into fists and held them in her lap. Six pulled the car over to an observation point, killed the engine, and looked over to Valentine. "What's next, Valentine Cash?"

"I have no idea." Her shoulders slumped.

Six said nothing. But the silence that fell over the car spoke volumes: Valentine had better figure out what was next and soon.

The silence got too much for her and Valentine stepped out of the car. She stretched and twisted her body, and her limbs slowly came to life with pricks and tingles. She stared out from the observation point over the water. The sun sank lower into the sky, not quite twilight but soon.

Something caught her eye. She turned, then tilted, her head. "What is that?" she muttered to herself.

"Wildhorse Island." Valentine hadn't heard Six get out of the car. "It's the island in the middle of Flathead Lake."

Valentine stared at the island. Something turned over in her chest. *There,* it whispered. *You need to go there.* "Can we go there? How?"

"By boat, I imagine." Six's words were dry. "As for permission, well, I think we're past that."

Valentine slid him a glance. "You know where we can get a boat?"

Six grinned. "Possibly."

Getting the boat was less difficult that Valentine expected. Six handed over identification and cash to the rental kiosk, then signed a liability waiver. The young man behind the counter eyed Six, then Valentine, with a dubious glance and she wondered what he thought of a middle-aged man in retro fashion and a teenaged girl in cowboy gear, renting a boat to drive on the lake in Montana. As usual, the young man didn't seem to see Church.

The trip to Wildhorse Island almost died on the docks.

"Six, do you know how to start this engine?" Valentine called out.

Six came over, each careful step rocking the boat a bit more. He studied the small engine, perplexed. "No. I've no idea, sorry."

After a few moments, Valentine reached for a cord handle and gave it a yank. The engine rumbled to life, and she heaved a sigh of relief. *Just like a lawn mower.*

Steering the boat took more concentration and skill than she expected but after a few false starts and turns, Valentine managed to keep the boat on a straight-ish path for the island. The water lapped from the boat in gentle ripples that spread far; the late afternoon breeze was cool with a bite to it. She could hear the rumble of other boats and people, families and college kids from the sounds of it, in the distance.

At the island, Valentine had to search for a place to land. With no discernible dock, she decided to aim for a long beach, pebbled with water-worn gravel and slicked in algae. A few feet away from the edge, the boat jarred to a stop and emitted a whine of protest. Looking over the edge of the boat, she saw that the engine had caught on the sandbar, the propeller blades sputtering in mud. She switched off the engine, then vaulted over the side of the boat. She gasped at the shock of the cold water but gripped the aluminum edge of the boat.

Valentine looked up at Six and Church. "We'll need to pull the boat in. It's too shallow here."

Six gave a distasteful glance over the edge of the boat. "I suppose you are right."

Valentine shook her head, then pulled forward. Her boots sank into the thick mud with each step; she had to wrestle free each time she lifted her foot, the accompanying squelch a punctuation of sorts to each step forward. The water had soaked her clothes to her waist, and she shivered from the cold. At last, she stepped free of the water. Valentine turned to pull the boat forward, further onto the beach. Church leapt out to run the length of the beach; Six stepped out, grimaced at his shoes in the water, and bent to help Valentine secure the boat to a nearby tree with rope.

"Where to now, Valentine Cash?" Six shook one foot, then another, as he tried to wring out the lake water from his shoes.

Valentine looked down the beach, then up at the forest that lined the edge of the pebbled stretch. She saw a small opening in the brush – and felt the clamp of the invisible grip on her sternum, icy and certain. She pointed. "That way."

Valentine led the way through the brush and into the forest. The daylight dimmed as they stepped under the canopy of the trees and gave the woods a twilit feel. With each step forward, Valentine felt the grip on her chest tighten, the cold deepening within. She thought she heard a faint melody in the distance but only a few chords, nothing more. The underbrush seemed to part way, to open a clear path for her. They were close. She knew it. Valentine lost track of the time as they wove around and over and through the woods. She simply followed the grip on her chest.

It grew tighter and tighter. The woods grew darker and darker.

Finally, they emerged from the woods into a small cove.

The small cove wrapped around a deep pool of blue green water, white capped wherever waves rippled against the rock. Grey cliffs and boulders rose up and encircled the pool, creating a small refuge from the rest of the island. The cold in her chest tightened, then disappeared.

"Here." Valentine pointed at the pool. "It's here."

Valentine scrambled down the embankment, sliding on her rear when necessary. She could hear Six behind her, muttering curses as he slid down on his tailored clothing. Church quickly passed her, barreling down the hill in leaps and bounds. At the bottom, Valentine stood and stepped away to make room for Six. As he stood, she scanned the cove and the water, looking for... something.

A thought occurred to Valentine. "What does the Flathead Lake Creature look like?"

Six straightened, brushing off his clothes. "No clue. No one I know has seen it in centuries."

Valentine sighed. *Of course.* "Do you know how to call it? Or if it responds to a summons?"

Six shook his head. "I'm afraid not."

Valentine studied the water. "Well, I guess we wait."

They sat at the edge of the water and waited.

And waited.

Night fell, almost all at once it seemed, and Valentine started to shiver with the absence of the sun. Her damp clothes and sodden boots stole away her own warmth, causing her teeth to chatter. Six gave her his jacket and started a small fire.

And still, they waited.

"What made you want to be a musician, Valentine Cash?" Six's sudden query broke the quiet dark. The flames of the fire cast long shadows on his face, the smoke further obscuring his features.

Valentine looked up. "I can't remember a time when I didn't want to be one," she said. "The music has always been there, in the back of my mind."

"Have you always been a songwriter then?"

"Yes? I think so." Valentine fed more wood to the fire, then settled back onto the ground. "Music builds a connection between people, you know? You write a story and a tune that suits the story, and play it, hoping that what you've put together has captured something that someone, somewhere in the audience, can understand. They listen and hear the truth you're trying to share. And then, maybe, the world is a little less lonely because someone else has heard that truth."

Valentine shifted, uneasy, and pulled the legend's jacket tighter around her shoulders. She hadn't meant to share so much. She snuck a glance to Six and found him studying her.

"Is that your goal, then? To make the world less lonely?"

Six's words resonated in her like a struck bell. They felt true, right, but too ambitious. Who was she to make the world less lonely? What right had she to try for something so precious and vital? Valentine gave a quick shake of her head. "I mostly want to pay my bills and have health insurance. Entertain people. Maybe retire someday."

Six didn't respond for a moment. Valentine stared into the fire and avoided his gaze, worried about what she might see.

Church gave a sudden growl, the ruff on his neck standing straight.

A sudden chill rippled through Valentine.

She scrambled up and faced the water. "It's here."

Valentine stared at the water at the edge of the cove, searching. She heard Six stand beside her. Church continued to rumble a low snarl. *There*, Valentine thought. A faint white gold light glowed from beneath the water's surface, moving at a steady clip towards the small cove. Valentine's heart beat an uneven rhythm in her ears. The crown that encircled her chest, shoulders, and back blazed in waves of heat and happiness, as if in recognition of the coming creature's imminent arrival. The emotion, foreign because it did not belong to her, sent goosebumps across her skin.

At last, the creature swam to the shallow depths. Out of the water, the bright glow of white gold light both outlined and obscured the edges of the creature. Valentine squinted against the light, and she saw that the creature stood on two legs. Fur wrapped across the body. Three eyes, each the blue-black depths of an abyss, traced across the creature's face above a long snout that resembled a wolf's.

The creature came to a stop. *Mortal. You seek me?* The deep voice felt like black velvet and filled up the corners of Valentine's head.

Valentine stepped forward. "I've been charged to return something to you."

What is it? Curiosity rippled through the voice.

"Your crown." Valentine pulled her shirt aside to reveal the tattoo on her right shoulder.

The creature closed its three eyes. Valentine was buffeted by several emotions at once: Relief chased by joy, and intertwined with a braid of anger, grief, and longing. She huddled into herself to escape the onslaught. The black velvet voice spoke again. *That belongs to me. Return it,* now.

Valentine stepped forward. "I want to give you your crown. I do. But I don't know how. How do I get this off my body?" She gestured at the tattoo, then looked back at the creature.

The black velvet voice came once more. *I can help you.*

The creature tilted its head — and Valentine was pulled under the water.

Valentine screamed at the sudden motion. Water chased the sound back down her throat and into her lungs. She coughed and twisted and fought to break for the surface, to breathe. Fear swamped her. She fought harder, lunging up and towards the sweet air. But she couldn't reach the surface. A sudden pain sliced through her, and she screamed again, on instinct. More water poured into her open mouth. Valentine opened her eyes, and despite the darkness of the night and the water, she saw the bone and gem and antler crown slip away from her body, like paint dripping from a canvas. The process took some time and Valentine still struggled for air, to break the water's surface. After a short time, she saw black first edge and then grow across her vision. When the last gem floated off her body, the pain stopped.

Valentine sobbed in relief, choking on the water.

She watched the crown coalesce into completion, then float towards the creature. The Flathead Lake Creature settled the newly assembled crown onto its head, elation clear on its face. Her task complete, Valentine gave a feeble kick and tried to reach for the water's surface. She did it. She delivered the crown. She just needed to breathe. She could do this. She *would* do this.

Then Valentine Cash died the second time in her short life.

Chapter Eleven

Valentine landed on the floor of the back room of the elegant casino with a hard thump. Stunned, in pain, she gasped and choked. She retched up lake water onto the lush carpet beneath her, then sucked in the sweet, welcome air in greedy gulps. *I'm alive, I'm alive, I'm still here.* She rested her forehead against the carpet. Tears slipped down her face.

"Welcome back, Valentine Cash."

She didn't answer. She simply breathed, grateful that she could. *I'm still alive.*

"You succeeded with your task, Valentine. Well done."

Valentine lifted her head. High John de Conqueror stared down at her, eyebrows raised. Paul Bunyan slouched on one of the chairs. When he met her gaze, he smirked at her sodden and distraught state. Dale stood next to the pink velvet couch, her face somber.

"Valentine Cash, pull yourself together. Get up," Paul Bunyan commanded. His smirk grew wider, his words edged in disgust.

"I just died, *Paulie*," Valentine snapped back. "Give me a moment, okay?"

The temperature in the room dropped by several degrees. Paul stood — and Valentine knew she had made a mistake. She remained on the floor, her head bowed.

"Listen, mortal. You are here on our mercy. If you cannot appreciate your good fortune, then you will die a final death." Paul's words were light, cheerful, and somehow that made the reprimand worse. "What say you? Are you ready to give up, mortal?"

Valentine shook her head. "N-no," she whispered.

"I can't hear you." Paul's words were edged with malicious glee.

Valentine lifted her head. "No." She tried not to glare at him. *Bully.*

Paul Bunyan's nostrils flared as if he had heard her private epithet. "Then get up and stop whining. No more disrespect — or we're done."

Valentine pushed herself up to a sitting position. She surveyed her body: Nothing seemed broken or mangled. Her skin stung from where the crown rested but nothing was bleeding. She forced herself to stand, grabbing onto a nearby chair to prop herself upright.

The double golden doors opened, and Six strolled in, unruffled and in a grey three piece with a patterned vest. Church walked at his side. "What did we miss?" Six asked.

No one spoke for a moment.

Dale stepped forward. "Are you ready for your next task, Valentine Cash?"

No. Never. Valentine forced herself to nod. "Yes."

"You are to contain or destroy a Hodag in Wisconsin."

Valentine swallowed a sigh of frustration. "Of course." She let a beat pass. "What is a Hodag exactly?"

Paul Bunyan grinned without mirth. "It's a beast up in Wisconsin. An enormous bull-like creature with horns and fangs. Likes to eat people."

Valentine met his gaze. *He's enjoying this. He wants me to fail.* Fear pebbled her skin with goosebumps. *What if I do fail? I'll lose my life, the music.* Her heartbeat stuttered at the pain of that thought. She lifted her chin and stared back at Paul. "Sounds like fun," she gritted out between clenched teeth.

Dale gave a sudden chuckle.

High John de Conqueror looked bored.

Valentine jumped as something pressed along her side. She looked down to see Church lean against her, as if shoring her upright with his strength. She rested a hand on his head. *Thank you.*

"Well, we should go," Six said. "Thank you, legends."

Valentine turned to leave but Paul Bunyan's words called out to her. "Valentine Cash."

She turned to look back at him.

He smirked. "Use the dynamite."

Valentine frowned. "I don't understand."

Paul Bunyan grinned wide and without mercy. "You will."

"Valentine, you seem tired."

"I wonder why, Six." Sarcasm dripped off her words.

Six sighed but didn't take the bait. He continued to drive them along the interstate that led to Wisconsin. They were in the slow lane. Cars and semi-trucks passed the new sky-blue mid-century convertible on a regular basis. Any speed above fifty-five made the car rattle in a disturbing manner. Church snored from the backseat. Valentine wished she could sleep, too. Instead, she stared out the window. Flat beige lands stretched out from either side of the highway, a grey sky above. Tall skyscrapers and short strip malls interrupted the landscape off in the distance. *Chicago.* She'd never been there. It seemed funny that she had had to die twice to make it there.

"Do you have any questions about the Hodag?"

Valentine shook her head.

Six lapsed into silence but Valentine felt his gaze on her now and again. She could tell he was worried, or irritated, or perhaps both. But she couldn't bring herself to reassure him just now. That dream of John and Emma, the second death, delivered without warning or concern by the Flathead Lake Creature — they broke something in her. When this had all started, when she first bargained with the legends in that back room of the elegant casino, Valentine had wanted her life back: The music, the contract with Defiance Studios, the tour, the fame, and everything that would come with it.

But the cactus cat, the Bloody Bones — it had all felt like a dream. An admittedly bizarre, richly detailed dream but a dream, nonetheless. She thought or maybe hoped that the tasks the gods set before her would be achievable, reasonable. That there wouldn't be so many of these tasks, or so damn dangerous. That they would make some kind of sense.

She hadn't expected to die.

Dying changed things. Her second death showed Valentine that the spoken and unspoken rules she had grown up with — work hard, do the best job possible, be kind and fair — did not apply in this realm. The legends and gods did not abide by the social contract between mortals; fairness and points for a good effort was a childish notion. She now played by a new set of rules, ones she didn't fully understand.

She only hoped she didn't die the final death before figuring them out.

And John and Emma. Valentine sighed and shifted in her seat, her forehead against the cold window of the passenger door. She grieved for them. An immense shame that weighed her down like an anchor. The same sensation she felt when pulled underwater at Flathead Lake — being held down, restrained, not able to breathe, water swamping her mouth and lungs — threatened to overtake her in that moment. Her seatbelt made an odd noose, trapping her in the car.

Oh, god, no. Please.

Valentine took several deep breaths to calm herself. After a minute, her heart rate calmed and slowed. A tear slipped down her face, and she wiped it away, hoping Six wouldn't see. She hadn't meant to kill them; she had only looked away from the road for an instant on that rainy night. *It wasn't fair, or right*. Valentine wanted John and Emma to live again, to pursue what made them happy - or as content as someone could be in this life.

The convertible rumbled over a pothole on the interstate and Church roused for a moment to growl from the backseat. Valentine stared out into the beige and grey expanse along the side of the highway, the leather seat cool beneath her legs. No answers awaited her out there, she knew. She wasn't certain there were any answers at all.

Valentine must have slept at some point because she awoke as Six drove them into Rhinelander, Wisconsin. She knew where they were because they passed a large sign that read in a cheerful font, "Welcome to Rhinelander, Wisconsin. Home of the Hodag." Valentine blinked and read the sign again. As they drove further into town, Valentine saw the same logo featured in many windows and even on the bus stops: a green monster that appeared to be a cross between a crocodile and a bull, with spikes down its back, a friendly smile, and eyes that twinkled.

Valentine shook her head. "Aren't we here to kill the Hodag?"

Six made a turn onto a busy yet bucolic street that looked like Main Street, America. Boutique shops lined either side of the road. "Kill or contain," he murmured, peering out the windshield.

"Yet the locals all know about this creature?"

"The locals have capitalized on the legend for tourism purposes. They made the monster more palatable and friendly," Six said. "The green cuddly creature you see in that window—" he pointed "—bears no resemblance to the original legend."

"Then what am I really facing?"

Six cast a pitying glance at Valentine. "A smelly, violent creature with a bad temper and enormous fangs."

"Great." Valentine sighed.

"Oh, look, a diner." Six brightened. "Are you hungry?"

Valentine stared down at her slice of apple pie with a slice of cheddar cheese over it.

"Valentine Cash, you have to at least try it," Six scolded. "It's a regional tradition."

"You know, you should get a host gig on the Food Channel."

Six rolled his eyes. "Funny."

Valentine took a bite of the sweet and savory mouthful.

Six waited, an expectant look on his face.

Valentine swallowed. "It's different," she allowed.

The legend's shoulders sank and he leaned away from the table. "Philistine," he muttered.

Valentine grinned at his obvious dismay, then took another bite. "Where does the Hodag live? And why do the legends want me to destroy it?"

Six sighed in bliss over his first bite of the cheddar and apple concoction. "The Hodag, the real one, not this cheerful beast the Chamber of Commerce has dreamed up, is a destructive creature who likes to eat human hunters who wander too close to its lair. The original Hodag manifested in Germany and when the immigrants settled in this area, another one — a new one — emerged, shaped by their worries about this new land and their nostalgia for the homeland."

"It's been around for a few centuries, then?" Valentine took another bite.

"Shortly after the first immigrants arrived, yes."

"So why now? Why do the gods want the Hodag destroyed?"

"Or contained," Six added. "Honestly? I think it's Paul Bunyan's idea of a joke. A bad joke, and a dangerous one. I don't think he likes you very much."

"I would never have guessed," Valentine drawled. "He's so friendly."

Six grinned at her. "If it's any comfort, most of the other legends consider him a prickly bastard at the best of times. But back to the Hodag: It can be contained, too. You needn't destroy it. I advise containment, if you can. Destroying the creature is senseless and for a mortal, near impossible."

Valentine pushed away her pie. "Containment? Like a trap?" She tried to imagine a trap that could restrain a magical monster. The cactus cat flooded her mind and she shuddered. Valentine doubted she could find something useful at one of the local sporting and hunting goods stores.

Six nodded. "A trap would work but only if imbued with magic. A simple hunter's snare won't work on a legend, or on anyone with a drop of magic in them."

"Has the Hodag been caught before?"

Six gave a slow nod. "Local legend states that an early band of mortals captured the Hodag and blew it up with dynamite. The sky turned black and it rained viscera and bile on that day."

"That's why Paul said, 'Use the dynamite,'" Valentine muttered.

"Yes," Six said. "However, the legend didn't mention that the creature manifested again later that day, in a different part of the woods. He then hunted down the band of mortals and ate them." Six shook his head.

Valentine blinked. "I don't want to be eaten."

Church rumbled from under the table. It sounded like laughter in the back of her mind.

Six gave a half-smile and his eyes twinkled. "That's a good goal to have."

"The dynamite is crap advice from Paulie, then. Figures." Valentine sneered his name. "Such an asshole."

Six cast a nervous look around the diner, as if looking for the tall and gruff lumberjack. "Valentine, hush," he muttered. "We're in timbermen's territory. These are his stomping grounds. Speak his name with respect or not at all."

Valentine gulped. "O-okay." *Now I have something new to worry about.*

"But yes, as the resident advisor and wayfinder, I do not recommend dynamite." Six looked over Valentine with interest. "Knowing that, what will you do?"

Valentine leaned back against the booth seat. "I think I have an idea."

The next day, Valentine found two instrument shops in Rhinelander, Wisconsin: a chain store she dismissed right away and a local one. She asked Six to drive her to the local place. Called Rhineland Winds, the shop was nestled between the boutique, tourist-centric stores just off Main Street. The store itself was small with a worn brick facade and large windows, the painting on which promised the best deals on back-to-school instrument rentals for parents.

"We'll stay out here," Six said.

Valentine looked at him in surprise. "You don't want to come in?"

"On every quest, the hero needs to select their weapon," Six explained. "You know what you're looking for. We would simply get in the way."

Valentine nodded, then headed for the entrance. A bell chimed as Valentine stepped inside. She inhaled, and almost smiled as she smelled polish and paper. Instrument shops had always been a home away from home for her.

A middle-aged woman dressed in plaid and denim emerged from the back of the shop. "Can I help you?"

"I'm looking for a mandolin or a guitar." Valentine wasn't certain which one yet.

"Either one, huh?" The woman nodded to the far side of the shop. "We have a selection over there. If you don't see anything you like, I have some in the back or I can order one for you."

"Thanks." Valentine wandered to the wall of guitars, ukuleles, mandolins, dobros, and a few other instruments besides. She scanned the wall, then handled a guitar. She tuned it, then ran her fingers through a few chords. Despite the soft and sweet sound, Valentine felt a metallic taste on her tongue. *Not this one, then.* Valentine placed the guitar back on the hook. She selected another guitar with a black backboard and abalone frets and did the same.

Again, same reaction: A sour taste coated her tongue and filled her mouth. She shook her head. *This might take a while.*

Valentine went through the wall of stringed instruments, one by one. She first started with the guitars. For a creature as large and ferocious as the Hodag, she assumed she would need a larger instrument to create a big sound. But none of the guitars *felt* right, and by the time she moved onto the mandolins, her mouth felt like she had sucked on a penny for some time.

Valentine then tried a few of the ukuleles and the two dobros. The sound was wrong, the shape almost foreign in her hands. The new penny taste deepened in her mouth, a metallic tang that made her wish she had some water. She immediately replaced the instruments back on the wall.

The mandolins were better – but still not right. The sweet sound that emerged tickled something in the back of her mind. *Right sound, wrong instrument.* There were four mandolins on the wall; Valentine went through each one. The third one that she tried, a mahogany affair with thick strings, might work. She laid that one aside.

Valentine took a step back and studied the wall. None of them were quite right. The mahogany mandolin might do well in a pinch but still. She was looking for something *more.*

Valentine was looking for magic.

Then she remembered what the other woman had said and made her way up to the front of the shop. The middle-aged woman had a name tag that read Desdemona leaned against the counter, reading a newspaper. "You said you have more in the back?"

Desdemona looked up. "I do. What are you looking for?"

"A mandolin."

The other woman nodded. "I'll bring what I have up front."

Valentine watched passersby outside the shop while she waited. The sidewalks were busy with foot traffic: Families and couples stopped at windows or wandered into shops. A line led out the coffee shop and bakery, almost around the corner of the block.

"Here we are." Desdemona's arrival jerked Valentine's attention back to the front counter. "I only have these two." She laid them on the counter.

Valentine examined the mandolins: One mandolin had an almost blonde wood, stained puce around the edges, the colors a striking contrast to one another. The tuners were polished chrome and the strings new.

Valentine looked at the other mandolin – and stilled. Her mouth flooded with the taste of honey and her sternum vibrated like a tuning fork.

This is the one.

The mandolin was small and black. A thin line of white – a shell of some kind? Valentine wondered – embroidered the edges of the wooden instrument. The tuners were bone white over chrome and the strings were new but unlike anything she had ever seen before. She pointed. "That one."

Desdemona handed it over without comment.

Valentine cradled the mandolin against her torso and quickly tuned it. Her fingers trembled as she went through her familiar routine. The instrument felt *right*, like an extension of her limbs. Like there was no separation between herself and the music. When she strummed a chord, she almost wept. She had to choke back tears; she avoided the other woman's gaze, her joy and astonishment too raw, too private, to share. Valentine stared down at the little black mandolin. The sound was unlike anything she had ever heard from an instrument but felt like an almost forgotten dream she might have had as a child, long before she had left her parents for Nashville: Familiar, loving, *right*.

Like a blessing she hadn't known that she needed.

She forced herself to stop playing, then looked up. "This one. I'll take this one."

Valentine emerged from the shop on shaky legs. She clutched the mandolin to her chest and walked out to the coupe, where Six and Church stood, leaning. Six sipped a coffee and held another in his other hand.

He held it out to her. "Did you find what you were looking for?"

Valentine accepted the offering. "Yes." Her voice cracked.

Six examined her with sharp eyes. "What happened?"

Valentine sipped her coffee, feeling exposed and raw. "I found an instrument. A mandolin."

Why are you so shaken, mortal? Church sounded curious.

Valentine shook her head, unsure how to explain. "I've... I've never heard this sound, this melody from an instrument before. It's... spectacular."

Six clapped her on the shoulder. "We should get going. Where to, Valentine Cash?"

She stared down the busy Main Street, not really seeing the tourists and the families as she listened for the answer. She looked back at Six. "Head north."

They drove out of Rhinelander after an enormous lunch (Six had insisted) and followed the road north. The woods had thinned around the edges of town but grew thick the further north they traveled. The late afternoon sun filtered through the evergreen and deciduous trees, dappling the ground below with golden freckles of light. All the while, Valentine cradled the mandolin in its case and strap in her hands upon her lap. She felt a sense of rightness, of homecoming, in this little instrument. She wondered if she would ever be able to show Loretta. Valentine felt a pang of sadness in her chest. She missed the older woman, with her brash sense of humor and unwavering belief in Valentine's talents.

Valentine hoped Loretta hadn't cried too much at the funeral. She wondered if she had even had a funeral, given the strained relationship with her parents. Would her parents bury her in Nashville? Or back home, in northwestern Tennessee?

Her dark thoughts scattered as the clarion sound of a bell rang through her. Valentine winced at the noise, then rubbed her chest. The invisible grip on her sternum was back; the spectral hand squeezed tighter, and she gasped.

"Six, pull over," she said. "We're here."

Without a word, the highway slipped the car off two lane road and turned off the ignition. Church disappeared from the backseat before they had even stopped, only to reappear outside the coupe. Valentine stepped outside and shivered; her thin white blouse with the anatomical heart stitched above her real one would hardly keep her warm in the evening. Likewise, her boots were not fit for hiking. But she knew the Hodag was out there, beyond the short embankment that led off the highway and into the woods.

"Valentine, here." At Six's voice, she looked up. He handed her a lantern, an old-fashioned kind with a translucent bulb with exposed copper wires. "You will need light to see the way."

Valentine led the procession into the woods, her mandolin strapped to her body crosswise, like a bandolier from the old Western films her grandfather used to watch, her lantern held high. She tripped over tree roots, banged into boulders, and caused more than one creature to skitter away in fright. Still, she pressed on.

The Hodag was somewhere up ahead. She could feel the grip on her ribcage pulling her forward.

At last, Valentine froze in mid-step. The lantern wavered in her hand.

She had heard something.

She crouched down and turned off the lantern. Six followed suit and without the light, the darkness seemed to rush in like a tidal wave of blue-black ink. She crept around the brush, squinting forward.

There.

In the faint starlight, a half-moon shone down on a small pond. Beyond the pond, the earth gaped open, a pitch-black maw darker than the surrounding forest, with boulders for fangs.

A cave.

The Hodag lived there, Valentine knew. She started forward, leaving the lantern off. Valentine walked around the pond and up to the cave entrance. She settled the lantern onto the ground and off to the side.

The earth moved under her feet.

Valentine froze.

The rumble came again.

The Hodag was coming.

Chapter Twelve

Valentine settled the mandolin against her body. She had tuned the little mandolin in the convertible, but she ran shaking hands over the instrument to make sure everything was in place, was right. She hoped this would work. She didn't want to be eaten.

A dull roar echoed up from the cave and through the forest.

He had arrived.

Valentine began to play the mandolin.

She chose sweet lullabies and soft songs a mother would sing to her child before bedtime. She sang old hymns about the peaceful hereafter, the ones she heard in Sunday School as a child. She sang songs about seeking respite from life's suffering. Valentine sang and played each song in threes, repeating the verses, the bridges, and the refrains so the strength of the lyrics and the melody wove together like a tapestry – or a net.

At the first song, the Hodag roared again, causing rocks and a pine tree to tumble down from the top of the cave entrance. Valentine flinched at the commotion but kept playing, chasing the chords in dogged determination. She couldn't stop. She knew that. If she stopped, the Hodag would consume her – and Valentine didn't know if she could survive that.

So, she played and sang and played and sang.

She played into the night. After the third hour, her fingers bled from overuse, the tips raw and then cracked, seeping red drops dyed black in the half moonlight. The blood caused her hands to slip against the frets and the body more than once, and she struggled to recover each time, to continue the melody and the magic uninterrupted. Still, she played.

The Hodag grumbled from the cave. More rocks tumbled from the entrance to roll to her feet.

Sweat gathered upon her brow and dripped down her face before seeping into her shirt below. Her hands and arms trembled from exhaustion and more sweat gathered there, chilling her in the darkest of night.

Still, she played.

From within the cave, the Hodag shifted – but did not emerge. No further rocks rolled.

Finally, the pain and the cold and the fear caused tears to slip down her face, the steady rivulets of emotion for which she barely had the names. Her heartbeat in tune with the melodies. Valentine sobbed out the lyrics, gasping for breath and fortitude. She felt drunk and delirious and ecstatic. There was no separation between her and the music. The melody was her body, the lyrics her skin.

Finally, dawn emerged over the eastern edge of the forest. The gold and pink color chased the fading lavender of the night, and in the middle of a hymn about an old churchyard, Valentine *knew*.

She had won.

Valentine played the final song a third time.

Then she slumped to the ground, weary. The music had held her up, seen her through the night. Without it, she slid to the ground and wept from fatigue, taking care to hold the mandolin in gentle, bloody hands to protect it from the forest floor.

She had done it.

The Hodag was contained.

Valentine leaned against the casino's bar, both elbows propping her upright on the gleaming coppertop.

"Want a drink?" Amaretto shook a silver tumbler in one hand. At Valentine's nod, she continued. "Anything in particular?"

"Surprise me."

"Feeling adventurous today." Amaretto grinned. "I like it."

Valentine shrugged. "Sure." She didn't quite care. She just wanted something for the pain. Her fingertips and hands, heavily bandaged, *ached* each time she moved. They hadn't healed this time when she had re-entered the casino. She wondered why.

She hoped it wasn't a bad sign.

"Amaretto Sour, such a delight to see you." Valentine heard Six before she saw. She felt Church lean up against her leg. "Valentine, hold the drink. The gods are ready."

Valentine pushed away from the counter. "Lead on, Mother Road." She nodded farewell to Amaretto.

The corkscrew curls bobbed as Valentine watched the other woman walk away before turning to follow Six across the casino floor. A pang echoed in her chest. When was the last time she had flirted with a girl? Felt a spark of possibility, the rush of connection? It had felt like forever, long before she had died. Valentine hadn't dated much in Nashville. She had worked too much, both at her day jobs and on her music, to go on dates. And while the alternate country music scene had a younger generation, there were still conservative threads that ran through the genre. Valentine hadn't felt comfortable in sharing her sexuality with strangers who stared up at her from the audience, with a white and hot beam of light focused on her. She had hardly pursued her sexuality off the stage. How could she discuss it in her music or with strangers?

Six opened the golden double doors ahead of them. Church glided in before Valentine.

The legends waited for her inside.

"Valentine Cash, you did good." Dale almost sounded gleeful as she rubbed Church's ears. The big black dog's eyes rolled back into his head and his tail thumped against the lush carpet underfoot. "The lullabies were a nice touch."

Valentine gave a half smile. "Thank you."

"I see you declined my advice." Paul Bunyan's wintry words cut through the room.

Valentine knew she had to tread carefully here. She didn't want to anger a legend who already didn't like her. She remembered the last conversation with him. "Well, I'm more familiar with music than dynamite. It seemed better to follow my talents."

Paul sniffed. He seemed... disappointed? Valentine couldn't quite read him. Still, she felt heartened. The legends seemed either impressed, miffed, or indifferent to her containment of the Hodag. Maybe she had a knack for this. Maybe, possibly, she could come through the other side of this with her life and future back. Valentine felt a swell of pride, and much more dangerously, hope.

It was short-lived.

High John de Conqueror stepped forward. "There is no time for celebration. Are you ready to accept your next task?"

Alarm drilled through Valentine. "Yes." She swallowed hard.

"You will slay a chupacabra that is attracting too much attention in South Texas."

Of course. It couldn't be easy, could it? "I accept."

Six growled, then shook his head. Church lifted his head up from Dale's lap. *They are dangerous.*

High John de Conqueror stared at the black dog. "And?"

Never mind. The dog leaned back into the country legend.

"Grim, she agreed to this penance." High John smiled and Valentine shivered. It was not a comforting gesture, full of teeth and anticipation. "A penance is a punishment – and those come with danger and sacrifice."

After leaving the back room in which the gods resided, Valentine wasted no time: She headed straight for the bar. High John's words had chilled her, knocked away the brief and small moment of confidence she had felt earlier.

Amaretto Sour met her across the copper bar top. "Ready for that drink?"

"Yes." Valentine sank onto the stool.

Amaretto returned with a complicated cocktail for Valentine, one she didn't recognize. "What will you have, Mother Road?"

"Whatever you're inspired to make, Amaretto." Six sat next to Valentine.

Valentine sipped the cocktail. The teal drink tasted of sweet nostalgia and bitter truths. "These won't get any easier, will they?" She didn't even know to whom she directed the question. Her shoulders slumped.

Amaretto set the highway's drink before him. "Thank you, Amaretto. You are simply marvelous." Six sipped the cocktail, a smoky grey drink with pink spirals. "Unfortunately, no," he said in response to Valentine's question. He tilted his head. "But you will become more practiced at dealing with hardship. You'll expand on your capacity handle more discomfort and difficulty, if that's any comfort."

"Build capacity to handle more stress and danger?" Valentine snorted. "Yes, that's very comforting."

"This gig isn't about comfort, Valentine Cash."

"The penance, you mean?"

Six shook his head. "None of it. This penance, your real life. Nothing about these journeys pertain to comfort. We are not here to be coddled and handled with care."

"Then why are we here?"

"On this penance? Or in life?"

Valentine met his gaze. "Both, I guess." She hoped the Mother Road had an answer.

Six smiled, and something changed in his eyes. Valentine watched as the usual bright cornflower blue of his gaze darkened into a sea with silver motes across his irises. His pupils seemed to deepen, to stretch into an unfathomable unknown far beyond Valentine's grasp. She shifted on her stool, uneasy. Six had been a comfortable companion and a true champion at times, on her behalf to the gods. When on the road, they had fallen into an easy familiarity that was equal parts of irritation from having to share close quarters with another person and gratitude for having a companion at all.

Valentine forgot that he was a legend.

He was not a man. He was the Mother Road of America, and as such, something beyond her own meager comprehension. To distract herself from her own discomfort, she swigged the rest of her drink.

Six finally responded. "Why are we here? I cannot tell you that. You must solve your own mysteries, Valentine Cash. We all do. That's the privilege and the obligation of our lives."

The dream came back.

It was different this time.

John baked chocolate chip cookies in the cozy kitchen that Emma had decorated in navy and gold colors. Flour dusted every possible surface. Cartons and bags of baking powder and salt and sugar were scattered across the countertops. A few chocolate chips littered the floor. Whenever John scolded Emma for swiping a few chips, she just giggled at his mock outrage.

"Are we having cookies for dinner then?" Emma asked, her voice rich with amusement and some resignation.

John pulled out a rack of cookies from the oven. The smell of warm chocolate and vanilla wafted over to Valentine, and her mouth watered. "Do you want me to pop in some chicken nuggets?"

Emma sighed. "We should have some kind of vegetable, right?"

"Sure." John grinned at her. "But vegetables always can wait until tomorrow."

"Fine." Emma chuckled. She began wiping down the counters and placing the baking supplies back into the cupboards. She shook her head at the mess. "You are a menace in the kitchen," she said. But her warm smile took the sting out of her words.

"Oh, you love it. You know you do." John slipped an arm around her waist and pulled her close, giving her a light kiss.

"I do." Emma leaned into the embrace. They rested together in the center of the kitchen, still for a moment. They seemed to draw sustenance and energy from one another, Valentine saw, like batteries charging. She looked away after a moment. It was too intimate, too soft.

"Get your proposal done?" John's words drew her attention.

Emma nodded against his chest. "Yes. This was a difficult one, but I think it will be worth it. Thank you for dinner."

John smiled against her hair. "Any time."

Emma pulled back. "Don't you need to run to the restaurant supply store? For the bakery?"

John nodded. "Yeah, I can fit that in tomorrow morning. I just need a few things — pans, muffin liners. The usual."

Emma glanced at the refrigerator, and following her gaze, Valentine saw a calendar. The month was heavily inked in appointments, events, and other details. "What do we have going on this week?"

John gave a short laugh. "A lot."

Emma sighed. "We need a vacation."

"It won't always be like this." John pulled Emma closer. "We'll find some peace and quiet soon."

Valentine turned away, guilt and shame and grief suffusing her.

She couldn't bear to watch them anymore.

It hurt too much.

Chapter Thirteen

Six had used another shortcut from the casino.

This time, they had stepped through a supply closet in the casino and emerged into a closed stacks section of a small public library. Outside, the car awaited them. It was a black convertible this time, and the gleaming dark chrome sparkled under the bright sunlight outside the library they had just left.

"Hey," Valentine said.

Six glanced over, a question on his face.

"I'll drive," Valentine offered. "If you want."

Six smiled, then tossed her the keys.

Valentine grinned, feeling a lightheartedness that chased away some of the blues that persisted from the dream. "So where are we going?" She slid into the driver's seat, and Church promptly appeared in the backseat.

"San Antonio." Six buckled in. "Chupacabras prefer warm climates."

"How will we find it?" Valentine asked. "What are we looking for?"

"Dead, mutilated goats."

Valentine stilled. "Ew."

Six nodded. "Exactly."

The small library had been in western Texas, so Valentine followed the highways that edged the U.S. and Mexico border. The land was dry and flat, and as Valentine drove, she weaved between desert and plains. Valentine wondered where John and Emma had lived. Did they live in Tennessee? Or had they finally found time for a vacation – only to die on that awful evening? Valentine tried to shake off the remnants of the dream but the sweet image of John and Emma in the disastrous kitchen, cocooned by the smell of cookies and the warmth of their affection for one another, stayed with her, haunted her.

The guilt felt like a boulder on her chest, heavy and immovable.

She tried to distract herself with the otherworldly radio stations that came through in the black convertible. Some of the music she couldn't listen to; the sound made blood trickle from her ears and nose before Valentine realized what had happened. Six had quickly reached over to change the channel. One station blared music that made Valentine want to strip off her clothes and dance naked through the desert until she dropped. The music wound her up, a toxic combination of feral delirium and delighted fury, and bade her to eschew her own identity to become part of the music itself.

Six had changed that channel, too, an irritated sigh on his lips. "Bacchanals are overrated," he had muttered.

Finally, Valentine found a station she could listen to without blood loss or going feral. The music felt *old*, the melody driven by percussion that sounded like the earth's heartbeat. The vocals were not human but still felt universal somehow. Valentine felt as if she had heard this tune in the back of her mind all her life and hadn't realized it until now.

She asked Six. "Who is this?"

Six peered up from the novel he read. *Dharma Bums*, Valentine saw. "Hmm?"

"This music. Who is this?"

Six listened for a moment. "Southern Russian witches, I think."

"Oh."

"If I'm remembering right, they are connected to Baba Yaga. Different iterations or something similar. Why do you ask?"

Valentine shrugged. "I like the music. I feel like I've heard it before but I'm not sure how that's possible."

"Music is its own kind of magic," Six said. "You saw that with the Hodag and when you repaired Pecos Bill's lariat. It's possible you've tapped into something in your mortal life without knowing it." Six studied her for a moment. "When did you start playing music?"

Valentine remembered precisely the first time she played in front of an audience: She was twelve, with her first mandolin (a used rental from the local shop) clutched in her arms. Part of a small ensemble that played old country songs at the local fair, the crowd had consisted mostly of family members and supportive locals, with polite applause and a few raucous shouts. They stood on a humble stage, dressed in country dressed that dripped with fringe and rhinestones, only three steps off the ground. The day had been hot, with the humidity like a damp blanket that had been laid over the fairgrounds. The awning had barely offered respite from the miserable weather.

Valentine remembered that the ensemble played four songs, growing more confident as each they segued from one song to another. But when the last song arrived, the oldest girl, who had volunteered for the solo, froze in fright. She quaked in place, eyes darting to and fro, immobile despite the hissed urging from the others. Valentine had stepped forward and began playing. She had practiced the solo before the county fair, had in fact practiced all the songs many times over, but hadn't volunteered for the solo because the oldest girl already had.

As Valentine played in front of the small audience, something shifted inside her chest, like a key finding its lock. As the sound of the sweet mandolin rose and floated out to the crowd, new knowledge had tumbled into place. She felt a connection with the other people in the room.

Valentine had always struggled to make friends at school. Even her parents felt like polite strangers on most days. But when she played on that afternoon for the crowd of strangers, she felt as though she finally found a way to talk with people. To connect with them. Words alone hadn't ever worked for her; she was bad at small talk and conversation. But the music — she could tell that they responded to the music. It seemed as though they knew what she was trying to say on that humid afternoon, surrounded by carnival rides, fair food stands, and livestock exhibitions, all only a few feet away. *We are connected. We are alive.*

Valentine stared out at the road that stretched out in front of her. "Twelve," she finally answered. "At a local fair in my hometown." She didn't look at Six as she spoke.

He didn't speak for a moment. Then, "You'll want to merge onto this next highway in a few hundred feet."

Valentine nodded and flicked on the turn signal.

They continued the journey in silence.

They arrived in San Antonio early the next morning. Six had urged Valentine to find a hotel and get some rest. Chupacabras were nocturnal; they would go hunting later in the day. She hadn't argued but slept poorly throughout the day, having tossed and turned in the heat. The day's bright light that had managed to seep through the dark fabric of the hotel curtains. The poor AC window unit had done little to cool the hotel room.

That night, they were in another diner.

"Are we looking for goat farms?" Valentine asked as the waiter set down a plate of food in front of her.

"That's the most likely locale," Six agreed.

Valentine placed a cell phone on the booth table. Six had picked one up on the way to San Antonio. "According to this, there are seven farms in the area – and that doesn't include the farmers who happen to have goats. Any advice on how to narrow the field down?"

Six emerged from the Hearty Farmer's Plate, fork in mid-air. "What kind of goats do these farms have? Chupacabras have a few favorites. Also, where have there been reports of livestock mutilations?"

"Nubians, Lamancha, Angora, Kiko..." Valentine trailed off, staring at the screen. "I didn't know goats were so... specialized. They're goats."

"Let's start with Nubians and Lamanchas," Six said. He cut into his country fried steak. Thick gravy dripped and spilled across the plate. "You grew up on a farm, right? You should know better."

Valentine shook her head before scrolling through the phone again. "My parents grew vegetables and raised chickens," she answered. "I don't see any reports of mutilations."

"Check the police blotter."

Valentine conducted another search. "Okay, here we go. A Nigerian dwarf goat farm reported the unusual – no further details – death of twelve goats." She shook her head, uneasy. "Twelve? That's...a lot."

Six nodded. "Chupacabras aren't known for restraint."

Church rumbled from beneath the table. *No wonder the gods sent you to stop this one. That is too unusual. The mortals will get suspicious.*

"Do we start there?" Valentine asked.

No. Church's answer was quick and definite.

Valentine peered under the table, met the black dog's glowing milk white gaze. "Why not?"

The chupacabra won't revisit the same place so soon. It has some self-preservation instincts, after all.

"Okay, a different farm then. Any advice where? And when do we start?"

"Let's try the Nubians. And after dinner." Six took an enormous bite of a biscuit.

Valentine sighed, then swiped a biscuit to sneak to Church. *This will take a while.*

The first farm specialized in Nubians, and was located about twenty miles outside of San Antonio. Valentine and Six drove by the entrance, then parked down the road and next to some brush to help disguise the car. Twilight had come, with the sunset a lavender and blood pink affair that sprawled across the western edge of the sky. Valentine pulled two high powered flashlights from the trunk; she had purchased them at a sporting goods store after dinner. They were easier to carry than a lantern.

Six grimaced but accepted his. "These lack drama and atmosphere," he muttered.

Valentine rolled her eyes, then focused on the farm. The lights were on within a large two-story home and within the windows she saw the silhouettes of people walking through the home. Two long barns ran parallel behind the home, the red and white colored a black and grey in the moonless night.

Valentine climbed over the chest high fence, then crouched low to jog forward. She kept to the shadows as best she could, hearing Six and Church on her heels. They reached the first barn and stepped inside. The smells of damp, hay, and animals swamped over her and she almost coughed. She peered into the enclosures as she walked down the aisle. Curious gazes stared back, and several of the braver goats came forward, likely seeking food or affection.

None of them seemed scared or injured.

Valentine, Six, and Church checked the other barn and found the same thing. They then walked around the edges of the farm, looking and listening for some kind of sign. A sudden thought occurred to Valentine.

"Church, can you smell these creatures?"

Yes.

Irritation and relief echoed through Valentine. *Why hadn't he said anything?* "Well, do you smell anything?"

No.

Valentine gave an irritated sigh. "Then let's go. We'll check out the others, see if we can find anything."

They struck out on the second, third, and fourth farms. The string of failures left Valentine irate and fatigued. Her clothes were dirty, her boots and pants were smeared with mud and other substances she didn't want to contemplate. She had lost her hat at either the third or fourth farm but couldn't remember. She was so tired, and all of the farms were so similar in the nighttime: Barns, goats, and hay. By the time they had reached the fifth farm, a small operation sixty miles southwest of San Antonio, dawn threatened in the eastern edge of the sky. Valentine parked the car at a nearby rest area, and they then hiked the remaining distance to the farm.

Close to the farm, Church stiffened, then lowered his head.

Valentine paused. "What is it?"

Church sniffed again, scenting the air. *It's here.* A deep growl punctuated his words.

Goosebumps rippled across her skin. "Do you know where?"

"It's close," Six answered in her ear, causing Valentine to jump. "You need to find a weapon. Or something. *Fast.*"

Valentine swept a wild glance around her. *What could she use? To defend herself from a chupacabra? Why hadn't she planned this better?* She saw a small shed next to the family home and started forward. She listened carefully as she started forward, not knowing what she sought but trying to be prepared. She heaved a sigh of relief when she saw that the shed didn't have a padlock and pulled open the door. When she peered inside, she flinched. In the darkness, the shed was something out of a horror film: Garden and farm tools hung from the ceiling and along the walls, the worn wooden handles over sharp metal that gleamed in the beam of her flashlight.

She reached for a short scythe, unhooked it from the wall.

"Church, where —"

A faint scream cut her off.

Valentine's head reared up. "What was that?"

The chupacabra. Church lunged and ran forward in ground-eating strides. Valentine and Six followed, past the shed and around a barn. Valentine slid to a sudden halt, and Six crashed into her, pitching her forward a few more steps.

"Oh god."

Valentine had never seen anything like this creature before. The furred monster paced forward with clawed feet, rippling with muscle and spattered with gore and viscera. A snake tongue emerged from its mouth and a pair of horns curled up from the crown of its head. The chupacabra stepped into the remains of several goats — how many Valentine couldn't tell — and then past them. A low sound, a combination of a hiss and a growl, emerged.

"Oh, no."

Valentine dropped the flashlight and gripped the short scythe with both hands. *I should have grabbed the pitchfork. Then I wouldn't have to get so close.* Nausea tickled the back of her throat and sweat seeped down her face. *Don't vomit. Focus.*

Six gave a sudden shout. Then the chupacabra was on Valentine, taloned paws grasping at her throat. She swung the scythe but couldn't get a good angle because the creature remained too close. Still, she managed a scratch and when the creature leapt back to growl at her, she lunged forward to land a deeper cut. The chupacabra howled at this new injury and lashed out. Valentine felt her chest open, then begin to burn with blood and pain. She choked out a moan, the pain sudden and shocking.

The chupacabra started forward. Valentine swung the scythe again and again, despite the pain. *Don't let him close.* She swung again. The creature grabbed the scythe in its maw, then wrenched it out of her hands. Valentine fell back, stumbling in her haste to get away. She cast a frantic look around, seeking something — anything — that would defeat the chupacabra. *There.* A shovel leaned up against the barn wall, the metal a dull matte in the dim light of dawn.

Valentine lunged forward to grasp the shovel. The creature followed, and Valentine screamed when she felt the talons slice across her back, tearing cloth and skin. Her hands landed on the handle of the shovel, and she whirled around, sending the spade in a quick arc for the creature's head. *Smack.* The impact jolted her hands and arms, but Valentine tightened her grip and started forward. The creature had stumbled back, roaring. The spade cut a diagonal welt across its face, and blood sprayed from the wound. She felt wetness on her face and could smell rotting sewage. She gagged.

Valentine swung again. The spade cut into the shoulder.

And again. This time, the creature's head.

Valentine swung and jabbed and beat down with the shovel. She kept on the creature, not pausing in her attack, not giving it time to recover. It howled and hissed and tried to dodge the sharp edges of the shovel, but Valentine didn't let up. Valentine saw an opening and gave a final lunge, her shovel aimed like a spear. The dual blades of the spade cut through the tender belly with a squelch, the sound and the feel abhorrent. Valentine continued forward until the blade pierced the back of the chupacabra.

The creature howled with rage and pain. It swiped at Valentine, too fast for her to dodge, and she felt the flesh open across her face.

She ducked under the talons to push the creature to the ground. When it fell, Valentine darted over to the discarded scythe. Returning to the chupacabra, she trapped one arm to the ground with her foot, then bent low to cut its throat. She sawed, the odd shape of the blade forcing her to work harder. Finally, she felt the spine of the creature against the scythe.

Enough. The Grim's voice rattled her focus.

"Valentine, enough!" She heard a shout and found Six before her, horror and concern and disgust wrapped on his face like a shroud. "Valentine, it's dead. Enough." Six glanced over to the farmhouse. Valentine followed his gaze and saw that a light had come on inside the home. A screen door banged open, and Valentine could hear a rifle being cocked even from that distance. "Valentine, we must go. *Now.*"

Valentine was half dragged, half carried back to the hidden car. Six led them in a punishing lope and Valentine sobbed with every step, the pain immense each time she moved. Blood, viscera, and sweat had matted her hair, and glued her clothes to her damaged body. Six's clothes were in a similar disarray, with blood splatter and dirt on his three-piece suit. His shoes were the worst: Torn leather dragged behind each staggered step.

Six deposited Valentine into the passenger's seat. She moaned as her open wounds hit the leather bench seat, then gritted her teeth. Everything hurt. She smelled awful. She was sticky. And she had killed that creature. But what most horrified her was her own violence.

What was the point of this task?

What am I becoming?

Is this worth it?

That was her last coherent thought.

Chapter Fourteen

Valentine woke with a cool, wet cloth on her face. She reached up to adjust the cloth to cover more of her face.

That was a mistake.

Pain burned along her face and down her body. Every movement seemed to amplify the pain, and Valentine gasped, tears smarting in her eyes.

Damn.

"Valentine, don't move just yet." She heard Six walk across the room to her bedside. "You need to let yourself heal."

Valentine cracked open her eyes. Six had stripped down to a button up shirt, sleeves rolled up his forearms, and trousers. He stood in socks, and she stared. She wasn't sure she had ever seen him so...undressed.

Valentine cleared her throat, then winced at the new wave of pain. "The chupacabra?" That was all she could manage.

"The creature is dead." A new note, something like wariness, entered Six's voice. "You did a most thorough job."

Valentine slumped on the bed in relief. She hadn't realized that she had been so tense. "But it's done? I did it? Completed the task?"

"I assume so. The legends are the final arbiters, though."

Valentine curled into herself. She was so tired. She didn't want to move, maybe ever again. "When do we have to go?"

"Go back to the casino?" Six asked.

"Or wherever." Valentine closed her eyes. *So tired.*

"We can stay here another day, which is for the best. You need to heal, to rest for the next task."

"There's another one?" Valentine couldn't prevent the whimper in her voice. *When would this end?*

Six sighed. "There are several more, if I'm not mistaken. You still have a long road ahead of you. These legends do not make easy bargains."

"I'm worried that I'm turning into a monster," Valentine confessed into her pillow.

After a moment, Six spoke. "Rest, Valentine Cash."

It was dark the next time Valentine woke.

She came to consciousness with a jolt, her eyes sandy and her breath rapid. Had she had a bad dream? What had awakened her? She didn't know. In a careful motion, she turned her head to one side to scan the room. When that movement didn't result in debilitating pain, she rolled herself to her side as gently as she could. She winced. The pain was still there, but muted. Valentine gave a sigh of relief.

She recognized the midrange hotel chain they stayed in, the two full beds with a dresser, a desk, and two chairs. Generic landscape portraits, a stormy sea and another at rest, stood above each bed.

Six emerged from the bathroom, dressed again in one of his usual suits. He adjusted a cufflink before meeting her gaze. An odd expression flashed across his face before concern settled in. "How do you feel?"

"Better." Valentine pushed herself upright, to a sitting position on the edge of the bed. She winced. The mattress was too firm.

"I'm relieved to hear that." Six settled across from her, on the opposite bed.

Valentine took inventory of her body. Her clothes were fresh and clean. She examined her hands and arms, seeing that the sliced flesh sealed. The wounds appeared several weeks old rather than a mere day. She touched her face and felt the taut edges of the cut. Again, closed. "How long was I out?"

"Sixteen hours or so." Six handed a pair of socks to Valentine. "I gave you something extra to heal your wounds more quickly. You can't go onto the next task wounded." He shook his head. "I'm not sure even the casino would have healed you sufficiently."

Valentine felt across her face, her fingers seeking the edges of the scar. "Is this permanent?"

"I'm not sure." Six's shoulders sank. "I'm sorry, kid."

Valentine gave a nod, then rubbed at her damp eyes.

"I received a missive from the gods," Six said. He pulled a note off the end table between the beds and handed it to Valentine. "Instructions for your next task."

Valentine accepted the piece of paper. "We're not going back to the casino?"

"No."

Valentine scanned the note, written in an elegant script on a heavyweight mauve paper.

Greetings Valentine Cash,

We recognize your defeat of the chupacabra. You have fulfilled the requirements of the task we set before you. Your next task is to defeat or banish the Bell Witch. You have one week.

Gold symbols in lieu of signatures lined the bottom of the parchment: An acoustic guitar, an axe, and a morning glory.

Valentine felt her stomach rise and then bottom out like she was on a roller coaster ride. She blinked up at Six. "The Bell Witch? Are we talking about *the* Bell Witch?"

Six had shadows in his eyes; his lips were twisted in worry. "I'm afraid so."

Valentine shuddered, then wrapped her arms around herself. She had grown up on stories of the Bell Witch in Tennessee. Mothers used to scold their children into good behavior with threats of the Bell Witch. A headache began to pulse behind her eyes. "How do I defeat a ghost?"

"Banishing a typical ghost is easier than most people think," Six replied, his voice apologetic. "But the Bell Witch will *not* be easy. She is an entity in another category entirely."

"Of course she is." Valentine rested her head in her hands. "When do we go?"

"Today."

Six ignored Valentine's offers to drive on the way to Tennessee when they left the hotel.

"You need to heal." His voice was firm.

Privately, Valentine was grateful. Her body ached with pulses of pain; headaches came and went, unpredictable and irritating. Six forced a tea on her at every meal, a noxious packet of herbs and flower petals. It seemed to speed her healing and help her scars. They were now only faint white lines across her body and face, rather than angry red and pink slashes. By the time she reached Tennessee, Valentine almost felt like her old self, only feeling the flickers of pain if she moved too quickly.

At the border of Tennessee and Mississippi, Six drove them off the highway and into a small town Valentine had never heard of.

"Where are we going?"

Six spared a glance at Valentine, a grim countenance on his face. "As your resident advisor and wayfinder, I advise you to seek out a banishment spell from a witch or root worker."

Valentine caught his meaning quickly. "Then who are we meeting?"

"An acquaintance." Six paused as he slowed to turn left onto a street. "Do you have anything to offer? As payment?"

"Like money?" Even as she spoke, dread pooled in her gut. Valentine knew money wasn't the currency Six referred to. It wouldn't be that simple. Not in this world.

"No. Like your firstborn. Or your hair." Six peered at Valentine again. "Well, maybe not your hair."

Valentine fingered her still shorn locks. Her hair hadn't grown since she had cut the blond lengths to repair Bill's lariat. "I'm not sure. I don't want children, but I won't give away a kid to a witch. I couldn't live with that." She shook her head and anxiety chafed at her insides. "I only know how to play music, Six. I'm not very useful."

"Hmm. Well, you'll have to think fast. We're here."

Here was a ranch style home in a suburban neighborhood. The house was blue with white trim and shutters. A cobblestone driveway led up to the house, edged by a manicured lawn. Rose bushes of every color lined the front of the house. The home seemed normal, with an ordinary beauty.

"Here? This is where the witch lives?"

"A witch, yes." Six stepped out of the car.

Valentine followed, closing the car door with a quiet thump. "But *here*? It's so...normal."

"Has nothing you've seen on this journey conveyed to you that appearances are deceptive, Valentine Cash?" Six shook his head as he walked up to the house. "You look like a good wind would knock you over. Yet you are one of the bravest and most resourceful mortals I have ever met." Six knocked on the front door and turned back to Valentine. "Don't operate on assumptions."

Valentine had no time to process Six's complimentary words. The door swung open, and a trim, petite blonde woman smiled at Six. "Mother Road, welcome. I'm humbled by your visit. Come in, please." Her warm drawl was pure South.

"Betty, it is delightful to see you. I hope all is well?"

Valentine followed Six and Betty further into the home and listened as they made small talk. The open concept home, dressed in whites, greys, and beiges, was something out of a magazine or a home renovation show. Betty settled onto a large sectional, leaned closed to a coffee table, and poured iced tea from a pitcher beaded in icy droplets.

"What brings you this far east, Mother Road? Your highway lies west." Betty sipped her tea, her eyes sharp as she took in Valentine, who sat next to Six.

"Betty, let me introduce you to Valentine Cash," Six said. "She is on a penance. I'm her guide."

Betty winced at the word *penance*. "That's a hard road to walk, no doubt about it. I wish you good fortune and blessings, Valentine Cash."

"Thank you," Valentine said.

"Valentine needs a banishment spell."

Betty's eyebrows flew up. "Oh? Can you share the identity of the deceased?"

Six shot Valentine a warning glance. *Don't say anything.* "I'm afraid not."

Betty shook her head. "That makes my job harder, Mother Road."

"I realize that. Can you help us?"

"Of course." Betty turned to Valentine. "Now what are you offering?"

"Uh, what is the usual price?" Valentine countered.

"Hair, teeth, bones, fertility." Betty shrugged. "I'm flexible – but not cheap."

Valentine fingered her shorn hair again and thought for a moment. "I have wisdom teeth," she offered. "Four of them. I'd have to go to the dentist to get them out, though."

Betty let out a tinkling laugh. "Oh, Mother Road, she is *adorable*."

Six gave a pained smile. "Is that an acceptable payment, Betty?"

"Yes." Betty turned back to Valentine with a gentle smile. "Hold on. This *will* hurt."

Pain ripped through her mouth.

Valentine fell forward, off the couch and onto the carpeted floor. Black floated along the edges of her vision as blood dribbled from her mouth, staining the wheat-colored carpet beneath her. *What the hell?*

Valentine must not have been unconscious for long.

She woke to Betty crouched over her. She flinched away but Betty ignored her. Turning her head, Valentine watched Betty set a stain remover into the beige carpet and begin scrubbing. The other woman muttered to herself as she scoured the carpet, her words too low for Valentine to understand.

Six helped her upright and back onto the couch. "Are you okay?"

Valentine tried to speak around a mouthful of blood but couldn't. She took several hard swallows, grimacing at the metallic flavor and the disgusting texture of her own blood. Finally, she could speak without dribbling blood. "Yeah," she croaked.

Betty stood up. "I'm going to let that set and do its job." It took Valentine a moment to realize that Betty referred to the stain remover. "Now you two wait here. I'll be back in a jiffy with your spell." The woman walked down a hallway and into another room. Family portraits (Betty apparently had a husband and three children), neutral landscapes, and floral paintings held up the walls of the room. A fresh bouquet of flowers rested on the whitewashed brick mantel of the fireplace. A discreet dog bed rested in the far corner of the room.

"Still think she's normal?" Six muttered. He seemed nervous, jumpy.

Valentine massaged her jaw. "I need some painkillers."

"We'll get you some on the road." Six flinched at a child's shriek of joy from the backyard.

"What's wrong with you?"

Six shook his head. "I'll tell you later," he muttered.

"Here we are!" Betty returned to the living room. Her cheerful voice and beaming smile reminded Valentine of PTA meetings and slumber parties. Betty handed a small leather pouch to Valentine, who accepted it with a ginger grip. Valentine could smell salt and something darker, earthier. She shivered. She didn't want to look inside.

Six stood. "We'll take our leave, Betty. Thank you for your wonderful and prompt work."

"A good journey to you, Mother Road and Valentine Cash." Betty paused as though a sudden thought occurred to her. "You know what? I have some freshly baked cookies – oatmeal cranberry. I'll put some in a container for you, to take on the road."

"Oh, you don't—" Six began to protest.

Betty waved away his concern. "It won't take but a minute. Hold on." She rounded the kitchen island and began packing a few cookies into a bag. Valentine looked from Betty to Six and back again. *What was even happening?*

Betty bustled back to them. "Here you go. I'll walk you to the door." She beamed at them again.

Valentine stood up, the pouch with its dearly purchased contents clutched tightly in her hands. She was more than ready to leave.

Chapter Fifteen

Six didn't speak until they were back on the highway and only then when Valentine prompted him.

"What is that woman?" Valentine asked.

Six shook his head. "It's almost better you don't know," he muttered. "The things you have to do to become that powerful, as a mortal?" He shook his head again. "She always gave me the shivers."

Valentine frowned. "Then why go to her?"

"Because we need every possible advantage over the Bell Witch."

"Why didn't you tell Betty about the Bell Witch?"

"Because Betty wouldn't have made the spell for us." Six sighed. "Many witches and root workers won't engage with that entity. I only hope Betty doesn't find out after the fact. I don't want a curse chasing us."

"Is that a thing?" Valentine swallowed hard, staring out the front window of the car. "Curses that follow you?"

"Oh, yes." She had never heard Six sound so grim before.

Great. Valentine sighed. *Just wonderful.*

They made good time to Adams, Tennessee. Well before Six drove over the county line, Valentine saw billboards advertising the Bell Witch Cave and Cabin. Shops and restaurants had Bell Witch wares, and brown historical markers referenced the Bell Witch often. With each new sign, trepidation grew within Valentine. She had heard stories about the Bell Witch as a child, in her hometown. Every campfire she'd attended, every slumber party her parents made her participate in, had a Bell Witch story. The Witch was named Kate, and she had pinched and punished John Bell and his daughter. The lore had it that Kate had poisoned John Bell, who died in 1820. Valentine clutched the pouch she had purchased from Betty. What could she do against such a creature? What were the gods thinking? And would the Bell Witch even show up?

Valentine stared out the window as they drove down Route 41. The familiar landscape tugged at her, reminded her of the times she had snuck away from chores to play the guitar or the mandolin behind the barn. Of the twilit evenings filled with lightning bugs that blinked on and off like a drained battery. From the comfort of the air-conditioned car, she knew the humidity would taste of mold and feel like a damp towel around her body. This land was so different from the flat plains in Texas, the blue and green forests of Wisconsin, the red and gold deserts of the Four Corners region. Valentine wondered what else she would see before all of this – the tasks, the penance – would end. She wondered when the penance would ever end. How much more would she have to endure before she could get her life back? And what about John and Emma? Valentine bit her lip, the guilt a sour taste at the back of her throat.

Would they ever get a second chance?

"We're here."

Six tilted his head forward and Valentine followed Six's gaze. *Welcome to the Bell Witch Cabin and Cave,* an enormous white sign with red ornate letters proclaimed. From the gravel parking lot, a well-maintained cabin rested in the distance on a manicured lawn. Off to the side, an arrow pointed the way to the Bell Witch Cave. In the daylight, the cabin and the well-kept grounds were so... *normal.*

"So now what?" Valentine said. "Will the Bell Witch appear in daylight?"

Six frowned. "I'm not sure but I doubt it."

Valentine glanced back at the sign. "Do you want to take a tour of the cabin and the cave? It's eighteen dollars for the combination."

Six gave a sudden chuckle. "Sure. Why not? Let's play tourist."

The tour left Valentine unimpressed. Clearly a replica based on reports from the original cabin, the interior was dusty and the mannequins creepy. The docent was a local, his drawl as familiar to Valentine as breathing. Clad in a trucker hat and loose denim held up by suspenders, he told several stories that Valentine had heard before and many she hadn't, each one more outlandish than the previous one. The Bell Witch was an active entity, he warned. He had cautioned them early on, "You may feel pricks and pinches. That's just Kate. You tell her to go on and stop it whenever that happens." This was followed by a wink, so Valentine assumed he wasn't worried about an appearance.

Valentine listened to the stories for a clue on how to contain or vanquish the Bell Witch but heard nothing useful. When the docent led them to the cave, she perked up. Maybe she would find an answer here. But her hopes were dashed quickly: The cave was well trod and easy to access. It was almost clean inside despite the dripping damp along the walls. Valentine got the impression that the cave was well-maintained by the tour operators; as a result, the cave felt empty of personality and danger.

At the end of the tours of both the cabin and the cave, Valentine's shoulders sagged in disappointment. She hadn't once felt a stir of recognition, a prickle of awareness, that told her the object of her penance was near. She hadn't felt the icy grip on her sternum, pulling her closer to her quest.

Above the ground again, Six and Valentine wandered, Church at their heels.

"Well, what do you think?" Six asked.

"I think we won't find the Bell Witch here," Valentine said. "It's too open, too many tourists. It doesn't *feel* right." Valentine rubbed her chest. The absence of the icy grip haunted her.

Six nodded. "I'm afraid you're correct."

Valentine studied the copse of trees that lined the property. "Where is the original cabin again?"

Six followed her gaze. "Somewhere in the woods, I heard."

Valentine felt a cold thrill near her sternum. "She'll be there — not in the middle of all this." Valentine waved her hand at the replica cabin and the grounds.

"What next, Valentine Cash?"

"We'll return tonight, after dark." A shiver chased down her spine. Valentine's hand wandered to her pocket, where she had stuffed the pouch from Betty. She hoped it would be enough.

The Bell Witch Cabin and Cave were much more ominous at night, Valentine found.

Valentine and Six had parked the car at a nearby rest area, then hiked through the surrounding corn fields to the cabin. The half-moon gave some light but not enough, and Valentine tripped and stumbled her way through the darkness, cursing under her breath; Six didn't seem to suffer the same fate.

They crept across the maintained lawn and past the replica cabin. They ignored the cave entrance and walked to the edge of the forest. The line of trees ascended like a castle wall in the darkness, thick and forbidding, and Valentine flicked on the flashlight. The forest was even darker than the surrounding night. The thick trunks and gnarled branches obscured the faint moonlight; the flashlight barely lit the way, the tight beam a thin needle of light in the abyss. Valentine picked her way across the ground with care. She didn't come all this way to break her leg through carelessness.

She felt an icy chill in her chest. She was going in the right direction.

Church's sudden growl ripped through the night.

Valentine flinched. Her eyes sought the cause for the growl. Her heart skipped a beat when she found it: A pair of red eyes gleamed in the darkness ahead of them. Valentine could make out the faint outline of a vast black dog, almost as substantial as Church.

Church lunged forward and his growl turned louder, a rumbling sound that broke the silence of the woods. *Begone, unnatural creature.*

The other dog hissed at Church. The red eyes were slitted, thin slices of fresh blood in the blackness.

Maybe it's not a dog. Valentine clenched her fist, trying to manage her fear.

Church's growl deepened; Valentine felt the sound vibrate in her bones. She peered at Church, then blinked. A gasp escaped her. She wasn't seeing things: She could see a ghostly outline of two other heads on Church, one on either side of his neck and all three identical in shape and size. All three heads snarled and snapped at the other dog-creature. As they growled, Church's body grew larger and larger, his ink black body eating more and more into the surrounding darkness.

With a final hiss, the other dog faded into the night, his red eyes the last to fade from sight.

Valentine tightened her grip on the flashlight, then took a deep breath. She watched the other two heads disappear from Church's body as he trotted back to where she and Six stood. "What was that?" she asked.

Better not to ask, came Church's reply. *It's an abomination.* Valentine could hear the disgust in his voice.

Valentine studied Church. She had so many questions but they didn't have the time. *Later. I'll ask later.*

They continued into the woods, listening hard and taking careful steps through the brush and fallen wooden debris. Church swung his head to and from, looking for the next adversary. Valentine stayed close to Six, his presence a comfort. She could hear her heartbeat in her ears. Her breath sounded loud to her ears, too loud for the quiet woods.

Valentine stepped around a massive oak tree – and screamed. She stumbled back, into Six, who caught her before she could fall.

A young woman in a green dress swung from a branch, a noose around her neck. Spanish moss dripped from her hair and clothes, and the light wind rippled through the fabric and greenery. As Valentine stared, the young woman opened her eyes and grinned down at them.

"Hello. Have you come to play?"

Valentine could taste bile in the throat. She pushed away from the scene, slamming into Six. "What do we do?" she muttered, her eyes fixed on the young woman, a child really, who chortled and whispered nonsense nursery rhymes to the wind. "Itsy bitsy spider..."

Six shook his head. In the muted light from the flashlight, his face was grim and sad all at once. "I don't think she can follow us. Let's keep moving."

Valentine nodded, then straightened. She continued forward, giving the girl a wide berth. The young woman's eyes followed Valentine, her grin manic and crazed. Her teeth were stained with a dark substance. Blood or dirt, Valentine couldn't tell. She shivered, then wrapped an arm around her torso. *What* was *this place?*

They hadn't taken more than a few steps before a cacophony unleashed: Several large black birds swooped down and around Valentine and Six, who ducked and raised their hands above their heads to protect their heads. The girl in the green dress wafted in the wind, cackling at the unruly scene before her. "Duck, duck, goose!" she called over and over as she burbled like a brook with unholy giggles. Valentine felt the birds pluck at her clothes, her hair. She yelped when one of the black birds yanked a chunk of her hair from her scalp.

Then the voices started.

Valentine couldn't make sense of what she was hearing for a moment or two – and then felt ice crystallize in her stomach. Her mother and her father spoke to her from the trees, their voices thick with scorn and disappointment. Valentine looked around, trying to find the source of the voices. But they seemed to come from everywhere, all at once. She tried to cover her ears, to repudiate the sound, but still, she could hear them.

"Good for nothing goddamn queer," her father muttered.

"You abandoned us and God, Valentine," her mother said. Valentine could hear the sadness and disappointment in her mother's voice. "And for what? A life of sin?"

"A musician?" Her father snorted, then laughed. It was an awful, demeaning sound. "You'll never make it – no one wants to listen to a queer."

On and on, her parents' voices berated her for being queer, for running away and for abandoning her duties to the farm, for seeking the sinful life of a good-for-nothing musician. Valentine shook her head, tears of frustration in her eyes. Nausea swirled within her stomach and shame warmed her cheeks. She hated hearing her worse fears spoken aloud by her parents.

Then a new voice came.

"You wasted all of our work, kid." It was Loretta, her manager. Her champion and advocate. "Got yourself killed, didn't you? That wasn't very smart."

Valentine shook her head. *Loretta would never say that. She is too kind. She loves me.*

"Shut UP," she bellowed.

The voices went silent.

Valentine heaved a sigh of relief.

But too soon.

New voices started up. Valentine listened, despite knowing better. She frowned, not recognizing them at first. And when she did, a quick sob escaped her.

John's voice came first: "Emma, where are you? Emma!"

"John?! Where are you?" Emma's voice furled through the wind, laden with unshed tears.

Tears slipped down her face, and she crumpled to the ground, curled up with her fists over her ears. *I wish it would stop.* She whimpered as the voices grew louder. Valentine shook her head against the noise, the birds, and the cackling girl who swung from the large oak tree. *What was I thinking? There's no way I can do this.*

A familiar icy grip on her sternum blazed through the noise and the pain.

Valentine gasped at the sensation. *What now?* She shifted on the ground, hoping that if she moved, the icy feeling might go away – and felt the pouch in her pocket, rubbing against her leg. The pouch that the Stepford Witch, Betty, had given her. *It's for the Bell Witch*, Valentine remembered.

Valentine reached into her pocket and yanked out the pouch. She stumbled to her feet, holding the pouch up high. "Enough!"

A sudden silence fell across the clearing.

The birds disappeared. The girl in the green dress swung a final time, then vanished. The voices ebbed away into faint echoes.

Six came to stand by Valentine's side. "Good thinking," he murmured. Valentine noticed tear tracks down the highway's face, smudged with ash or dirt.

"Are you alright?"

Six grimaced. "No."

Valentine looked around. "Where is Church?"

"Banished, I believe."

A new voice with an odd accent came from between two oak trees. "You are correct. I don't like those creatures. Never have."

An old woman with slate grey hair stepped forward. Her eyes were black and bottomless, her skin parchment thin and just as pale. She wore a brown dress with petticoats and an apron. Her hands hung at her side, gnarled from age and hard work. Her lips sneered open and she spoke again.

"What are you doing on my property?"

Valentine held the pouch up higher, uncertain what to do next.

The Bell Witch looked over the pouch, then scoffed. Mirth crinkled the corners of her eyes and her lips split open to reveal stained, yellow teeth. She started to laugh and didn't stop. She laughed and laughed and laughed.

Valentine swallowed hard. Dread and fear twined around her limbs and then crawled up her spine.

"What is *that*, child?" The Bell Witch cast a derisive glance at Valentine. "Am I to quiver in fright? To beg for mercy? All because you sought out a sister to provide you with a banishment spell?" The Bell Witch chuckled. "I think not."

The pouch caught fire, the sudden flames licking and burning Valentine's hand. She screamed, then dropped the pouch on the ground. Valentine backed away, cradling her injured hand against her chest. She could smell the burnt flesh, and the rotten remnants of whatever had been in that pouch. Fear hammered at her. *Now what?* What could she do?

The Bell Witch stepped closer, then stilled. "Is that the Mother Road? My, my. What are you doing so far from home?" Surprise and delighted anticipation wove through her words. Valentine shivered. Would she hurt Six? *Could* she harm him?

"Greetings, Bell Witch." Six nodded to Valentine. "I accompany this one on her penance."

The delight on the Bell Witch's face melted into disgust. "A penance?" she sneered. "How dull. Mortals are such silly, weak creatures, doing anything to cling to their precious life." She sighed, then fixed her attention on Valentine. "What is it, child? What quest have you come to fulfill?"

Valentine swallowed and didn't answer.

"Speak up!" The words cracked like a thunderbolt. Valentine flinched.

"I-I killed someone. On accident," Valentine stammered out.

The Bell Witch sneered. "Accidental murderer, is it? And now you've come to seek an absolution by disturbing me? Foolishness. The gods should have better things to do." The creature spread her arms. "Well, you've found me. What was your task again?"

"To b-banish you." Valentine couldn't stop shivering in the darkness; her teeth rattled together.

The Bell Witch laughed again, the sound like cut glass against skin. "No."

Valentine flew the air and slammed into the trunk of a tree. Pain blazed down her back. She thought she heard something crack. Her breath stuttered out of her, and she gasped, trying to seek air. She started to slide down the trunk but stilled when Spanish moss and vines curled around the trunk and over her body, wrapping her in a tight and unwanted embrace. Valentine struggled and twisted but she didn't budge. The bonds held her tight against the tree trunk and wrapped around her neck, holding her head in place. Valentine flinched as she felt pins and pricks across her entire body. She watched the Bell Witch approach, fear coating her insides.

"You won't defeat me, child. And you will fail your penance." The Bell Witch sneered on the last word, then turned to walk away. After a few paces, she seemed to melt into the trees, to disappear like vapor in the half moonlight.

The vines twisted around Valentine's body, tighter with each loop. Anxiety caused her to gasp for breaths that wouldn't seem to come, and she wondered if this was the end. If this was the night she died a final death.

She had failed.

The gods wouldn't be happy. *Well, Paulie will be.*

Valentine almost snickered but it hurt too much.

The dawn first limned the edges of the treetops. Light filtered through the leaves and dappled the ground beneath; the vines loosened their grip. With a sudden give, Valentine slid to the ground and stumbled forward onto her hands and knees. A rock on the forest floor cut her left knee and Valentine hissed, gritting her teeth.

A pair of feet clad in Oxfords came to stand in front of her. Valentine peered up. Six stood over her, worry creasing the lines of his face.

"Let's get you up, kid." He extended a hand to Valentine.

She accepted the hand. The movement jarred the injury on her back, and she winced as pain lanced through her ribs. "Six, I failed."

"It happens to all of us, I promise."

"But what will happen to me?"

Six didn't respond at first as he led them out of the woods. "That's for the gods to decide," he finally answered.

CHAPTER SIXTEEN

No one saw them as they crept back to the car in the early dawn. Once back in Adams, Six dropped Valentine off at a bar that was improbably open. "I need to make a call. Get something to eat. I'll be back soon." Valentine didn't need to ask who he would call. She knew that he had to report on her failure, if they didn't already know. Then the gods would condemn her to a final death.

After all, she had failed the task before her.

The dim light inside the bar caused Valentine to blink against the darkness a few times. Once her eyes adjusted, she saw an ancient bar top with a few stools nestled underneath and several tables spread throughout the room. A small stage, barely a dais raised a foot off the floor, held a mike and a stool. The smell of old beer, roasted meat, and peanuts enveloped her like an embrace. Valentine relaxed for the first time since leaving the grounds of the Bell Witch.

She had played in places like this as a musician; some had been better, some worse. It felt familiar, like a place she returned to again and again. A home.

"You need anything?"

"A burger and a Coke?" She doubted that they served breakfast here.

"Sure thing. Sit where you like."

The bar was empty. "Okay."

Valentine chose the table closest to the stage. She recognized the microphone brand; decent but not one of her preferred ones. She saw three guitars hanging along the hallway, signatures scrawled on the body. She recognized a few of the names, local and regional musical legends in her old life, having seen them from a distance on the circuit. She usually played the opener's opener, so she had never really had contact with the bigger folks.

"You play?" The barkeep arrived with her burger.

Valentine nodded.

"Play if you want to. If you're terrible, you gotta stop when other customers come in."

Valentine cracked a grin and regretted it when her chapped bottom lip split open. "Okay."

Valentine didn't feel like eating but knew she should. She didn't want to face her final death on an empty stomach. The burger was fine; the soda unexceptionable. After she finished, Valentine sat back in her chair. She eyed the stage. *Maybe I should play something*, Valentine thought. *Just in case it's the last time.* Valentine stood up, then walked over to step up onto the stage. She chose one of the guitars, handled it for a moment, and then hung it back on the wall. Valentine selected a second. She preferred the weight, size, and feel of this one. She tuned the old instrument as she sat on the stool, the worn wood surface a testament to frequent use over the years. Valentine plugged the guitar into a small amp at her feet, then flipped on the mike. Static rippled through the small room. A fragile joy uncurled inside her.

And Valentine began to play.

She started with her favorites first, old traditional ballads that were the direct ancestors to the music she wrote. Valentine sang in a soft voice, then louder as the familiar melodies and rhythms wrapped around her like a child's favorite blanket. She moved onto the blues and gospel songs she loved. In mid-tune of one song, Valentine had started in shock when she realized that she was playing a song written by Dale Wright. *I wonder if she knows. If she can hear me now.* Valentine continued to play, wandering from the King to the Outlaws from the 70s country scene. Johnny Cash featured heavily, as did Willie Nelson. Valentine's fingers wandered away from them and into contemporary alternate country, the Steve Earles and the Neko Case tunes.

Finally, she played her own work.

She paused to re-tune the old guitar. But the sweet, mellow sound that emerged was worth it and a good match for her soprano-contralto range. Her fingers flew over the strings as she played what she privately referred to as her angry songs first. The words and the diction were harsh, the attitude within two middle fingers extended at the world. The anger faded and a yearning stole over her. Valentine switched to a song she wrote after she had realized she was queer – and then realized she couldn't tell anyone, especially not her parents.

Valentine's last song wasn't quite a complete tune. Not yet. She had heard tendrils and faint echoes of the song in the back of her head around the third task during the penance but hadn't had time to chase down the melody, to solidify the lyrics. She did that now. She listened, her head tilted, as she strummed a series of chords, then backed up to replace a few notes with new ones. She played again and again, her tongue chasing and tripping over different words. At last, she thought she might have it. Valentine played it through, her voice gaining strength and emotional depth by the second chorus. She sailed into the bridge of the song and away into the sunset of the finish, satisfied and relieved that she had captured it.

An applause interrupted her absorption. Valentine blinked, then gazed around. Six and Church sat at the table closest to the stage but the bar behind them had filled up. Looking over the crowd, Valentine recognized no one. Nonetheless, they all felt familiar to her. She had seen these folks at her shows, had grown up alongside them. Even though they were strangers, she knew them.

Valentine stood. "Uh, thank you. That's it for today."

"Free Bird," a man hollered out. A scattered chuckle swept the small room.

Valentine rolled her eyes. She switched off the mike before she sighed. *There's always that one.* She stepped off the stage, waving away the applause. Sitting next to Church, she reached out to rub his ears. She finally glanced at Six, her heartbeat in her ears and fear like a vise around her throat.

"Well?" she asked.

Six reached across the table. "They have decided that you will continue onto your other tasks."

Relief washed through her like cold water on a hot day. "What? But why? I failed. Badly." Valentine didn't understand.

Six shook his head. "Apparently, they didn't expect you to truly succeed against the Bell Witch." Bitterness had seeped into his tone; he seemed to choose his words carefully. "She's almost a god herself, given her strength. Paul Bunyan insisted that you try, though."

Valentine sagged against her chair. She knew she should feel joy. But after the relief passed, she just felt numb. She shook her head. "I'm not going to die? For now, I mean," she amended.

A relieved smile bloomed across Six's face. "No. You won't die today, Valentine Cash."

Valentine studied Six for a moment. "You were worried."

Six leaned back in his chair, then straightened his shirt cuffs. He avoided eye contact when his gaze swept the bar. "Weren't you?"

"Of course, I was. I was terrified." Valentine rubbed Church's ears once more. The black dog let out a rumble of pleasure and leaned against Valentine, heavy yet comforting. "This seems too... easy. Why did they make an exception? Paul hates me. Loathes me, really."

Six nodded at the bar staff who had arrived with a large plate of food. "Um, not sure. Who knows why the legends do what they do?" He didn't meet her eyes as he spoke but instead focused on the table.

He's not telling me everything, Valentine realized. *But why?* "What's the next task, then?"

"Well, I suspect you have several more tasks," Six murmured. "The gods don't give opportunities like this often – or easily. But yes, you have another task."

"What is it?"

Six shifted in his seat, picked up his utensils, then set them down again. He fiddled with the drape of his jacket, brushing off nonexistent dust and debris. Valentine waited him out, her worry budding into full blown fear by the time he spoke. What would scare him so?

"The Wild Hunt." Six finally met Valentine's eyes, a mute and grim apology within them. "Your next task is the Wild Hunt."

Valentine had never seen Kentucky before, despite having grown up in Tennessee. Her parents didn't travel, and she hadn't been able to afford a tour in the region. She had mostly played in Nashville.

Kentucky had blue-green forests and plenty of rolling hills. The land alternated between rich farms and working-class spreads, the difference obvious between the gleaming white fences that lined considerable acreage versus the weathered wood-and-barbwire boundaries that popped up alongside the highways. Valentine could even see the wealth disparity in the very roads and infrastructure of the towns they drove through. The difference was as plain as the contrast between gleaming ivory and plain pebble rock. It made Valentine uncomfortable, like wearing an itchy, ill-fitting sweater.

Church leaned over the bench seat. *I need food.*

Six snorted. "We'll be in Lexington soon. Just wait."

Valentine stared out the window. "Can you tell me about the Wild Hunt again?" She had never heard of it and based on what she had seen of the other tasks, she knew she wouldn't enjoy it.

The legends weren't kind.

An ancient punishment for evil deeds. Something like satisfaction curled through Church's words. *If a human commits an unforgivable sin, the Wild Huntsmen chase the culprit through the heavens and on earth, drawing succor from the human's fear and horror. It is...an event.*

Valentine stilled. "What kind of sin?" She thought of John and Emma. Would she be suitable prey for the Huntsmen? Would they punish an accidental murderer with a Wild Hunt? Her heart beat a little faster.

"Cold-blooded murder, abuse, assault — the heaviest crimes," Six answered.

Valentine relaxed a bit. "The Wild Hunt is a supernatural punishment for villains and bad guys?"

Church tilted his head. *Yes and no. Sometimes innocent humans are in the wrong place at the right time and they, too, get swept up into the hunt, despite their innocence.*

"That's comforting." Valentine snorted to herself. "And I'm supposed to, what, ride with the Wild Hunt? Is that the task?"

Six nodded his head. "In short, yes. You must stay on the horse for the duration of the Hunt. You cannot let go of the reins nor lose contact with your mount. You also cannot protest the actions you will see for it is not your domain."

Valentine thought for a moment. "I don't think I've ridden a horse before."

Church rumbled in amusement. *You won't be riding horses. Not really.*

"It's much harder than that. The Wild Hunt is not merely active or rigorous by human standards. It is *legendary*. It will traverse realms you've never heard of before, let alone seen. You will be both tempted by beauty and struck by horror on a scale you cannot yet comprehend. And when you witness those things, you will need to ignore your desires and fears. You will have to stay mounted until the Hunt is finished."

That sounded difficult, if not impossible. "They chose something this hard because I failed with the Bell Witch, didn't they?"

Likely. Church shifted in the back seat. *I'm still hungry.*

"Great," Valentine muttered.

"No, no, this is an opportunity, Valentine Cash—" Six began but Valentine cut him off.

"I'm tired, Six." She turned her head to stare at him, sadness weighing down her shoulders. "I'm tired. I know this probably isn't half finished and I know I need to carry on. I made this choice; I'll do it. But I don't need more pep talks. Just tell me what I need to do."

A silence fell over the cab.

Valentine felt a stirring of shame in her chest. Six and Church had only ever helped her. Six, especially. He didn't deserve that. It was their fault she had gotten herself into this mess. For all she knew, Six and Church were just as stuck as she was on this trip. She shifted in her seat, once, then twice. Finally, she spoke. "I'm sorry. I shouldn't have said that."

Six nodded, his eyes on the road.

"You talked about an opportunity?"

Six accepted the peace offering. "The Wild Hunt has a loophole, a clause, for the event of accidental inclusion of mortals. If a mortal survives the Wild Hunt, they may ask for a boon from the Huntsmen."

"A boon?" Valentine echoed. *A favor? From supernatural creatures — oh.* She felt silly and naive. *The legends want the favor.* "What do the gods want me to ask for?"

Six gave Valentine a half grin. "You're catching on very well." His voice was thick with approval. The grin faded as he continued to speak. "They want you to ask for the next foal, born from the Huntsmen's stock, to be delivered to the legends."

"A horse?" Valentine shook her head, incredulous and irritated. "Someone wants a pony? That's the task?"

Church barked. *There's a restaurant. Right there. Pull over.*

"Church, you will not starve. Patience." Six looked over at Valentine. "It's not simply a case of getting a pony. You should know that by now. If you have a mount from the Huntsmen's stock, you can travel across several realms. You have access to worlds previously denied to you." Six shook his head. "Who wouldn't want such a steed?"

Valentine turned her head to stare outside the passenger window, thinking over Six's words. Valentine didn't especially like horses or livestock. She had also seen enough of the supernatural to know that possession of such a creature would come with its own burdens and strife. Magic always did. No, if she could ask for the boon for herself, Valentine wouldn't request a legendary horse. She didn't need to travel across several realms.

She only wanted to go home.

CHAPTER SEVENTEEN

Despite Church's growing protests, Six didn't pull over until they reached the north side of Lexington. He pulled into the empty parking lot of a rundown diner. Valentine was unimpressed by the exterior and less so by the interior. *At least it's clean. Mostly.*

Church bounded past Valentine, and to her surprise, straight into the arms of the fry cook, an old man with a robust combover and a stained apron. The man hugged and tussled with Church; the black dog growled back, playful and talkative.

"Is this why we stopped here?"

Six smiled. "Yes."

"Who is he?" She nodded at the cook.

"You can call me 'Cook,'" the old man answered as he came over to shake Six's hand. He studied Valentine with sharp eyes before turning back to the other man. "Mother Road, you're looking good as always. Always so spiffy." He chuckled.

"Cook, a pleasure." Six gestured at Valentine. "This is Valentine Cash. She's on a penance."

Cook winced. "Sorry to hear that."

"Um, nice to meet you."

"Sit, sit, you fools." Cook ushered them to a booth. "Church tells me you're starving him?"

Six rolled his eyes. "Hardly."

Church let out a sharp bark; Cook chuckled. "Let's get you some food before this place fills up."

Valentine cast a surreptitious glance around the diner. No one else was there.

Cook caught her glance, then gave a grin. "Just wait. You'll see."

After a half hour, Valentine had to admit it: Cook had been right. The diner had filled up, and fast.

Had she never seen the casino before the diner, Valentine would have been astonished by the denizens. None of them were mortal, for one. The diner seemed reserved for the special use of gods, legends, and other creatures. A chartreuse woman dressed in veils and glittering scales sauntered by with a saucy look at Valentine, who stared back and then blushed violently as Church barked with laughter. Six had hidden his smile behind a napkin. Two squat men in harlequin costumes and smeared stage make-up, tumbled and bounced and leapt over one another through the dining room. They seemed incapable of walking, let alone in a straight line. An androgynous creature with spikes alongside their arms and back slithered by, their multifaceted eyes flickering in the light.

As the diner had filled up and more creatures had arrived, Valentine saw that the worn Formica tabletops, the cracked black and white checkered tile, and the split vinyl bench seats for the booths had somehow faded from her vision. Or maybe she simply didn't care about it as much. Now the ceiling had transformed into a celestial nightscape: Stars, moons, and planets beamed down on them, and the silver and golden light gave a gentle glow limned the creatures below. Weather patterns wafted around the dining room, mostly ignored but sometimes cause for complaint, such as when a jagged lightning bolt connected with a fork and shocked its handler, a red imp with a stub of a tail and three horns.

Valentine finally turned away from the scenery before her. "What *is* this place?"

Six smiled. "We call it the Last Stop Diner."

It's a watering hole for creatures like us. Church's voice was garbled. From under the table, Valentine could hear the obscene noises he made while eating the feast Cook had brought out to him a few minutes earlier. She tried not to wince.

"The line between realms and existences is thin in this area," Six explained. "It makes visitation easier for most creatures since family and friends have an easier time getting here."

Valentine scanned the room again. Cook was reassuring the irate red imp about the lightning bolt. "Is it a family reunion?"

Church chuckled in the back of her mind. *That's appropriate. This place contains the same amount of drama.*

Six smiled into his post dinner coffee.

Valentine studied the highway for a moment. He was relaxed. Happier than she had ever remembered seeing him. The topmost buttons of his tailored shirt had been loosened and his shirtsleeves were rolled up, his cufflinks tucked away in his vest pocket. A few locks of hair had escaped his pomade and fell across his face. He grinned wide and easy each time someone had greeted him or came over to clap him on the shoulder.

"You really like this place, huh?" Valentine asked.

Six paused, fork in midair. "Yes, I do. This place is a refuge."

"Why is this place different from the casino?" Valentine swept a glance around the room. "It's got the same folks — supernatural, powerful. I'd think you'd be equally as comfortable in both places."

Six seemed to consider his words before he spoke. "The casino is the legends' arena of choice. It is their domain for contracting with you, theirs to manage and control as they see fit." Six nodded to the cheerful bedlam in the dining room. "This is neutral. Simple. Everyone is here for the same thing: food, friends, and the latest gossip. There are no games and no nonsense in a place like this."

"What you see is what you get," Valentine murmured.

Church paused his noise beneath the table. *Yes and no.*

"Church is right. It's not that simple but you're right in the essentials."

Why ask about our preference for this place? Church asked.

"You seem happier here, more relaxed."

"Well, of course. Mom and Dad are out for the night, and the babysitter invited her girlfriend over to hang out." Six grinned. "We're free from scrutiny and checks. It's time to raise some heck."

Valentine laughed at the mischievous twinkle in his eyes. Then a motion caught her attention. A short, heavily muscled man with the blackest hair and greenest eyes she had ever seen stood in front of the table and stared down at them. She cast a quick look at Six. Did he know the man?

Six waved and a chair floated up to the table from somewhere beyond the short man. "Malcolm, sit. Thank you for joining us. Can we buy you dinner, or a refreshment?"

"A beer would be good." Malcolm sat down, then leaned into the back of the chair. "You're the Mother Road."

Six nodded. "And this is Valentine Cash. She is on a penance."

Malcolm stared at Valentine before giving her a wordless nod. She nodded back, uncertain. The man turned back to Six. "I hear you need something."

Six swept a casual glance through the dining room. "Yes. Should we wait to discuss our needs?"

A loud crash, followed by a gout of flame, across the diner distracted them for a moment. Valentine could see the red imp in the midst of the debacle, shouting at his companions who roared with laughter at his expense.

Malcolm shook his head. "Ain't nobody going to overhear us in this crazy din."

"I suppose you're right." He nodded to Valentine. "This one needs a bridle, custom made."

Malcolm sat up straight. Interest gleamed in his eyes, and he rubbed his hands together. "Oh? What are the specifications?"

"It needs to withstand the Hunt," Six muttered.

Malcolm's head snapped back in shock. He blanched, surprise filtering across his face. He cast a pitying glance at Valentine, then shook his head before turning back to Six. "Anything else?"

Six's eyebrows raised. "You can do it, then?"

Malcolm snorted. "I can make the thing. I can't guarantee she won't still fall off. I'm a stable hand and tack master, not a miracle worker."

"When will you have it ready?"

"Hold up." Malcolm shifted his gaze to Valentine. "What will you give me in return for the bridle?"

Valentine's gums pulsed in pain as she remembered Betty's casual and abrupt removal of her wisdom teeth. She tried to think of what she could offer him. "Um, I'm not sure. I don't have any children, nor do I plan –"

"Ew. No. I don't want your children." Malcolm seemed queasy. Valentine watched his Adam's apple bob as he swallowed hard. "Gross."

Church snorted from under the table.

Valentine blushed at her gaffe. She tried to think what she could offer to the surly stable hand. "I can play music. I've trapped animals. Well, an animal. I've repaired a lariat. I've killed a Bloody Bones –"

Malcolm held up his hand. "Stop. I don't want anything that complicated. Just come work for a week at my stable and we'll call it good." He shot an irritated glare at Six. "Are we done?"

Amusement gleamed in the legend's eyes. "I think so."

Malcolm stood. "Then I'll see you at the stables tomorrow morning, 6:00 a.m. Be there on time and wear clothes that can get dirty." Valentine gave a start when he disappeared into thin air. She had expected the big man to walk away.

Valentine turned to Six. "Am I... cleaning a stable tomorrow?"

Six grinned outright. "Yep."

Valentine sighed. "Great."

Shortly after dawn, Six and Valentine drove out to the stables. Church had elected to remain asleep. After about a half hour's drive northeast of Lexington, Six pulled to a stop in front of an ornate gate flanked by white fences on either side. "Here you go."

Valentine rubbed her face. She needed more coffee. "You're not coming?"

Six's jaw dropped, aghast. "No. *I* am not mucking stables. *You* are."

"Great." Valentine peered through the passenger window. "This looks awful."

She heard the grin in his voice. "It probably is."

She cast him a withering glance. "I'm glad you're enjoying this."

"Have a good day." Six almost choked on his laughter.

Valentine stepped out of the car. "Asshole."

As Six drove off, Valentine turned to study the spread. The stables were enormous. Each building ran long and wide, the aisles within large enough to drive a vehicle through and were painted in no-nonsense shades of green with white trim. A grand house, surrounded by a courtyard, stood off in the distance.

"Hey!"

Malcolm waved her over across the courtyard. Valentine pushed past the gates, then walked up the drive to the stablemaster.

"You're late."

Valentine didn't think she was but didn't want to argue. "I'm sorry."

"Let's get started."

Malcolm led her to the first building and gave Valentine a whirlwind tour. He pointed out the tack room, the stalls, the food and the hay, and the tools. In this last room, he pulled out a shovel, a pitchfork, and a wheelbarrow. Malcolm then cast a disparaging glance at Valentine's boots. "Those won't work. Use these." A thump echoed his words as he threw a pair of rubber work boots into the wheelbarrow.

Malcolm then led Valentine to one end of the stable. "Put your boots on, then muck each of these stalls."

Of course, it wasn't that simple.

After Valentine struggled to get the work boots on, Malcolm had had to show to approach the horse in the stall and secure the creature before cleaning the space. Neither Valentine nor the horses enjoyed being around each other. They were so big; she was wary of being stepped on, pinned, crushed, or any number of anxieties currently running through the back of her mind. And they seemed to sense her discomfort. They dodged her tentative hands, backed away from her approach, snorted and huffed as she drew close.

This doesn't look good for the Wild Hunt. She tried not to think about the task that awaited her and how she would likely fail it, given how abysmally she handled these regular horses.

Somehow, despite her own misgivings and several missteps (she'd never seen a man turn that exact shade of puce-y rage as Malcolm), Valentine fell into a rhythm. She worked her way down one side of the stable, then the other, her feet slipping inside her too large boots. Still, she was grateful for the borrowed shoes – it was so *muddy*. Once she had mucked the stalls, she had to feed the horses. Many of them had special diets; all of them got an apple, and Valentine had enjoyed that part. After that, came cleaning and conditioning the tack. That was her favorite activity so far: Sequestered in a small room, the smell of soap and leather wrapped around her like an embrace, and away from Malcolm and the horses. It ended too soon, and then Valentine was back on mucking duty.

She was so tired that she almost tripped into the car when Six picked her up at the end of the day. As Valentine settled into the polished retro sedan, Six gasped at the smell and leaned away from her. He quickly rolled down a window, taking a deep breath of the cool evening air that wafted into the car. Valentine felt a petty satisfaction at the sight. If she had to suffer, so should he.

"Dear god," he said when he could breathe again.

"It can't be that bad," Valentine retorted, her tone irritable.

Six cast a horrified glance at her. "Can you *smell* yourself?"

"Just take me to the hotel."

Six sped back to their hotel, exceeding the speed limits for the first time since Valentine had known him during their entire acquaintance. He kept his window down. Valentine turned away and grinned at her reflection in the passenger window.

After the best shower of her life (and her death, for that matter) and equipped with a fresh change of clothes, Valentine and Six had a quick dinner at the Last Stop Diner again. The unusual creatures and legends made the usual appearance in the diner, the cheerful noise and occasional fireworks enveloping the room. Despite being what appeared to be a small space, the room accommodated an enormous crowd of different sizes and shapes within. Valentine assumed it was magic.

Cook came by after a moment. "The usual, Mother Road?"

"Yes."

Cook turned to Valentine. "And you?"

"I want chocolate cake." Valentine was starving.

Cook grinned. "A whole one?"

"A slice to start with."

Cook shuffled away.

Valentine stared at Six as a sudden suspicion grew within. "You know, I never asked. Why are you doing all of this?" Valentine waved a hand around the Diner.

"This?" Six gestured at the Diner. "Or this?" He gestured between himself and Valentine.

"All of it," Valentine replied. "Why be a wayfinder and advisor for me? Have you done it before?"

Six shook his head. "No, I've never advised someone on a penance before." He shifted on his bench seat, refusing to meet her eyes.

"Then why now? Why me?"

Six cleared his throat, then shifted in his seat. "It's complicated."

Valentine felt her eyebrows rise. She could feel his reluctance from across the worn Formica table. "I'm listening."

Six sighed. "I've told you before how legends come about, yes?"

Valentine tilted her head, trying to remember one of their earliest conversations. "Hope and imagination, right? Or something like that?"

"Imprecise but accurate enough for our purposes." Six fiddled with the sugar and salt packets on the table. "When I came into being, the humans at the time had such scope of imagination, such a determined zest for life and something better, that I burst forth like a sunrise. I surprised others with my sudden arrival, disturbed the mostly settled firmament of the other American legends and gods with my noisy debut." Six shook his head. "Despite what the others thought, I didn't mean to appear with such noise and vigor. I just... became."

"The first decades were sweet and kind," Six continued. "Humans were happy and drove along my highways, fueling my existence with their dreams and desires. I was content, happy. They offered me joy, and I believe I offered the same thing to them. Well, more, really: Beautiful vistas, replete with gorgeous scenery where memories were made, little restaurants where families and couples ate and fought and yet still carried on together."

"The subsequent few decades were...," Six paused, seeming to search for words. "Well, things had changed. The humans began to build interstate highways, ugly and efficient roads that carved through the least attractive land in the continental United States. Whatever my opinions on its lack of beauty or romance, these new interstates *were* practical. This infrastructure created opportunities for commerce, jobs, and the American way."

Six paused for a moment as he removed his cufflinks. He rolled up his shirtsleeves, then leaned back into the bench seat. *He looks sad.* She felt an answering twinge of sympathy in her chest and reached up to rub her sternum.

"Well, the rest of the story is a bit more obvious, I'm afraid. As humans began to use the interstates more and more often, they began to drive my roads less and less. With fewer humans on my roads, I experience less joy. Less grief and road rage and screaming children who perennially ask if they have arrived yet —

yes, I mourn even them — and all of those emotions I've become accustomed to witnessing. I... miss all of them. I feel... grief at their absence."

Six cleared his throat before continuing. "As long as my roads exist and humans continue to dream and imagine the possibilities they could encounter on the open road, I exist. But I'm not what I once was. I'm... less vibrant, more worn down, I suppose. And I worry about oblivion. I don't want to be forgotten. I'm not expecting a return to my early golden years but I want... remembrance of some kind." Six studied his hands, the edges of his mouth turned down.

Then Valentine knew. "What did the gods offer you?"

Six flashed a half smile. "A celebration. A flashy event like a bicentennial or some such, seeded within the dreams of humans so that they could foster nostalgia and a return to my roadways for at least a short while. The gods, they were convincing. Dale especially."

Valentine studied Six. She felt as though she should be upset. Upset that his motivations weren't centered around her success on this penance, that he had personal motivations for engaging in this endeavor. But she couldn't drum up a sense of betrayal or anger. She understood. Oh, she wanted something different, a return to her old life and the possibilities within – the music, the connection to others, maybe a wife and a family someday. But really, she and Six were the same.

They were lonely.

They both wanted a connection. Community.

"Okay, Mother Road, here is your usual." Valentine startled as Cook's cheerful voice jarred her thoughts. "And a slice of the best chocolate cake east of the Mississippi for Valentine Cash." Cook gave her a wink.

"Thank you, Cook," Six murmured.

The cheerful man bustled away.

A silence fell over the table.

"We should eat." Six offered a small smile to Valentine. It was clear he wanted to change the topic. "You have a busy week ahead of you."

CHAPTER EIGHTEEN

*V*alentine winced to herself.

She dreaded these dreams. They hurt too much. Nevertheless, she made herself turn around and look.

John and Emma were older, with gray that stained their temples and laugh lines etched into their faces. They had two children, and Valentine studied the children, at once eager and sad to see who they could have been. The daughter was John's lookalike; she saw more of Emma in the son, with his father's nose and his mother's hair.

They were at a party, Valentine realized. A graduation party.

Balloons and banners draped across the cozy backyard of a large suburban home. The barbeque had been fired up; Valentine could smell roasted meat and sweet corn. The tables were laden with food and drinks over festive tablecloths. Relatives and fellow graduates filled the backyard, the noise genial and filled with warm laughter. A few children ran through the adults, laughing off the scolds tossed their way.

Near the doorway, Valentine watched John and Emma's daughter. She wasn't a child anymore. She wore a college graduation gown with honors tassels attached to her lapel. She beamed as family members and friends came by, one by one, to congratulate and hug her. Many of the older family members offered a small envelope, colorful and neat. Emily looked thrilled and grateful with each gift.

Valentine looked away.

The daughter's happiness was too much to bear, too painful to witness.

Valentine knew that the other young woman would never get her chance to live.

Her eyes found the son next, gathered in a group of young men. They laughed at jokes and jostled each other. After a stern look and nod from John, Valentine watched the son break away from the group to assist Emma with gathering trash. Emma kissed her son on the forehead, pleased by his help.

This is what they should have had, *Valentine thought.* They should have had the chance to see their children grow up, to make mistakes and to succeed. To live.

Tears slipped down Valentine's face.

I did this. I stole this from them.

She turned away. Her sobs were soon the only sound she heard.

CHAPTER NINETEEN

The next four days were a blur of horseshit, mud, hay, and rain for Valentine.

Each night, she stumbled out to the polished sedan and slid into the bench seat with a moan of relief, as her aching muscles stilled. Malcolm had grown progressively less grumpy with each subsequent day, satisfied that Valentine knew enough to do the job and would not harm his horses through her inexperience. And Six had learned his lesson from the first evening: He always had the windows down before Valentine got into the vehicle.

It was miserable.

And Valentine still didn't like horses.

Near the end of the fifth day, Malcolm came by the stall she mucked out. "Hey."

Valentine paused with her pitchfork in mid-air. "Yes?"

"Finish this, then come find me in the tack room." Malcolm walked away. Valentine finished as quickly as she could.

In the tack room, she found Malcolm holding a box lined in black crushed velvet. He held the box out to Valentine. "This is yours now."

Valentine accepted the box. "May I open it?"

Malcolm waved an irritated hand. Valentine took it as an affirmative.

The inside was lined with cream satin, a stark contrast to the black velvet exterior that glowed in the light. Within lay a bridle unlike anything Valentine had ever seen: Copper links, lined with white down fur and studded with moonstones, formed a halter for a mount's head. Silver white strands of hair, woven into long braids with jet and carnelian beads, served as reins. It pulsed in her hands like a heartbeat and glimmered in the light.

Goosebumps crinkled her skin. "It's beautiful."

Malcolm preened. "I know."

"So... I'm supposed to catch a horse?"

Malcolm shook his head.

"The Hunt begins tomorrow at midnight." He handed a folded piece of paper over to Valentine. "You will find them here. Try not to be seen or too obvious when you arrive. Select the smallest mount you can find – you'll have an easier time of it during the Ride. Ask for permission to ride the creature, slip on the bridle, then offer thanks for the acceptance."

"What do I offer as thanks?" Valentine asked. "Apples and sugar lumps?"

Malcolm stared at her with a curled lip, his disdain obvious. "These are not normal horses. They will not accept mundane bribes." He reached into this jacket pocket to pull out a small packet wrapped in parchment paper and twine. "Frankincense and myrrh."

"Okay." Valentine couldn't help the defensive edge in her voice. Malcolm didn't have the best interpersonal skills. "Do I need to come back here tomorrow?"

Malcolm snorted. "No. Please don't."

Oh, thank god. "Well, thank you." Valentine lifted the box. "For this and the instructions."

Malcolm nodded. "Good luck."

She could hear his unspoken words: *You're going to need it.*

Dinner was again a noisy affair at the Last Stop Diner. From what Valentine could gather, a troll draped in a cape of pebbles woven into lichen and moss was celebrating a birthday or anniversary. His comrades slapped the table and let out intermittent roars. No one else paid them any mind.

Valentine handed the folded piece of paper to Six. Church bumped against her legs under the table, then grumbled as he settled onto the floor. "These are the directions from Malcolm. They look like latitude and longitude but... they're different."

Six scanned the crabbed handwriting. "It *is* a set of latitude and longitude coordinates – along with an astral and a chronal location," he murmured before looking up. "The Hunt exists in and beyond this world."

"So where are we going?"

"A local spot southwest of the city. The Hunt starts at midnight which means we'll need to be there earlier, to give you time to find a mount." Six looked up from the piece of paper. "Do you have an appropriate tribute? For your mount?"

"Malcolm gave me a packet of frankincense and myrrh. Will that work?"

His brows flew up, impressed. He gave a nod. "That's smart of him. Yes, that will work very well."

Valentine studied the food in front of her. Starving from the hard day's work in the stables, she had opted for a big meal: Steak, potatoes, and cornbread. But she thought about the Hunt, and her appetite waned. Worry trickled through her. What was she *doing*? Would this even work? What would happen to her if she failed – the final death? Or something worse? She rubbed the back of her neck.

"What's wrong?"

"Thinking about the Hunt. Do you have any advice?"

Six grimaced. "I swear I'm not being flippant but... stay on the horse."

"That's not helpful. Thanks."

Six winced at her dry tone. "I'm utterly serious, I'm afraid. What if you fall off your mount in another dimension? Or on the other side of this world? At best, you will fail the task. At worst, you'd end up in a hell somewhere. You cannot afford to fail this task, not after the Bell Witch."

Valentine's shoulders slumped; she picked at her cornbread. "I know," she muttered.

Use your knees.

"What's that, Church?" Six asked.

You won't have a saddle during the Hunt. Those creatures won't tolerate a saddle. So you will need to use your knees and legs to hang on.

"No saddle?" Valentine echoed. "That's... not ideal." She shook her head. "I'm going to fail," she muttered. "This is impossible."

"Valentine."

She found Six watching her.

"You can do this. You *must* do this. Otherwise..."

She finished his sentence, filling in the words he couldn't bring himself to speak. "Otherwise, I die."

The drive out of Lexington and to the rendezvous was tense and silent. Church, who normally slept in the back seat, sat upright and stiff as he had scanned the road ahead of them. Six had gripped the steering wheel with white knuckles. He had chain smoked slender cigars all evening. Valentine could still smell the tobacco on his clothes, his hands.

Valentine worried.

She didn't pray because she wasn't the praying kind and in this instance, she didn't even know who to beseech. Who did the dead pray to? Who would listen to the dead? And what would she ask for? A saddle? Steady knees? And what would be the cost of such a boon? Valentine knew enough about the afterlife to know that magic, boons, and gifts had a price.

Nothing is free, in this life or any other.

Six pulled over. "We're here."

Valentine felt a frisson of fear dance down her spine. "Okay."

"This is where we leave you."

"Of course." It was too much to hope for companionship, for comfort, before the Hunt.

"Do you have the bridle? The tribute?"

"Yes."

"Then good luck." Six paused. "We will be here when you return."

Valentine heard what he didn't say. *If you return.* "Thank you."

She stepped from the car, then stilled when she saw it. The mound was enormous, a large swell of pyramidal turf whose base was even larger. The grass fluttered in the faint, cold wind, and the full moon above illuminated the grounds and cast long shadows. The skies were clear, and the starry skyscape stretched from horizon to horizon.

Valentine started forward. She walked to the base of the mound, then around the perimeter, looking for any sign of the Hunt. She found none. She checked her phone: Twenty minutes to midnight. She walked around the mound again, and again, searching for some sign. Anything at all that would lead her to the Hunt. Upon the close at the third circle around the mound, Valentine saw them.

The Huntsmen had arrived.

They were all large, dressed in furs, leathers, and thick boots. The men had thick beards and braids; the women either wore braids or had shorn hair. All of them wore armor of some kind, with runic designs upon their crests. Ghost green flames danced and kissed across their skin. As Valentine watched, she saw that their skin flickered and faded in the moonlight, alternately translucent and opaque. During the translucent phases, she saw their skeletons underneath.

She shivered.

Then, beyond the Huntsmen, she saw the mounts.

They were stunning.

Each horse shimmered, dressed in golds and silvers, blues and violets, coppers and moonlight. They were enormous, with hooves the size of dinner plates and lush manes that draped across the starlit skin. Valentine watched as they huffed, stamped their feet, and half-reared. They were *ready*, she could tell. They wanted to hunt, to chase.

She heard Malcolm's prosaic voice in her head. *Choose the smallest mount.*

Valentine scanned the herd. *There.*

The smallest mount glowed like a golden fire in the moonlight, with a silver mane. Compared to the others, this one was dainty, almost delicate. Valentine cast a quick glance at the Huntsmen, then started forward, crouching low to avoid notice. As she moved forward, she draped the bridle over her shoulder, then pulled out the packet of frankincense and myrrh. She poured it into her hands, then crept forward. She stopped before the golden creature, a good six feet away. Though this mount was smaller than the others, it was by no means tiny.

When Valentine stilled, the horse raised her head.

What do you want, mortal? The voice sounded like a crack of lightning in her head. The eyes glowed with violet flame.

Valentine heard the words float out as though she weren't the one speaking. "I wish to ride the Wild Hunt. May I ride with you?"

A mortal on the Hunt? The horse snorted. *Leave while you still can. You will die otherwise.*

"I'm already dead. And I have my own reasons for riding the Hunt. May I ride with you? Please?"

The horse stepped forward, sniffing the air in delicate huffs. Valentine made herself stay still. *You are dead. How unusual.*

"May I ride with you?" Valentine repeated her request a third time, then waited on bated breath for the answer.

The horse studied her. *What can you offer me, unusual mortal?*

"I offer you frankincense and myrrh." Valentine held out her cupped hands.

Acceptable. Pleasure suffused the creature's tone and her mane rippled in delight. *You may ride the Wild Hunt with me.*

Valentine started when the frankincense and myrrh disappeared from her hands.

The mare came forward. *I see you have a bridle. That is wise. It may help you stay on.*

"May I place it on you?"

You may.

Valentine took a step forward, then another. After a week of working in the stables, she knew how to approach a horse with gentle hands, to place a halter over the head. She administered this new knowledge with unsteady hands, knowing that this creature was something more than a mere horse, something far more dangerous. The golden mount smelled of ozone and the sea tang of a distant ocean, an otherworldly blend of starstuff and salt. When the last clasp clicked into place, Valentine wrapped the reins alongside the neck and crossed them over the mare's back.

It is comfortable and it accents my beauty well. Thank you for your consideration.

"You're welcome." Valentine paused for a moment. "Um, how should I get up? On your back, I mean?"

I kneel for no one. Lightning crackled across those words.

"No, no, I understand." Valentine cast a panicked look around the clearing. There, a stump. "Would you mind standing near that stump?"

Valentine heard the creature sigh. *Fine.*

With the stump, Valentine clambered up onto the mare's back, trying not to kick or flail. She mostly succeeded, though she heard the mare give what sounded like a derisive chuckle in the back of her mind. Once mounted, she sat upright to settle into the withers of the mare, extending her legs around the ribcage. She wasn't comfortable but she felt steady in her seat.

For the moment.

"Oh ho, what have we here?"

The words plucked at Valentine. She swallowed hard, then made raise her gaze.

The Huntsmen surrounded her and the mare.

"It's a mortal."

"Not quite. A *dead* mortal. She's not alive."

"Alive enough."

"*She* wants to ride with us?" A shout of laughter greeted this statement.

A mountain of a man with braids on either side of his face leaned on a glaive, the sharp blade at the top limned in moonlight. "You wish to ride the Wild Hunt, mortal?" He smirked.

"Yes." A belated thought prompted Valentine to continue. "In exchange for a boon. A f-favor."

More laughter, raucous and disbelieving. It stabbed at her like knives. Valentine gritted her teeth together and made herself hold the gaze of the mountain.

"A boon?" The man smirked harder. "You are lucky to be here, whole and in one piece, with your sanity and health intact. And you have the audacity to seek a boon?" The man laughed. "The balls on this one."

Valentine pushed through her fear and growing anger. "It is the lore. If a mortal rides the Wild Hunt, they get a boon. Right?"

"Aye, that's right." The man cast a lazy glance over her. "But you won't make it, little mortal."

"I would like to try." Valentine tried to make her words firm.

The man shook his head. "When you fail, do not beg for mercy. You will not get it." He turned his attention to the mare. "And you? What did she give you to cause such a fall from dignity, letting a human ride you?"

That's between her and I, Huntsman. I do not answer to any of you. Valentine could hear the scorn in the mare's words.

The mountain stepped back. "I will enjoy watching you fall from the sky, mortal." He turned to the others. "Kinfolk, mount up. We have worthy prey to chase tonight. A murderer, who chose to end several lives for financial gain." The men roared their disapproval; the women howled their disdain. They stamped their feet and their weapons into the ground, shaking the earth, as the mountain continued to speak. "We are called to show this execrable creature the error of his way. We will show no mercy nor quarter. We will chase and harry and hound and *hunt* this man into an everlasting hell of his own making."

The Huntsmen howled in fury and delight. Several of the mounts half-reared and many more trumpeted their glee at the forthcoming chase. Her own mount scuffed the ground with an impatient hoof, vibrating with barely restrained energy. Valentine gripped the braided silver hair reins in her hands, her knuckles turning white. She felt a burn lance down her palms, and she saw that reins had cut into the flesh, leaving several slender lacerations that seeped blood, staining the silver hair like ink on paper.

A scream distracted her.

Valentine followed the sound with her gaze.

A pale man, white and blonde in the silver moonlight, in a tattered business suit crouched in the center of a loose circle, surrounded by the Huntsmen. He gibbered in fright, as snot and tears and blood streamed down his face, while the Huntsmen jeered, lunged at, and mocked him.

"Who are you?" the man cried. "Why are you doing this?"

"Quiet." Though he didn't shout, the mountain's voice carried across the grounds, deep and authoritative. "William VanderDoen, do you know why you are here?"

The tattered man straightened while anger and contempt marred his face. "This is an outrage. I will not be harassed in this manner. I demand that the police be called. I am an important man!"

The Huntsmen howled with laughter and glee.

"William VanderDoen, you are dead." The mountain sneered these words. "In your one precious life, you stole, cheated, and murdered for personal gain. You have no redeeming qualities, and you gave nothing of value to this world or any others."

Valentine saw that William realized the gravity of his predicament.

The man gave a hard swallow, then straightened his suit jacket. "What do you need? Hmm? There must be something you want and I'm in the position to get it for you. I have connections, wealth –"

The Huntsmen began to heckle the tattered man.

"Ooh, the bargaining. That's original."

"He has wealth, did you hear that?"

"What could that creature possibly give us? Ha!"

"Quiet."

The Huntsmen fell silent at the command; William almost swallowed his words.

The Mountain continued. "William VanderDoen, for your crimes you are sentenced to suffer the Wild Hunt. No bribery nor begging will free you. We do not show mercy." The Mountain whistled and the largest horse Valentine had ever seen strolled through the herd to stand by his side. The Mountain swung up. His mount reared in eagerness; his eyes shot with bloodlust.

"William VanderDoen, you should *run*."

The tattered man froze for a moment. Valentine shivered and gripped the reins with white knuckled hands as the howls rose from the Huntsmen and horses. As more and more Huntsmen mounted, William seemed to realize, finally, that this was real. That he would be chased and run down.

He turned and fled.

"Hold!" After a moment, Valentine realized that Mountain spoke to the Huntsmen, not to the tattered man. "Let's give him a head start. It's only sporting." He chuckled as he hefted the glaive in one hand. He had to restrain his mount from leaping forward; Valentine had the same problem. The mare beneath her danced with impatience, her breaths heavy and loud in the night. Valentine saw the anticipatory glee, the eager bloodlust in the other Huntsmen. She shook in equal parts of fear, sympathy, and relief atop her own mount.

She was grateful she was not the object of the Hunt.

After a few moments, the tattered man was a distant figure in the night.

"Let the Hunt begin!" The Mountain howled. Ululating cries from the Huntsmen, filled with joy and anticipation and purpose, echoed in response; the horses trumpeted their relief and excitement. Valentine's mount lunged forward to follow the others, the sudden motion causing her to slide down and back, her seating precarious. Fear shot through her. Would it be over before it had even begun?

No. You can do this. You must do this. Valentine leaned forward, shifting her weight along the withers of her mount. She clamped her legs around the ribcage of the mare like a vise and wrapped the ends of the reins around her hands multiple times, ignoring the new and old cuts, and buried her fingers in the mane of her mount. *I must do this.*

The Huntsmen surged forward, a spectral wave of retribution and revenge. The cries changed in tone as they crept closer and closer to the tattered man. Taunts replaced joy, mockery and threats replaced eagerness. The wind and her horse's mane cut against her face, stinging and raw. Her arms were already sore from the tense grip on the reins; her legs trembled with the effort needed to stay mounted.

All too soon, they caught up with the tattered man.

William, after a fleeting, terrified look over his shoulder, shot forward with a new burst of energy, his fear a heady fuel for his flight. But it wasn't enough: The Huntsmen caught up to him. They stayed at his heels, forming a loose half circle, as they harried him. Valentine watched, horrified, as the Huntsmen took turns harassing the tattered man. One of them rode up to his heels, then shoved him forward with a lance.

"William, where's your money now? What can you give me?" The Huntswoman mocked.

Another Hunter rode in tight circles around William, cutting him off, forcing him to stumble in new directions. "Was it worth it, William? Murdering for *money*?" The man sneered; his mount, a blood red creature, reared as if to echo his rider's disgust.

"William, William, William!" The Huntsmen chased the tattered man through the night. From the back, Valentine watched them herd the frightened William in one direction, then another, their laughter and mockery ribboning through the night.

Suddenly, Valentine's mount leapt into the air. The mare continued to run into thin air as if it were the solid earth beneath them, her strides covering great distances with each leap and bound. Valentine screamed, then bit her tongue to silence the noise. She gripped the reins and clamped her legs tighter around the horse. She felt herself slide down the back of her mount and squeezed her eyes shut. *Please don't let this be the end. Please.*

The mare beneath her evened out and Valentine slumped forward along her neck at the sudden movement, banging her nose against the mare's neck and mane. Pain flared, then caused stars to dance across her vision, different from the ones that surrounded her in the sky they rode across. Blood burst from her face and streamed down her lips and onto her neck. Valentine ignored the blood and the pain; she would have to ignore it. She didn't dare let loose of the reins.

Her seat secure, Valentine watched the tattered man continued to stumble and charge forward, even in the air. She could see the whites of his eyes from where she crouched upon her mount, the fear and the incredulity rippling across his face, fighting with exhaustion and despair. The night sky was largely cloudless. Starlight glowed brighter up here, in green and violet and blue fire. The wind up here was a painful, bitter cold. The earth lay far below, a patchwork quilt of farms and cities and roads.

As they rode through the night sky, the tattered man attempted to hide behind a lone cloud. The Huntsmen threw javelins and spears at the wisps, dispelling them in a single burst. William stumbled forward, then continued to run. His business suit, already rumpled before the start of the Hunt, hung in pieces of fabric from his frame. Cuts bled and bruises had bloomed. Valentine saw that he had lost a shoe somewhere during the flight.

The night sky shimmered around Valentine and she tensed, wondering what new horror awaited William. The air turned arid, with a dry wind that whipped at her skin and sucked moisture from her lips and eyes. Below them, a desert of silver and red sands spread far and wide, no green or blue in sight. A scream, filled with a new kind of fear, pulled Valentine's gaze from the desert below and back to the tattered man.

She watched as he fell through the sky, gaining more and more speed until he slammed into the sand below with a sickening thud. He didn't move and Valentine wondered if he had died a final death. *It would be a mercy.*

But the tattered man moaned. Feeble sobs escaped him as his limbs jerked and flexed and moved, the broken bones and organs knitting themselves back together to make William whole and healed.

Ready to resume the Wild Hunt.

Oh, god, he has to continue.

Horror swamped over Valentine. Bile rose in her throat and she swallowed several times until she choked it back down. She didn't think her mount would stand for a mortal upchucking upon her.

When the tattered man realized that he had to continue, he cried a piteous wail that made Valentine's bones ache in sympathy. The Huntsmen roared with laughter, the sound ugly and mean.

"Oh little lad, you didn't think it would be that easy, did you?"

"Get up, murderer. You're not done."

"Look at the pitiful creature cry."

The Mountain moved forward on his mount. "William VanderDoen, get up. Your sentence is not yet complete."

William continued to sob, ignoring the man.

"Get. Up." The words rippled with power, and like a stringless marionette, the tattered man was yanked up onto unsteady legs, then drawn forward in stilted steps. His cries wracked his frame and he folded into himself, hunched over in misery and grief.

"Now *move*."

The tattered man whipped forward, one foot in front of the other, in a staggering gait. His remaining shoe slipped off his foot and he stumbled, almost falling, until pulled upright by the magic within the Mountain's command.

The Huntsmen howled in triumph and glee, eager to resume the chase. Valentine swallowed back the nausea that threatened again. Tears slipped down her face and she made no move to wipe them away; she could not, would not, let loose of the reins. She knew the tattered man to be a murderer and for the worst of motivations. According to the Mountain, he wasn't a good man. Still, she could hardly stand to watch the broken man stumble forward as the red and silver sands burned his feet, his skin leaching moisture from the bright glare of the sun, his tears the only liquid in this arid wasteland.

It was painful to witness such justice. She wondered if it was more akin to revenge.

And then the Hunt resumed.

William staggered, fell, crawled, ran, and fled from the Huntsmen across the desert. Like a mirage, the desert soon shifted into a swamp and the tattered man swam and stumbled across the dark depths of a green jungle, crying out when snakes bit him and alligators gave chase. He drowned in a swamp only to emerge into an alien darkness that smelled metallic to Valentine. He screamed as he fought his way through the darkness, unable to see anything.

All the while, the Huntsmen continued to harry and prod, to mock and threaten.

Valentine just hung on, her legs tight and then tighter around her mount. She could no longer feel her fingers wrapped in the blood-stained reins. She felt crusted blood and mucus, dried from the wind, on her face. She wondered when, or even if, the Hunt would be over.

She wondered if she would survive.

The Huntsmen chased the tattered man into the sky once more. Lightning crackled a spiderweb across the night sky and thunder boomed, causing Valentine's bones to vibrate and her ears to ring. William no longer cried but only stumbled forward, exhaustion and despair writ upon his face. His clothes were gone, lost in the swamp where he drowned. Deep lacerations were lanced across his back and legs; the skin and the flesh of his feet had worn away during the flight, leaving only broken blood-stained bones that gleamed in moonlight.

William fell through the sky once more, hitting the ground with another thud that caused Valentine's heart to leap up into her throat. As the Huntsmen rode towards the ground, Valentine could see a faint smear of red gold light along the eastern horizon.

Dawn had come.

Valentine jolted as her mount hit the ground. She slid forward, then back, careful to hold her head to the side so she wouldn't break her nose anew. The mare came to a stop beside the other Huntsmen, her breath huffing from exertion. A quick glance told Valentine that they were back at the original location in Kentucky.

Is it over? Please let it be over.

She studied the tattered man in the distance.

This time, it took longer for William to piece himself back together again. But he did, the jerking limbs snapping together with a pop that made Valentine hunch over in sympathy. As he snapped back together, the Mountain moved his mount forward.

"William VanderDoen, you are sentenced to hell. You will go there henceforth and await the next full moon. We will come for you then and the Hunt will continue." His pronouncement was greeted with howls of glee; the horses stamped their feet and blew their breath.

William sobbed with a new fervor as he disappeared, his wails echoing after him. Valentine shuddered at the fading cries. She had never heard a man make that sound before, hopelessness and despair and fear all in one.

She hoped she never would again.

"Valentine Cash."

She gave a start, then shivered when she realized that the rest of the Huntsmen had circled her. Some wore expressions of grudging respect, others shock. "Yes?"

"You survived the Wild Hunt, little mortal."

"I did." *Barely.*

"What did you think of William VanderDoen's punishment?" The Mountain's gaze was challenging.

"It's not my place to judge. I am only a simple mortal." Valentine did *not* want to upset him by passing judgement on his sentence. "I am only here for the boon."

The Mountain snorted. "Whatever else you are, Valentine Cash, you are not merely a simple mortal. Let's have it. What is your boon?"

"I ask that the next foal born of this herd be delivered to Dale Wright, High John de Conqueror, and Paul Bunyan."

Loud murmurs rippled through the gathered Huntsmen and Valentine flinched. Had she said the wrong thing? Would the Huntsmen kill her for effrontery and audacity? Had the legends set her up to fail?

"Meddling gods," the Mountain finally muttered to himself. "Very well. Your boon will be fulfilled. The next foal of this herd shall be delivered to those gods. Shall we fail our obligation, we forfeit our right to the Wild Hunt for a twelvemonth." A silver horseshoe, studded with gems, appeared in her hands. "Here is a symbol of our promise."

Valentine nodded. "Thank you."

A silence fell over the clearing. After a moment, the Mountain raised his brows. "This is where you get off, little mortal. You can't come with us." His deep chuckle was echoed by the others and Valentine felt ice along her spine. No, she didn't want to go with them. She began to unwrap the blood-soaked reins from her hands and whimpered when they parted from her palms, causing fresh blood to seep. Holding onto the mane, she slipped, then fell off her mount and tumbled into a heap on the ground, her legs bloodless from lack of movement and a too tight grip around her mount.

The Huntsmen laughed at her frailty.

Valentine gritted her teeth, then pushed herself upright from the ground. She tucked the horseshoe into her back pocket, then removed the bridle from the mare with shaking hands. Finally, it was off the mare's head and Valentine let her hands slump down besides her torso.

"Thank you for allowing me to join you."

Good luck on your penance, little mortal. The mare turned away to follow the departing Huntsmen. They whooped and hollered and fled into the morning sky, then faded from view.

Valentine turned and started towards the road, her limbs leaden with weariness. Her lips were chapped from the wind, and she licked them, tasting salt from the tears that were whisked away by the ride. Horror and sorrow wrestled within her. The Wild Hunt was an inhuman kind of justice, one untempered by mercy or expectations of fairness.

She walked towards where she thought the road would be. She only hoped Six and Church waited for her.

Chapter Twenty

They found her near the road.

When Valentine saw them, she stumbled in relief and almost fell. She kept herself upright by sheer stubbornness. She watched the emotions flicker across Six's face: Shock, worry, and then pride. Or maybe it was affection, she couldn't tell. The small smile chased by warmth in his eyes felt a hug, one she could use.

She was so tired.

Six grasped her by the arm, slid one arm around her, and helped her to the car, Church at their heels. She barely remembered the hotel but did remember the shower. The water stung her cuts and bruises like bullets. Finally, when the water had run cold, she stumbled out of the tub and into fresh clothes.

To her surprise, Six took them back to the Last Stop Diner.

"Are we getting breakfast?"

Six shook his head. "Not here. Do you have the horseshoe?"

Valentine nodded.

"Then we're ready."

Cook beamed at them as the trio stepped inside the diner. "Good morning. Here for a meal?"

Six shook his head again, this time at Cook. "Transport, if you'll let us."

Cook stepped aside. "Of course. Use the blue door in the kitchen." He studied Valentine for a moment, then grinned. "Little mortal, did you truly ride the Hunt?"

"Yes."

Cook laughed, throwing his head back. "I won my bet. Thanks, Valentine Cash."

Six rolled his eyes, then pulled Valentine forward and past Cook. "Thank you, Cook."

"Anytime, Mother Road. Valentine Cash, best of luck to you."

"Thanks," she called back. She turned to Six. "Bet?"

Six sighed. "Your penance is now well known among certain circles. Some of the ruder creatures are taking bets on the outcomes of each task."

Valentine frowned. "I don't think I like that."

Six shrugged. "We get bored." They wove between kitchen equipment and ducked past line cooks and bus boys before reaching the blue door. "Here we go."

The casino remained the same.

Dim light, gorgeous interiors, and low laughter filled the room. Valentine had to pause for a moment, to let her eyes adjust. A man with black bouffant hair bopped and twisted around the stage; Valentine knew his name, his legacy, but couldn't speak it for some reason. Six deposited her by the bar. "I'll announce us. Get a drink."

Valentine sank onto the bar stool. She laid the celestial horseshoe on the bartop with care, keeping a hand on it at all times. After all that she had done to retrieve the boon, she couldn't afford to be careless with it.

"Whiskey?"

Valentine smiled at Amaretto Sour. "Nah."

Amaretto smiled. "How goes the penance?"

Valentine shrugged, then winced as the motion pulled something in shoulder. "Okay. I think." *I hope.*

Amaretto set a glass of water in front of her with a smile. "Meet any interesting people?"

Valentine took a sip. "Too many."

The other woman laughed. "What's next then?"

"The gods will tell me."

"No, I mean—"

Six appeared, cutting off whatever Amaretto was about to say. "Valentine, they're waiting. Amaretto Sour, lovely to see you again."

The woman smiled back as Valentine gulped the last of her water. "I'm well, Six, thank you for asking. See you later." She winked at Valentine.

Valentine stood, holding the horseshoe in hand. "I'm ready."

The back room was the same.

Dale Wright sat on the pink velvet couch; the cactus cat slept on a fringed pillow beside her. Paul Bunyan paced the room, impatient and restless. High John stood next to the couch, unreadable, with his hands clasped in front. Valentine studied them for a moment, uncertain about what nagged at her when she watched them. Were they... smaller? Had someone gotten a haircut? She couldn't put her finger on it, but something was different.

Valentine stopped before them, then held up the horseshoe. "The Huntsmen have promised to deliver the next foal from the herd to the three of you, or they forfeit the right to the Wild Hunt for a twelvemonth. Here is a symbol of their promise."

Dale clapped her hands together. "Excellent."

The horseshoe disappeared from Valentine's hand.

To her surprise, High John de Conqueror spoke. "How did you find the Wild Hunt, Valentine Cash?"

Valentine rubbed her hands together to quell her nervousness. "Monstrous. Stunning."

High John smiled. Valentine blinked at the warm expression.

Paul Bunyan scoffed. "Oh, sure."

Dale continued. "Your success on the Hunt more than makes up for the lapse with the Bell Witch, especially combined with what Six has given us."

What? "I don't understand. What did Six give you?" *What did he do?* Dread seeped into Valentine, and she rubbed her sternum.

Dale shook her head. "I do not discuss other people's business. Six has the instructions for your next task, though you'll need to retrieve a unique weapon to fulfill the task." The legend grinned wide, her white teeth gleaming against ruby lips. "Good luck."

As she left the room, Valentine glanced at the clock with the many hands that dripped time into the lower half of the hourglass. *It's getting full.* She swallowed hard. *I'm running out of time.*

And then they were on the road again.

"Where are we headed?" Valentine asked. She turned her face to the wind, welcoming the dry wind.

Lookout Mountain. It's in Colorado. Church rolled over to a more comfortable position in the backseat.

Valentine frowned. "Why are we headed there? Aren't we looking for a monster in Maryland?"

You need the rifle.

"A rifle?" *Of course I do.* "What rifle?"

"The creature you need to kill can only be destroyed by a supernatural weapon, one owned by another creature. A legend."

Valentine thought for a moment. *A legend?* "Then who are we going to see?"

Six smiled. "Buffalo Bill Cody."

Valentine drove past the Red Rock Amphitheatre at sunset and continued up the winding highway that wrapped around Lookout Mountain. The dry land gleamed red, coral, and gold in the fading light, only interrupted by spare vegetation and the accompanying shadows. Six and Church napped in the car next to her. She hadn't realized the Mother Road needed sleep. *Do legends dream? What do they dream of?*

She pulled into the parking lot of the small museum nestled at the top and parked. She glanced at the dashboard of the sun yellow mid-century convertible they were in. 4:36 p.m. The museum would likely close soon.

"Six. We're here."

"Hmph?" The man barely stirred.

"Six." She raised her voice. "We're here. Wake up."

With a groan and a wince, the highway straightened in the cramped car seat. "At Lookout Mountain?"

"Yes." Valentine peered through the windshield and saw a sign that confirmed her suspicions. "It looks like they will close soon."

"Oh, that's all right."

Valentine cast a puzzled glance at Six. "What do you mean?"

Six smiled back. "We're breaking in, obviously."

Over dinner, Six explained that they couldn't steal — or borrow, he had amended — Buffalo Bill Cody's rifle in front of museum visitors or staff. They might object, he added with a conspiratorial smile. Valentine nodded through the explanation, commented in the right gaps of the conversation; otherwise, she ate her dinner. Grilled cheese sandwich. She was tired, she realized. Tired of all of this. If — and that was a huge if — she were successful in completing the tasks for the gods, and she returned to her life, would it be worth it? Would she want the same things? The album deal with Defiance Studios? The shotgun home somewhere in Nashville?

How much would she change?

A chill rippled through her. How much had she already changed?

Valentine squelched those misgivings, kept them private. How would she even begin to explain to Six and Church? She would sound ungrateful for the chance of a penance, childish and defiant at reality, at the basic fact that nothing in life is free.

"Valentine, are you ready?"

"For Lookout Mountain?" At Six's nod, Valentine pushed back her plate. "Let's go."

Six drove this time, parking the very visible convertible down the road from the parking lot. They slipped past the gate, ignored the vista platform, and walked around the small building, searching for an entrance. "There," Six pointed out. Valentine peered around him and saw that a small window had been left ajar.

She glanced back at Six. "You can't be serious."

"It's this, or we try to jimmy a lock." Six shrugged. "Do you know how to pick a lock?"

Valentine sighed. "No."

Six was much stronger than he appeared, Valentine discovered. He hoisted her with little effort up to the window and almost sent her sailing through the small opening. Valentine braced her fall onto a counter below, kicking a coffee maker in the process. She winced at the awful racket, then listened for an alarm. Hearing none, she made her way out of what was the kitchenette and to the back entrance, where she opened the door for Six and Church.

"Where do you think the rifle is?"

"Must be in the museum," Six muttered as he swept a glance through the gift shop they now stood in. "We won't find it here."

Once in the museum, Valentine wandered from exhibit to exhibit. She saw period dress, trunks, furniture, jewelry, and several revolvers. Taxidermized animals with unfortunately askew expressions. The undignified statues made her uneasy, and she avoided looking at those whenever she could. Finally, she came to a stop.

"Six?" She called. "Is this it?"

Six came over to stand beside her. "Yes."

"What are you doing here?"

Ice trickled down her spine as the new voice spoke, the rough sound of gravel and threats. Her heart rate tripled in a second. Valentine took a deep breath before she turned around. *Had they missed a security guard? How would they explain their presence?*

A tall man with dark eyes and in a deer hide jacket with fringe stared at them. He wore a hat with the brim folded back on one side; his mustache draped over his face, and his beard was shaped to fall just from the chin. Loose curls fell to his shoulders. Valentine saw that he had a pair of revolvers strapped to his thighs.

"I'll ask again. What are you doing here?"

Six stepped forward. "Buffalo Bill Cody, I presume? It's a ple—"

The other legend waved his hand.

Six disappeared.

"Six." Valentine shouted. "Six!" She whirled towards Buffalo Bill Cody, her fists clenched. "What did you *do* to him?"

"Hold your horses." Bill waved aside her anger. "I just put him outside. I know a showman, a smooth talker when I see one. I used to *be* one. I don't want to listen to pretty lies so I suggest you tell me what you're doing here."

Valentine swallowed hard, then scolded herself. *You rode the Wild Hunt. You defeated a Bloody Bones and returned the crown to the Flathead Lake Creature. Stand up straight.* "I need to borrow your rifle. Please."

Bill stared at her, disbelief etched on his face. Then he threw his head back and roared with laughter. "That all? You want my hat, too? My revolvers?"

Valentine felt wary. He didn't seem upset but... amused? Disdainful? She couldn't quite read him. "Will you let me borrow your rifle?"

Bill had stopped laughing. "What do you need it for?"

"To kill a monster in Maryland," Valentine replied. She felt a bit foolish saying the words out loud. "It's killing people. Children."

"And you're doing this out of the kindness of your heart?" Skepticism edged the legend's words like razor blades.

Valentine shook her head. "I'm on a penance," she confessed.

Bill snorted. "I figured."

Valentine scowled. "I need your rifle to destroy the creature. I'm told it's the only one that will do the job."

"Who told you that?"

"The Mother Road," Valentine said. "Dale Wright. High John de Conqueror. Paul Bunyan."

"Hmph. You got a lotta people telling you to come get my gun."

"I need it for the task."

"How many tasks have you completed so far?"

Valentine glanced down at her wrists. Seven gold music notes glittered in the dim light; one black blemish splashed across the inside of her left wrist. "Eight. No, seven." The Bell Witch wasn't a success.

"Failed one, huh?" Bill grinned. "Can't win them all. What are you going to do if you complete your penance?"

"Go home. Go back to my life." As she spoke the words, Valentine frowned. The words felt different this time; they didn't fill her with calm, like a mantra. Instead, they felt... hollow.

"You don't sound so sure."

"I am." Valentine glared at Bill.

"Take it easy, little pistol." Bill held up his hands. "I'm only saying what I see."

"I want to go home. I want my life, my music, back," Valentine repeated. That sounded firmer but still empty. *What is wrong with me?*

"Music?" Bill perked up. "You're a musician?"

"Yes."

Bill nodded. "Okay, little pistol. You can borrow my rifle on one condition: Write a song about me."

"Now?" Valentine didn't understand.

"No, not now. I suspect you're under a time constraint and the gods don't like to be kept waiting. But after all of this, when you're back home or finally dead, write a song about me."

How can I write a song if I've died the final death? But Valentine didn't ask, just nodded. She could do that.

"You do anything else besides music? Got a family, loved ones?"

Valentine's face heated with embarrassment. "No. Not really."

"Well, that's a sad life." Bill shook his head.

"Thanks." She couldn't keep the sarcasm out of her voice.

"Don't get worked up. I just think companionship and family are worth something. It makes life a little easier. Well, sometimes."

Valentine thought of her parents and the silence between them. Why had they called that night? Did they miss her? And who did she have, back in Nashville? Loretta was a friend and a mentor, yes. Was she family? She was the closest Valentine had ever had. Valentine gave an angry shake of her head. She didn't have time for this. She'd worry about family after all of this – if there was an after.

"Thank you for letting me use your rifle," Valentine said. "I will return it to you, and I owe you a song."

Bill shook his head. "Return the rifle to Miss Dale. She'll see it gets back to me, safely."

"And the song?"

"When you get to it." He gave a gentle smile. "You've more pressing things to deal with for now."

Valentine nodded, then moved towards the exhibit to reach for the rifle in front of her.

"What are you doing?"

Valentine sent him a puzzled glance. "You said I could borrow your rifle?"

"Oh." Bill shook his head. "That's a rifle I used in my mortal life, yes, but that's not my *real* rifle. You'll want this one." He reached over his shoulder and pulled out a long, gleaming rifle from a scabbard Valentine hadn't noticed. Bill hefted the gun in his hands before handing it to Valentine. She saw that it was inlaid with gold and ivory, with designs of bison and flowers worked into the metal.

She accepted it with gentle hands. "Thank you."

Bill nodded. "I'll walk you out. I want to look at the sunrise. No matter how long I've been around, I never get tired of those."

CHAPTER TWENTY ONE

They found Six pacing in the parking lot. "Was that *really* necessary?" he demanded of Cody as they approached.

Cody chuckled. "I didn't want to waste my time. You talk a lot, Mother Road. This one got to the point, and quickly." He jerked his head towards Valentine.

Six glared at him. "Rude. That's very rude."

Cody ignored them, turning to the east. "Here it comes."

The sunrise filtered over the eastern ridge of the mountains. The light gilded them in golds, marigold, and butter yellow, and reds, coral and peach. Valentine studied the glowing ridgeline, purples and blues beneath the rising sun. She felt a faint warmth on her face and closed her eyes, enjoying the respite from the cool winds of the fading night.

Cody turned to them. "I wish you luck, little pistol."

The drive to Maryland was uneventful. Valentine took a turn driving and made good time, clearing four states in a single day. Later that evening, Six and Church regaled her with a list of their favorite tourist stops along the Mother Road over dinner.

Six loved the drive-in movie theatre in Carthage, Missouri. "It is a historical site, a monument to an era." Six leaned over his usual dinner, an enormous breakfast. His eyes took on a dreamy cast and a lock of hair fell out of its pomaded curls as he gesticulated with both hands. "The drive-in theatre is emblematic of a new world, driven by technology and possibility."

Church snorted. *A drive-in theatre is a glorified parking lot.*

"*Church.*" Six was scandalized. "How can you say such a thing?"

Very easily. Church rumbled with laughter in the back of Valentine's mind. *You want impressive? Try the National Petrified Forest Park. Alien landscape, cool trees, and ancient. That's where it's at.*

Valentine listened to them with half an ear, thinking.

Their debate on the merits of so many different locations had made her realize how much she hadn't seen in her short life. In fact, she realized that she had seen and done more in her afterlife than when she had been alive. Valentine shifted in her seat, uncomfortable. She had spent so much time pursuing a career in music, to the exclusion of anything else — friends, fun, a community of some kind. She had told herself that she had to work that hard to support herself, to pay her bills and her dues, to make it as a musician. But... Was that true? Couldn't she have carved some space out for something, or someone, else? And if she were successful at this penance, something she doubted, what would she do when she returned to her old life? She wouldn't be the same person.

So who would she be?

Valentine picked at her food for the rest of the meal, uncomfortable with her thoughts.

When they arrived in Frederick County, the Snallygaster practically advertised its presence. Valentine soon saw the headlines in the newspapers and missing children posters that lined the shop front windows. Once parked, she studied the posters for a moment. In the past three months, five children had gone missing near the headwaters of the river that wended through the town. No one had seen or heard from them since. A flutter caught the corner of her eye: A newspaper abandoned on a bench ruffled in the breeze. Walking over, she picked up the paper and scanned the headlines.

Two more children, a pair of siblings, had disappeared the day before. The local authorities suspected the same abductors were behind this.

Six approached with two cups of coffee and offered one to her. Behind him, Church choked down a donut. Valentine held up the newspaper. "The monster is likely at the headwaters. He, or it, took two more yesterday." Valentine paused for a minute, afraid to ask her question. She forced the words out. "Are the children still alive?"

"I hope so." He didn't sound optimistic.

Valentine sipped her coffee. "Do we track the monster along the river?"

"That seems like the best strategy," Six agreed.

"Church, are you able to sniff him out? Or does that violate the rules?"

Church had cinnamon sugar dusted across his snout. *I'm not permitted to help. The gods made it clear.* Valentine could hear the apology in his words.

"Great," she sighed.

Valentine stepped through the underbrush that lined the river's edge. The banks were muddy, the ground unstable, and she had slipped more than a few times. Her boots were coated in mud and damp leaves; dirt streaked her clothes. She had strapped Cody's rifle to her back and carried the bullets in a sack. She used her free hand to grab the foliage for stability. Valentine heard Six and Church behind her, stepping with care to avoid the places she had tripped or slipped.

She cursed as she stumbled again.

She took a deep breath, let it out, and then continued forward. *Keep going. You'll find it. It has to be nearby.*

As if summoned by her thoughts, a garbled cry echoed down the river.

Upstream. It came from upstream. Valentine plunged forward, scrambling over boulders and crashing through bushes. Branches reached out to trap her clothes, tear at her face. Valentine ignored it, trying to move as fast as she could through the forest. A drizzle had started and Valentine had to blink against the damp mist which further obscured her vision. After a few more stuttered steps, Valentine fell past a small tree and into a clearing that lined the river.

The Snallygaster was there.

Valentine stared at the creature across the river, shocked into immobility. It was huge, the size of a small house. A snake's body, green and blue scales, twisted and coiled around the body of a little girl, unconscious or dead – Valentine couldn't tell. Enormous, blood-red feathered wings reached toward the sky and a silver beak rested beneath cold, intelligent eyes.

Her heart rate tripled in her chest, then stuttered.

Another body, a little boy, lay half in and half out of the river.

"Valentine!"

She started at Six's shout. "What?"

"Shoot it!"

"Right. Yes." Valentine swung the rifle around her body, then knelt on the muddy bank. The cold and the damp seeped into her clothes; she ignored it. She loaded two bullets into the rifle, then cocked it. She lifted, then took aim, sighting down the barrel. *Where should I shoot? The head? The torso?* She shook her head, frustrated at herself. *It doesn't matter. Just start shooting.*

She aimed at the head. She pulled the trigger.

Nothing happened.

What the hell? She pulled back, looked over the rifle. The bullets were loaded. The rifle cocked and ready to go. She lifted the rifle, aimed again, and pulled the trigger a second time.

Still, nothing.

"Six, what the hell? What do I do?" Urgency and fear graveled her voice. She hardly recognized herself.

"It probably needs a tribute of some kind." Six crouched down, his face worried. "Blood or tears should work. Do you have a knife?"

"No." Valentine scrabbled across the ground for something, anything. She saw a black rock with a jagged, sharp edge. She threw herself forward, grabbed the rock. Scrambling to an upright position, Valentine pressed the jagged edge of the rock against her palm – and pulled.

It hurt.

She grunted as the sharp edge cut through her skin, her body fighting against her mind's command. Finally, blood seeped through, then rushed forward. Valentine smeared her bloody palm against the length of the rifle, coating the gold and the ivory with red. The rifle pulsed in her hands, once, twice, and then a third time. The blood disappeared – and the barrel warmed in her hands.

Valentine lifted the rifle, sighted down the barrel at the creature, and fired.

The Snallygaster bugled a scream that hurt Valentine's ears as the two bullets tore into its neck and face. It whipped its head back and forth, its wings beating a forceful gale across the river. Metallic blood, copper and silver, seeped down the creature's scaled skin. She trembled as she lowered the rifle; Valentine then dropped two bullets into the mud. She ignored those and gathered new ones from her sack, then reloaded the rifle. She swung up, took aim, and fired.

Again and again and again.

Valentine kept firing until she ran out of bullets.

She didn't know how many times she had shot the monster.

With a final bugle that caused her left ear to give an unpleasant pop, Valentine watched the creature slump forward and crash into the river. Water rained down on both sides of the river from the splash and the stream clouded with its blood, the monster's eyes still and staring at nothing.

Valentine stood, then staggered to the side.

Six braced her upright. She nodded across the river. "We need to get those children to a hospital. If it's not too late." Her heart skipped a beat at those words. She shook off her fear and examined the river, looking for an easy path across.

There.

A few feet upriver, the stream was narrow and fast but didn't look too deep. Valentine slung the rifle across her back and stumbled up the bank. She took a few steps into the water, testing out the slick rock beneath. Her footing was stable enough, so she continued forward.

Valentine stumbled and slipped and pushed her way across the river, getting waist deep at some points. She saw Six and Church materialize across the river, next to the children, and envied them that ability. Finally, she staggered up the bank and down to the children. Six and Church pulled the boy out of the water. Valentine made for the little girl, still trapped in the creature's coils. She lifted a coil, straining at that weight of the thick muscle and scales. A pained grunt escaped her; the scales had further cut her bleeding palm. Valentine tugged and shoved, twisted and pushed, and finally the coils were loose enough to free the little girl.

Valentine lifted the child up and away from the Snallygaster. The blonde girl was still. Too still. Valentine felt for a pulse, holding her breath.

A faint beat trembled beneath her fingers.

A sigh gusted out of Valentine. She looked up at Church and Six. "Is he okay?"

Six nodded. "He's still alive, at least."

Valentine sagged against the girl she held in her arms. After a moment, she pulled herself up. "We need to go. They need medical attention." She looked between the boy and the girl. "Six, I can't carry them both. Are you allowed to carry one of them?"

"You completed the task. I can help you get these children to a hospital," Six said, his tone grim. He stood with the little boy cradled in his arms. "Let's go."

The trek back to the car was painful. Valentine staggered through the woods, the girl clutched to her body. Her arms ached from the strain; her palm tingled and burned from the cut. She shivered from the cold; her clothes were caught onto her body by sweat, river water, and blood. She bled on the girl and felt guilty for it. Cody's rifle banged against the back of her head with every step and she felt the beginnings of a headache come on. As she tripped over logs and rocks, Valentine dreaded falling. She didn't know if she could get back up.

Valentine cried silent tears of relief when she saw the sedan on the gravel road, a mirage in the deep forest.

Another task done.

Valentine barely perceived the drive to the hospital; she only focused on holding the girl. As they stumbled into the emergency room with the children, the staff on duty leapt into action. Valentine gasped in relief as two nurses lifted the little girl from her arms and onto a nearby gurney. She stumbled and pitched forward without the extra weight as ballast. Six reached out to steady her, having been relieved of the little boy.

"What happened?" One of the nurses, an older man, demanded.

"We found them. At the river," Valentine replied. She didn't say anything about the Snallygaster. Who would believe her?

The man's eyes sharpened with understanding. "These are the missing Rackner children," he breathed. Valentine watched him step away from the children and over to the nurse's station, where he had a murmured conversation with another nurse. They peered at Valentine several times with deepening frowns, and she knew what they saw: A bloodied young woman with shorn hair, coated with mud and river muck, who just appeared out of nowhere with a rifle strapped to her back.

Hardly the picture of trustworthiness.

Six leaned over to her. "We should leave." Worry cast his face in hard lines.

"Yes. Now?"

"Now." Six grasped her hand and led them to a nearby closet door.

"Excuse me, miss, where are you going?" Valentine heard the nurse call out. Fear tightened her stomach.

Time to go.

Six opened the closet door and Valentine coughed at the stench of cleaning agents and bleach that wafted over them. He pushed past through the carts and mops and brooms, and led them to a second doorway at the back of what turned out to be a housekeeping closet, Church close on their heels. Six pushed through the door — and they entered into the casino hallway, the lingering smell of bleach in the air.

Valentine flinched as she felt her clothes dry against her body with an audible *whoosh.* The mud and the dirt disappeared, the blood evaporated. Her palm stung and burned as the flesh knit itself back together. A wave of relief and fatigue stole over her.

Valentine took a deep breath. She was back, safe for the moment.

Six let go of her hand to straighten his vest and suit jacket. He swept a hand over his hair, settling the disheveled locks back into place. "Ready to report in?"

Valentine nodded. "Let's get this over with."

They walked towards the back of the casino, dodging the usual denizens and ignoring the games of chance only a few feet away. After everything she had seen, after all the magic she'd witnessed, Valentine realized that the stakes at these games were much higher than mere currency. She shivered at that thought. Soon they were at the familiar double doors, golden and ornate.

Six knocked, then pushed through.

Inside, the gods awaited them.

Dale stood behind the pink velvet couch with a purple cocktail that cast smoke and shadows in her hand, her dress an elegant silver concoction. High John rested on the couch, an ankle on his knee and his arms crossed against his chest. Despite his watchful gaze, he seemed almost relaxed to Valentine. Paul Bunyan paced behind the couch in a tense and tight stride, only stopping as Valentine, Six, and Church came in.

Valentine swung the rifle off her back and lifted the strap over her head. She held it up. "I'm supposed to give this to you, Dale, to return to Buffalo Bill Cody."

Dale shared a ruby and ivory smile. "I will see to it, child."

Valentine nodded. "Thank you."

Paul Bunyan stepped forward. "May I see the rifle?"

Valentine cast a puzzled look at Six, then Dale. "Uh, yeah? Sure."

Paul took the rifle from Valentine, a small and somewhat silly grin on his face. He handled the rifle with care, running gentle hands over the barrel and examining the trigger and cocking mechanism with a close gaze. He caressed the floral and bison designs etched into the stock and the metal, then whistled to himself. Out of the corner of her eye, she saw High John roll his eyes before exchanging a knowing glance with Dale. The female legend chuckled. It took her a moment but Valentine realized that Paul Bunyan was *impressed* with the gun. He was... giddy with excitement from holding Buffalo Bill Cody's famed rifle.

Valentine swallowed a smirk and stared at the lush carpet on the black marble and gold floor. She didn't dare let him see her amusement. He'd probably tack on additional tasks as a punishment.

"Paulie, are you done?" Dale drawled.

Valentine looked up in time to see Paul scowl. "Yeah," he said, his voice gruff. "Here." He handed the gun to Dale, who settled the rifle next to her seafoam acoustic guitar.

The gods turned to examine Valentine. She wanted to squirm under the weight of their collective gazes but held herself still.

"Valentine Cash, you have survived the Wild Hunt and vanquished the Snallygaster," Dale said. "Despite your failure with the Bell Witch, you have done well. You have two final tasks before you."

Valentine jerked in surprise. Relief, elation, and fear coursed through, her thoughts chasing each other like greyhounds on a racetrack. "Two more? That's it?" Her tone betrayed her caution and wariness.

High John gave a sudden chuckle. "You are right to be wary, child. Your next task is this: You will retrieve golden grapes from the Vesper's Vineyards along the California coastline. After you retrieve the grapes, and for your final task, you will escort a hellhound back to the Underworld."

"Oh." *Where would she find a hellhound?* Valentine stiffened her shoulders against her disappointment. *Of course it wouldn't be easy*, she scolded herself. *Nothing about this is ever easy.*

High John continued. "Should you prove to be successful on these final two tasks, return to the casino a final time. We will discuss your reward at that time." He smiled and uncrossed his arms to spread them wide, his eyes steady on Valentine's face. She met his gaze, unable to read him. Behind him, Dale sipped her cocktail while Paul ignored her and others, looking at Cody's rifle once more.

After a moment, Valentine nodded. "I will."

CHAPTER TWENTY TWO

They left the room. Without a word, Valentine made her way across the casino and to the bar. She needed a drink to celebrate her good fortune. *Only two more tasks. Don't get too excited. Don't get cocky. Remember the Bell Witch.* Valentine saw that Amaretto Sour waited behind the bar with a welcoming smile.

The other woman leaned on the bar top. "I hear you both have something to celebrate."

Valentine tried to swallow the smile that threatened to take over face. "I hope so."

Amaretto peered at Six. "Are you excited about your celebration? After her penance is complete?"

Six stared at the crowd in the casino. "Plans have changed, unfortunately. The celebration won't be going forward."

Valentine's head jerked towards to the legend. "What? Why not?"

"Circumstances change." Six gave a shrug.

Valentine frowned. "I don't understand. This is why you agreed to guide me. You wanted a splashy festival, a celebration of the highway and your history. Why isn't it happening?"

"Let it go, Valentine." Six swallowed his drink quickly.

Valentine rested on her heels, stunned. She had never heard that tone from the legend before. *What is he hiding?*

"You know what? No, I'm not letting it go." Valentine shifted from the bar to face Six squarely. "Why aren't you having the celebration? I can't do any of this without you – it's only fair you get something out of this... effort."

Six smiled down at Valentine, his eyes crinkled in the corners and his earlier coolness gone. "Kid, I appreciate your indignation. I will be fine. I promise."

"Oh."

Valentine had forgotten about Amaretto behind the bar. "What?"

The woman gave Six a pitying glance. "Did you do it for her?"

Six frowned at Amaretto. "Stop. At once."

"What does she mean?" Valentine demanded. Her heartbeat banged against her chest. Worry gnawed at her insides as she tried to take a deep breath. *What did he do?*

"Nothing. She's mistaken." Six stared at Amaretto with stern eyes and a frown, as if willing the woman to stop talking.

Amaretto shook her head, a frown on her face and a furrow between her brows. "You did the right thing. She deserves to know."

"I deserve to know what?" Valentine's gaze swung between the two. "Come on, *tell me.*"

Six sighed. "I didn't want her to find out. She's been through so much." Six finally glanced back at Valentine. "You remember the Bell Witch, of course."

"It's not something you forget," Valentine scoffed. Anxiety crawled through her like a snake, weaving a tight hold on her chest. "What about it?"

"You didn't complete the task."

"Believe me, I know." *Where is this going?*

"You would have died."

"I know." *Oh god.*

Six shifted from one foot to the other, then cleared his throat. The legend seemed to be searching for the right words. "You were going to die, kid. I couldn't let that happen. So I traded my celebration for another chance. For you."

Valentine staggered in place. She grasped the bar top with a numb hand, and tried to process what she heard. *He saved me. I was going to die, and he saved me.*

Six stepped closer, a deep frown on his face. "Kid, say something."

Valentine shook her head, trying to clear the racing thoughts. "Why? Why would you do that for me?" Sadness seeped through her as another realization kicked in. "Your celebration is completely canceled? Gone? God, Six, I'm so sorry."

Six stepped even closer and before Valentine realized it, the legend had swept her up into a hug. She stiffened at first. She couldn't remember the last time she had been hugged. Maybe Loretta? After a moment, her arms crept up and around Six. Valentine rested her head on his chest. Tears slid down her face. "I don't want you to be lonely. To be forgotten," she whispered. "Why did you do that, Six?"

"Kid, I couldn't let you die." Valentine could hear the unshed tears in the legend's voice. "You are *remarkable*. Tenacious, and a good person. I couldn't let you go without a fair chance to try again." Six cleared his throat again. "I would make that decision again and again. You are worth it, Valentine."

Those words broke her. Valentine tried to muffle her sobs against the fine clothes the legend always wore. She wasn't successful. She tried to stop crying but could not. Everything that had led to this moment — the tasks, the stress, everything she had seen — seemed to weigh on her at once. Her feet felt leaden and her shoulders sagged as she leaned into Six and cried. She didn't know how long they stood next to the bar of the unearthly casino.

She only knew that Six held her as she cried.

The mood in the car on the drive to California was different. Strange. Valentine and Six took turns driving like usual but bickered over the radio station.

"Can't we put something on that won't literally make my ears bleed?" She had protested.

Six had given an irritable sigh. "You've survived ten tasks set before you by the gods. I'm sure you'll be fine."

Church whined and chortled at this sally from the backseat.

Valentine was not amused.

Unable to agree on a radio station, they left it off.

They fell into now familiar patterns: Six gassed up the car, this one a black convertible with a leather cream interior, while Valentine foraged for snacks and treats in the convenience shop. She knew which snacks to seek out: Six predictably was partial to old-fashioned sweets like taffy and bubblegum; Valentine and Church preferred salty and cheesy snacks. She made sure to purchase separate snacks for Church, too. The one and only time she had thought to share a bag of chips with Church had left an impressive memory of curled lips and utter disdain.

She hadn't done it again.

They stopped for meals at mom-and-pop restaurants along the road to California. Valentine didn't care where they ate but Six loved the old timer cafes and diners. He seemed to thrive off of the nostalgia of these places, and she couldn't bring herself to ask him to go to a fast-food joint. She could only imagine the horror and distaste he'd express.

They drove on the Mother Road most of the trip. Valentine felt surreal at times when she remembered that the highway was driving along its own roads. As for Six, the legend glowed with an inner peace and a relaxation she had only ever seen at the Last Stop Diner. He whistled while he drove. He stopped at tourist landmarks so Valentine could see them, giving impromptu lectures on the *real* origin of the attraction. He chattered almost nonstop, really, about anything they saw. But Valentine didn't mind. She could see that he was happy, content, to be back on his own lanes. She listened, offering a few sporadic words, knowing that their time together would end soon.

One way or another.

She didn't let herself examine that knowledge too closely. She pushed it away for the moment.

On the three nights it took to drive to California, they stopped in hotels along Route 66. Each of these were kitsch, with decorations and branding that were aggressively on theme. These places delighted Six, who pointed out the little details: Alien salt and pepper shakers at the continental breakfast bar at the Area 51 themed hotel named Lost in Space. Leopard print and jungle themed bedding and interior decoration at a safari themed motel in Nevada. Wild West memorabilia at the Silver Dollar in eastern California. Each night, Six asked Valentine to play music for him.

The first night, she was surprised. "What?"

Six had leaned against the headboard of the bed, Church sprawled next to him. He didn't meet her eyes as he rubbed Six's head. "Play something for us."

Valentine thought she understood. Six also realized that they didn't have much time left together. "Any requests?"

Six had shaken his head. "Play anything. Everything." Church rested his head on the legend's knee.

Valentine pulled out the black mandolin and tuned it. Then, she played. Old ballads and her own work blended together, filling the small hotel room with sounds that felt tangible, like she could hold them in her hands. She sang sometimes, her contralto growing huskier from prolonged use as she slipped from one song to another. But mostly she played, her fingers chasing notes and melodies across the frets in a different kind of Wild Hunt, one of her own creation.

Each night, Valentine played.

Each night, Six and Church listened. They offered no praise or requests. None were needed. The nightly ritual formed a communion between the trio, a celebration of their trials together.

It was also a farewell.

But no one spoke of that.

Not yet.

The California coastline gleamed in the bright sunlight and ocean breezes. The ocean formed a blue road that stretched across the horizon, a different sort of highway than the ones they had recently traveled on. Valentine studied the blues and greens, inhaled the salt tang, and felt the wind ruffle her hair. It was the first time she had seen the Pacific.

She turned to Six. "What are we looking for again?"

Six pointed to a cove at the base of the cliff they stood on. "We're seeking directions to Vesper's Vineyards. We need to ask the Old Man in the Sea."

"You don't know where the Vineyards are?"

"It may surprise you, Valentine, but I don't know everything."

She almost rolled her eyes. "What is the Old Man in the Sea like?" She paused. "Or rather, who is he? Really?"

"Local water god." Six grinned at her. "He's kind of salty."

Valentine did roll her eyes then.

An hour later, they arrived. The cove was a small half circle of sand and pebbles. A small cavern was nestled into the cliffside to the right, the black depths within the only darkness that blotted the bright day. Dense vegetation lined the edges of the cove, almost obscuring a short trail that led from a small parking lot at the base of the cliff. To Valentine's surprise, no one was present. Not a single person or car marred the space.

At the end of the short trail, Six pulled off his brogues and rolled up his pants before stepping into the damp sand. "Come on," he urged. "It feels great."

Valentine paused to pull off her boots, then stepped into the sand. She smiled as the sand wedged between her toes and sprinkled her skin. It felt cool on the bottoms of her feet. Valentine continued forward, up to the edge of the ocean. The tides had deposited kelp and seaweed, sand dollars and even a starfish. Old twine fishnets, coated in green sludge, rested a few feet away. Polished pebbles twinkled in the sunlit waters.

She smiled as the foam-crested waves swept over her feet. "How do we contact him?"

Six stepped forward to stand next to her. "He's already coming. He'll be here soon."

As he finished speaking, Valentine noticed movement out in the ocean.

She squinted against the sunlight, a hand over her eyes to shield them. Closer and closer they came, until Valentine realized at last what she was seeing: A large man riding a horse among the waves, a trident in one hand. They lunged forward with the crest of every wave, disappeared for a few seconds, then rose again with a new one. Soon, the rider and the horse were close to the shore and Valentine saw that this horse had fins for a mane and tail, scales instead of a hide, and long legs with additional fins. The eyes faced forward, ocean blue, and were as cold as a shark's.

Valentine shivered.

A few waves out, the rider slipped off the horse's back to glide through the waves. He strode forward. His dark skin gleamed in the bright sunlight over a large, muscular frame. Salt had crusted his hair and beard into locs, with charms and precious stones woven into them. Bottle green eyes swept over Valentine first, then Six and Church. A half smile edged across his handsome face as he stopped a few feet away.

"Mother Road," he called out in a greeting. "It's been a while."

Six stepped into the waves. "Enki, it's good to see you again. You're far from home these days."

"As times change, so must I." The legend and the god embraced. "What brings you to my stretch of ocean?"

Six nodded to Valentine. "She's on a penance. We need directions. We were hoping you'd help us."

The bottle green gaze studied Valentine. "What's your name, penitent?"

"Valentine Cash."

Enki turned back to Six. "Where are you headed?"

"We need to find Vesper's Vineyards."

Enki laughed. "The golden grapes? Again? The gods are so predictable."

"It's hard to argue with the classics," Six said with a shrug.

Enki glanced back at Valentine. "What do you have to offer me?"

"I can play music," she offered.

Enki shook his head, swept a hand out to the sea. "Under these waves, I listen to the primordial sounds of this world. They have sung a song of power and of creation for eons. What use do I have for mortal music? No, I'm afraid you'll need something better than that."

Well, I'm all out of wisdom teeth. Valentine studied the god before her. *What can I offer him?* His locs were adorned in gems and shells, his eyes lined in kohl. His loincloth, the only clothing he wore, was a fine sea-green fabric lined with metallic threads. Rings flashed across his fingers and his nails were painted in gold and copper. *He likes adornment. I need to give him something attractive to wear.*

"I can offer adornment to you and your mount." The words poured out of Valentine like they belonged to someone else.

Eyebrows flew up on the sea god's face. "Oh? Are you an artisan, too?"

I'll have to be. "Y-yes," Valentine said. She hoped her uncertainty hadn't betrayed her.

Enki studied her for a moment. "You have until tonight," he stated. "I will return then. If I find the tribute lacking, you will get no help from me." *Don't waste my time,* his tone warned.

"Agreed." Valentine made herself nod.

I hope I can do this.

Chapter Twenty Three

Valentine got to work as soon as Enki strode back into the waves.

Six and Church wandered across the sands, bound by the usual restrictions against helping her, and watched as Valentine gathered the sand dollars, starfish, sea glass, and polished rocks scattered across the cove. She picked up the old twine fishnet and a few strands of seaweed, then searched the caverns, where she came away with a few weathered bones.

Once she gathered everything, Valentine began.

She took the fishnet and tore a rough triangle out of the cloth. Using the remainder of the twine, she wove a half cape fit for the sea god: A collar of sand dollars rested across the shoulders, with a starfish clasp. Polished pebbles and sea glass formed a firmament of color and texture through the net, twinkling in the sunlight. She added smaller starfish to the seaborn tapestry for extra adornment, certain that the god would want something *more*. For the mount (a kelpie, Six had told her) Valentine wove a wreath of seaweed, glass, and sand dollars.

Valentine hoped it was enough.

The time ebbed and soon, too soon, Enki rode his kelpie across the waves to the edge of the ocean. He glided with the tides up to where Valentine stood, her feet buried in the damp sand. She held the shawl in her hands; the wreath lay at her feet.

"Well, penitent?" Enki asked. "What do you have for me?"

Valentine offered the shawl in her hands to the sea god. "I have made you a cape for your travels. This tapestry is made from the very elements of this cove, designed to accent your beauty." She gestured at her feet. "I also offer a wreath for your mount, if it pleases them."

Enki accepted the shawl, looking it over. Surprise, then satisfaction, filtered across his face as the sea god took in the precise pattern Valentine had worked across the old fishnet. After a moment, he settled the cape across his shoulders, testing out the weight and feel of the garment on his body. The starfish clasp settled into place; the sand dollars lay nicely against the firm shoulders. The woven net shifted and swayed within the wind against his arms and torso.

Valentine picked up the wreath, and held it in her hands, waiting for the sea god's response.

Enki peered up. "This is acceptable."

A sigh gusted through her and she grinned from relief. She offered the wreath to the sea god. Enki let loose a sudden sharp whistle that hurt Valentine's ears. She watched as the kelpie gallop from the waves, pausing several feet from the shore. Valentine gave a hard swallow, then stepped further and further into the ocean, until she came to a stop before the creature. This close, Valentine saw the intricate layers of scales and skin on the kelpie, painted in a myriad of greens and blues and purples. The ocean tugged and gusted against her body, waist-deep. She was cold.

"May I?" Valentine held up the wreath.

In response, the kelpie lowered its head.

Valentine took a deep breath, then laid the wreath on the creature's neck, taking care not to scratch or jostle the kelpie. She backed away at once, towards the shoreline.

She found Six and Enki in conversation.

"...far along is she on the penance?" Enki asked.

"Two more to go," Six replied. "She's a tough one."

Valentine staggered out of the waves, coming to a stop next to Six. She shivered. The adrenaline hadn't left her yet.

Six pulled off his suit jacket and draped it over Valentine. "Enki has given us the directions. We should go soon before the location changes again."

Valentine nodded. "Thank you," she said to Enki.

He preened under his cape, the sea glass and shells clinking together. "This isn't terrible, mortal. I like this."

Valentine grinned at that.

Enki nodded at Church, then strode back into the water. He vaulted onto the kelpie and together, they disappeared into the horizon.

"The location is only ever temporary," Six said as he navigated the narrow two lane highway along the coastline. "That's why we needed to ask for directions. Last week's location would be useless to us."

"I'll have to sneak in, right?"

Six chuckled. "Well, I wouldn't announce our presence, no. We can see what the situation is when we arrive, then adapt."

Brilliant plan. Church yawned from the backseat.

"Oh, like you have a better one?" Six said over his shoulder.

Valentine ignored the bickering. She leaned forward, peering through the windshield as Six slowed the car and pulled to the side of the road.

They had arrived.

Vesper's Vineyards rested at the top of a valley, golds and greens that stretched across south-facing slopes and down to the valley floor. The neat rows of short, wiry trees were laden with full fruit, almost bursting with abundance; brown furrowed earth interrupted the golds and greens in a precise pattern. A stone mansion rose at the pinnacle of the hill, with gables and turrets, a castle among the moat of the vineyard. Several long green barns lay around the mansion, outstretched like petals on a flower. *Where the wine was made, perhaps?* Valentine couldn't be sure. She knew nothing about wine.

They climbed the small hill to arrive at a clearing beside a faux rustic barn, the kind Valentine had seen featured on home decor magazines. Inside, bulb string lights with Edison coils draped from the ceiling to the walls, a charming chandelier of sorts. Whitewashed wooden walls gleamed with artwork and pithy platitudes in ornate lettering. Long, chest high tables with open bottles of wine and stemmed goblets lined the tabletops.

The barn was *crowded*.

But as Valentine studied the faces among the crowd, she realized something: These weren't just people. They were gods, legends, and creatures. Her gaze skipped and hot-scotched around, trying to take in everything at once. She saw a recently deceased celebrity, whose name blazoned across her mind but wouldn't cross her lips. She saw a man with cicada wings and a troll arguing over wine a few tables away; a centaur shook his head as he listened to the two argue. Everywhere she looked, Valentine saw something unusual and magical.

Valentine bumped into four people on her way inside, the last of whom – a horned man with a green tinge to his skin, his antlers a full crown above his head – did a double-take when he glanced at Valentine. He seemed startled, then wary, before he stepped away from her. Valentine examined her clothes and arms. *Do I smell? Am I wearing something offensive?*

Six bumped into her from behind, then steadied her before she could stumble. "We should get what you need, then leave." His brow furrowed as he swept glances around the thick crowd. *He looks worried*, Valentine thought.

"Six, are we at a... wine tasting for the gods?" Valentine couldn't quite keep the disbelief from her voice.

Six nodded. "Gods, legends, and creatures, yes."

"Oh. I didn't know that was a thing."

"Valentine, these creatures are the original drunkards and bacchanals." She could hear the exasperation in his voice. She watched him continue to scan the crowd with watchful eyes. "Of course they seek any excuse for a party."

"Six, who are you looking for?"

He winced. "I'd rather not say —"

"Route Sixty-Six? Oh my gods, it *is* you."

A buxom blonde dashed up to Six and threw her arms around him, the force of her sudden embrace causing him to stagger backwards a few feet. Valentine took a step away, to avoid the crossfire. A high pitched squeal emerged from the blonde and the sound ricocheted off the barn walls. Five others, a mix of men and women, of skin tones, body shapes, and hairstyles, materialized from the crowd to cluster around the blonde and Six, burying them in a tangle of limbs and color and noise.

Valentine winced. *A lot of noise.*

"Mother Road, it's been *so* long."

"Too long. Shame on you."

"But you came back. We'll take care of you."

"Still so handsome."

Valentine could hardly find Six underneath the affectionate swarm of young creatures.

Church chortled in the back of her mind.

"So he knows them?"

Yes. He knows them very well. Church burbled.

Valentine snorted. "And they clearly miss him."

He left rather... precipitously the last time. Church shook himself. *They can be... clingy.*

"Who are they?"

Nymphs and tritons. They run Vesper's Vineyards.

"Hmm."

What?

Valentine grinned at Church. *I think this is a good time to get some grapes.* She watched to see if he could hear her.

Church grinned, white and sharp teeth gleaming in the string lights. *An excellent time.*

It was child's play to slip out of the crowded barn and across the clearing to the neat rows of the vineyard. Valentine swept glances behind her, searching for someone who would stop her or at least question her presence. But every creature ambled about, loose limbed and flush with the bright sunlight and flowing wine. No one paid any attention to the dead mortal girl and her large black dog stealing away into the vineyard.

Among the neat rows of turned earth, lush golden green leaves sprouted from thick, gnarled trunks that reached waist high on Valentine. The grapes were pitch black and blood red, as round as her thumb was long, and plump against the vines. Valentine walked along the row, her fingers tracing the cool, round grapes and the slightly fuzzy leaves. Her fingers tingled, causing her to stop before a particular tree. *This is the one.* Valentine studied the vine, then reached forward to snap a first bunch off of the limb. She pulled two other bunches in quick succession, using her shirt to form a half pouch to house the grapes.

As she laid the third and final bunch into her shirt, a klaxon sounded above her head.

Valentine flinched at the sudden, jarring noise. Her hands fumbled with the grapes in her shirt, almost spilling them onto the ground. She saved them from a fall at the last moment. Her head reared up and she swept a quick glance around the vineyard.

"What is that noise?"

An alarm. Obviously. Church whined at the noise, shaking his head. *They know you're here.*

"Shit." Valentine gathered the grapes close to her body. "I'll meet you back at the car."

Valentine started to run. Crouched low, she ducked behind one green barn, then another. *Please don't let them see me.* The alarm continued, growing louder and fiercer, until the noise rattled the bones in Valentine's body. She ignored it as best as she could and continued forward. *Got to get to the car.*

"There she is!" A female voice, deepened by rage and determination.

Uh-oh.

Valentine gave up any pretense of hiding and ran as fast as she could to the parking lot. *Get to the car, get to the car, get to the car.* The mantra became a rhythm, urging her forward without caution or care. *Almost there.*

Six materialized out of thin air next to her.

Valentine screamed, darting sideways in fright. Somehow, impossibly, she held onto the grapes. "Don't *do* that." She slid to a stop before the passenger side of the vehicle. "Let's go. We have to go." Valentine plunged into the car as Six slid in. He started the vehicle, whipped out of the parking slot, and wrenched the car down the road.

Valentine shuddered in the seat, trying not to burst the grapes in her lap. Then she noticed a new barrier.

"Six. The gates. They're closing!"

The car slammed through the closing gates that guarded the vineyard entrance, knocking one of them askew. Six didn't slow down; instead, he pushed the vehicle faster down the narrow lanes. Valentine adjusted her hold on the grapes and freed a hand to hang onto the strap above the passenger door. Six whipsawed them down the mountain, a journey that felt like hours to Valentine. Bile rose up into her throat and she swallowed it back down. *You can't be sick right now,* she scolded herself.

At the base of the mountain, where the narrow lanes merged into the coastline highway, Six finally slowed.

Valentine expelled a deep breath. "Thank you."

Six gave his own sigh. "Damn." His clothes were mussed, half undone. Lipstick of three different shades smudged the edges of his collar and traced up his neck and over his jawline. His hair resembled a bird's nest, so unlike his usual coiffed style. "Are you okay?"

Six gave an exuberant laugh, then shook his head. "I'm fine. The nymphs and tritons are... darling. I miss them."

Valentine leaned back into her seat. "I got the grapes."

"Well done. Only one more task to go."

Valentine snorted. "Tell me. Where do I find a hellhound? Much less escort it back to hell?"

Six studied the rearview mirror for a moment. "You'd be surprised."

CHAPTER TWENTY FOUR

Six drove them along the coastline. After an hour, Valentine made him stop for an ice box. She needed something to house the stolen grapes. When Six turned left from the coastal highway and headed inland, Valentine frowned.

"Where are we headed?"

"Death Valley."

The land changed the further inland they drove, from coastal forest to desert scrub and cacti. The bright sun shimmered over the cloudless azure sky and the heat shimmered in waves over the horizon. Often Valentine thought she spotted a car in the distance but it only turned into a mirage, shadows that flickered and folded between the heat waves in the distance. They reached Death Valley National Park by late afternoon. The heat outside overwhelmed the air conditioning within the car. Valentine felt sweat slip down her back and bead on her forehead.

Six drove until they reached Hells Gate, then pulled over to park. The sun had started to set, painting the sky in fiery hues. To the east, Valentine could see the first stars emerge. She jumped when Church materialized next to her, not waiting for Six to let him out.

"Church, what's the –" Her voice faded as he hurtled into the east, his fast pace churning the ground beneath him in long strides. Valentine glanced at Six in surprise. "What's this about?"

The corners of the legend's smile dipped down. She had never seen him so sad before. "We should follow him."

Valentine peered after Church, a black speck in the distance. "We'll never catch him."

"We will."

Valentine studied the legend as they crossed the road and stepped into the desert. He seemed miserable and remote, a contrast to the usual easy smile and affable attitude. "You're being weird tonight."

"I know."

Valentine shook her head, then led them away from the car and into the barren desert, after Church. They walked further and further into the night, the golds of sunset fading into the navy scene of night. The stars were bright, larger and clearer than anything Valentine had ever before seen, and dusted across the sky like spilled sugar on a cosmic kitchen countertop. Valentine stole glances up at the sky whenever she could but mostly had to watch her footing. The new moon didn't provide any light for them to walk by. Instead, Six had pulled out an old flashlight for Valentine.

They walked.

And walked.

The air rippled around them and flickered, creating airborne gaps through which Valentine could see glimpses into different landscapes beyond: More deserts, similar but with red sand and striking stone formations. Forests, tropical and temperate. Sandy beaches that embraced ocean shores. Rivers, thick and thin, crisscrossed a delta.

Still, they walked on.

Valentine crested a small summit and swept a glance around the now cool desert. It was empty – no sign of Church anywhere. She heard Six come to a stop besides her. "Where is Church?"

"We'll find him."

They continued on.

Valentine walked on, her footsteps mirrored by Six behind her, the crusted desert ground crunching beneath their feet.

This is the last task. If I can find the hellhound, and somehow get him home, I get my life back. I get to be me, to make music and to live.

She shivered in the darkness. She wanted her life back, the normalcy of music and work and performing on stage. Then she thought of John and Emma, and her heart ached. Despite all the tasks she had completed during the penance – the pain, the hardships, the injuries – she still felt... undeserving. The tasks, they had been at the gods' direction and designed by them as some sort of remedy for her trespasses. But Valentine couldn't help but wonder: Did any of the tasks serve John and Emma? The children? What kind of restitution did they get from her penance? How could she gladly accept her life when they were still gone?

How could she live in a world that was poorer for the loss of that family?

"Valentine." Six's voice interrupted her thoughts. "Look."

A cloaked figure knelt in the distance, Church writhing in its arms with frantic joy.

"Who is that?"

As Valentine spoke, the figure turned its head towards them.

She froze.

Even at this distance, she could see the gaunt, skeletal face. The eye sockets were empty, black, and the bones glowed blue silver despite the lack of moonlight. A rich robe, a collar of stars and fabric woven with threads of glimmering light, flickered in an arrhythmic pattern. Even without eyes, Valentine knew the creature could see them.

Church broke free from the creature — *Death*, her mind whispered — to dash back to Valentine and Six, sliding to a dusty and abrupt stop before them.

Valentine Cash, I need to go home now.

"Home?" Valentine echoed. Something clicked and she felt foolish, stupid. "Church... you're a hellhound?"

She could almost hear him shrug. *We get a bad rap.*

"You're going home? You're leaving us?" Shock, grief, denial kaleidoscoped through her. *No.* Her heart turned over in her chest.

Yes. It's time. Church stared at Valentine. *You're a far better mortal than I expected. I will miss you. Please eat cheesy snacks for me.*

Valentine choked on her laughter, wiping at the tears that slipped down her face with dusty hands. "I will."

She knelt to hug him, weaving her fingers into his thick fur as she wrapped her arms around him. His hot breath smelled like sulfur and brimstone, his body solid with muscle.

Church swung his head to Six when Valentine stood again. *Mother Road, it's been an honor. I will miss you.*

Six knelt and swept Church into a hug. "Thank you for your companionship, Church Grim." He spoke terse words through his tears. Valentine's heart twisted again in her chest; she could hear the unspoken emotion, the heartache, in Six's words. How long had they traveled together? When would they see each other again?

Six stood again. "Goodbye, Church."

Church smiled, all ivory fangs and sulfur breath.

He turned around to trot away, gaining speed until he galloped up to Death, who still knelt for him in the desert. They embraced again, then Death stood. He waved a single hand — and a rip in the fabric of the night appeared. Through the rip, like peeking past torn satin, Valentine saw a gate with double doors. The gates were made from the bones of long forgotten creatures, pitted and ossified, with gemstone handles and circular patterns across the surface. The trim around the gates flickered and sputtered like candlelight on a windy night, and after a moment, Valentine realized what she saw.

Memories.

The gates were held together by memories. Scenes, like a silent film reel, flashed across up and around the door's edges. Some were in color; others were not. Some were familiar to her: dinner with loved ones, road trips with family as a child. Valentine studied the shifting tapestry of other people's memories and her heart leapt into her throat. Were John and Emma there?

Valentine watched as the doors swung open. Beyond was a landscape that glowed in aurora borealis colors and filled with creatures that defied her ability to describe them. Death and Church walked through the gates and the doors clanged shut after them, a soft swish in the desert night.

Her heart cracked open as the doors shut.

Valentine bent double, sobbing in earnest. Her tears salted the desert beneath; her shoulders shuddered with each breath she tried to take. She hadn't known how much Church had meant to her. He had been with her and Six for every task, for every fight and joke and breakfast for dinner. She didn't want to say goodbye, to lose him – perhaps forever. Loretta, John and Emma, the children, and now Church. Valentine didn't know how much more she could stand to lose.

She was so tired of goodbyes.

CHAPTER TWENTY FIVE

The casino was the same.

The usual denizens swanned across the black marble floor, calling out to the others they knew. Raucous games of chance echoed across the room, accented by the music played by the band in the corner. At the bar, Amaretto Sour served a drink to a patron. When she caught a glimpse of Valentine and Six, she waved with a smile.

Valentine smiled back. The expression felt foreign on her face. The trip back from Death Valley, from Church's departure, had been quiet and sad. After Six and Valentine had helped each other across the desert that night, she had driven them to a hotel before stumbling into a bed. Outside of the hotel room, she had listened to Six sniffle over a cigarette. She had cried herself to sleep.

"Valentine?"

"Yes?"

"Are you ready?" Six didn't have to clarify what he meant.

"I think so. Maybe." Nerves spiked and roiled in her stomach, undermining her own words.

"Then let's go, kid."

Valentine clutched the plastic icebox with the grapes to her chest, grateful to have something to hold onto. They made their way across the casino floor and to the ornate double doors. Six knocked, then pushed open a single door.

The gods were the same. Valentine doubted that they ever changed.

Dale Wright sat on the pink velvet couch, her seafoam acoustic guitar and ornery cactus cat nestled next to her. Paul Bunyan paced the room, barely sparing a glance at Valentine as she entered. High John stood behind the couch, still and observant, his hands clasped behind his back. The tall urns with the pampas sheaves graced the corners; the lush carpets and art deco finishes remained in place, unchanged.

"Valentine Cash, welcome back. Mother Road, it's always a pleasure." Dale beamed at them. High John merely nodded. Paul Bunyan ignored them but stopped pacing, his gaze fixed on Valentine with unswerving attention. She shifted, uneasy.

"Dale, thank you." Six came to stand next to Valentine. "You of course know this but Valentine –"

"Has completed every task," Paul interrupted. "Yes, yes. We know." His irritation at her success was clear, and Valentine felt a petty pleasure at upsetting his expectations. "Dale, this is your show. You're the patron of musicians."

"Valentine Cash, you have fulfilled the original terms of your penance," Dale spoke from the couch. "You have completed additional tasks to compensate for the times you received a minor degree of help. Now you are entitled to return to your old life, exactly as it was prior to the night of your death. Are you ready?"

A silence fell over the room.

Elation soared through her like a bird in flight. Her breath stuttered in and out of her. Was she ready to go back to her life? Her body rippled in drastic shivers, and she hugged herself, trying to contain everything that whirled within. A small voice whispered from the back of her mind.

But what about John and Emma?

What if… what if she asked the gods to intervene? The gods didn't do anything for free so she would have to give them something of value, something precious to her. Like her music and the album deal at Defiance Studios.

Valentine swallowed hard. Could she do that? Was she brave enough?

"Can I have a moment? Please?"

Dale glanced at Paul Bunyan, then High John de Conqueror. Something unspoken passed between before Dale turned back to Valentine. "You have one hour, Valentine Cash."

Valentine didn't quite remember getting back to the bar.

Six poured her into a chair, then took one for himself. "Amaretto, two whiskeys when you have a moment."

Valentine heard the words at a distance. Her mind reeled. Her emotions buffeted her. She felt like a hurricane raged within her body. She could hardly keep up with her thoughts. *Can I do this? Can I give up my music for them? But I worked so hard. I did everything they told me to do. I just want my life back.*

A small voice within spoke back. *John and Emma didn't ask to die, either. They didn't get a choice. At least you have a choice.*

She shivered. When Amaretto set the whiskey before her, Valentine gulped a mouthful, then coughed. The burn and the warmth ached down her chest, dispelling some of the chill that had settled over her body.

I don't want to lose my music.

Valentine thought of Loretta, shepherding a lost young woman through the industry and through Nashville itself, having run away from home. She remembered her parents and wondered why they had called that fateful evening. She thought of Cara at the Hoity Toity, who she never got to ask out. To kiss. But mostly she thought of her music.

She never had the chance to share her music with a wide audience, to make a connection and form a community. She wanted that, so badly that her hands trembled as she reached for her drink again. The possibility of losing her music, of giving it up, cut like a knife.

I don't want to lose my music.

Valentine sipped the whiskey this time. It still burned but she didn't cough. Another sip, then a breath. She thought of John and Emma. Of John baking with the kids at home, then going into his professional bakery to shape and present pastry, breads, and cookies. Emma, rushing to and from throughout the house, tripping over toys, despairing of ever having a clean house. Valentine remembered the graduation party, the one that hadn't happened but could. It was a possibility – which was better than nothing. She remembered the calm contentment and peace she had seen on John's face as he manned the grill; the pride that glowed across Emma like morning dew on grass. They would never have that moment.

Unless she asked the gods the intervene.

Valentine sighed, resting her head in her hands.

But I don't want to lose my music. I need it, the album deal and everything. Don't I?

Though... hadn't Valentine lived a great deal in her own afterlife? She thought over the tasks she had completed for the gods, the penance that had felt too long and now too short. She had lamented the bother, the injuries, the inconvenience. But there were treasures, too, to be had along the journey. Church, and his love for cheese snacks. Six, and his steady, unwavering guidance and care. The sacrifice of his celebration, of his renewed power, for Valentine after she failed with the Bell Witch. The Last Stop Diner, the Wild Hunt, all of the magical, horrifying, and remarkable events she had witnessed, or caused. The tasks themselves – no one else had lived those experiences, had survived those challenges.

But she had done it.

She suspected that she had truly *lived* more in her afterlife than most.

I don't want to lose my music... but I don't want them to miss out on life. I've had enough and more than many get.

"Valentine?"

She saw Six

"Talk to me." Six leaned forward. "Let me help."

Valentine shook her head but a half-smile crept onto her face. "You can't guide me out of this one, Mother Road."

"I'm worried about you, kid." He sighed, then sipped his own whiskey. Sadness marred his face, and worry lined his brow.

Valentine studied her own reflection in the mirror behind the bar. Dark circles marred her pale face beneath the shorn, ragged locks of her hair. Faded bruises lined one side of her neck. The hollows beneath her cheeks were deep, her face skeletal. She had skipped a few meals over the penance but hadn't realized how much weight she had lost. It didn't look good on her. But the worst were her eyes. Dark, empty, and sad.

She was so *tired*. Grief and fatigue had made her a stranger to herself.

I don't want to lose my music.

But I want them to live.

Valentine straightened from the bar. "I've made my decision."

Valentine Cash stood before the gods one last time.

Dale stood up from the pink velvet couch. "You're ready then?"

"Almost. I have a request." Valentine took a deep breath. "I wish to trade my music for John, Emma, and their children. I want them to live."

Six gasped. "Valentine, no!"

Satisfaction gleamed in Dale's eyes and a wide smile spread across her face like molasses. Behind her, High John looked surprised: His brows lifted, then settled down again. His face then cleared, his gaze inscrutable. Paul Bunyan, who stood to Valentine's right, snorted. But his tattoos flickered and crept across his skin in urgent hops and skips. Valentine suspected he wasn't as calm as he pretended.

Dale nodded. "Very well. We accept your offer."

Valentine swallowed hard, fighting to steady her limbs. They trembled and shook. Her body warred with her mind and heart. *Why are you* choosing *this?* a small voice whimpered within. She shoved it down, took several deep breaths. *It will be okay. It will. This is the right decision.*

"When will I go?" Her voice cracked.

Dale offered a sympathetic smile. "No time like the present, Valentine Cash."

Oh, god. Valentine turned to Six. "Will you d-do me a favor?"

Tears streamed down the legend's face. "Anything." His voice trembled on the last syllable of the word.

"Hold my hand? When I go?" Tears slipped down her face. She couldn't see his face through the blur. "It's... I'm scared," she confessed.

Six gasped out a small sob, then stepped forward to kiss Valentine on the forehead. "Anything for you, Valentine Cash. It's been an honor. I will never forget you, kid." His hand fumbled for hers, then squeezed the captured hand.

Valentine turned back to the gods. *Steady. This is the right decision.*

Dale seemed happy, almost proud. High John looked interested in the proceedings for the first time since she had met him. Paul Bunyan half-pouted, a grumpy toddler whose favorite toy had been taken away. *Well, I won't miss him.* She took one last, deep breath and squeezed Six's hand, an anchor among the storm.

"I'm ready."

Everything went black.

Chapter Twenty Six

Valentine Cash slammed into her body.

It *hurt*.

The force knocked her off the barstool on which her body was perched, and onto the floor. The commotion of her arrival caused a stir, then a silence. Other folks in the bar stared at her, then whispered to one another.

Valentine sat on the floor, stunned, trying to place where she was. Her senses flooded with too much information: She could smell alcohol and greasy foods, hear live music (neo-traditional country, not her favorite), and feel the hardwood floors littered with spent peanut shells beneath her. Were was she?

Glancing around, Valentine recognized the Hoity Toity, the bar she and Loretta had left the night she first died. She shook her head. Was the Hoity Toity in the afterlife? God, she hoped not.

"Miss?"

Valentine flinched at the gentle query.

Cara stared down at her with a concerned look, her brows pleated. "Are you alright?"

Embarrassment began to creep into her shock. "I don't know." She pushed herself to a kneeling position, then stood upright, testing the steadiness of her legs. She reached out to the bar to anchor herself. The bartender watched her with a skeptical eye from across the bartop.

A thought occurred to her. "Where's Loretta?"

Cara and the bartender exchanged puzzled glances. "Who?"

"Last time I was here, I was with an older woman, big blonde hair, pink business suit?"

The bartender frowned. "Yeah, your friend left a few minutes ago." He nodded over at a table.

"Oh." Valentine followed his gaze, then stared at the plate that held her tater tot nachos and the empty cocktail glass left behind by Loretta. That had been her last meal before the penance. Had she ...had she *returned* to the night she first died? What was happening? She wished Six were here to explain, or Church. A pang of grief echoed in her chest like the gong of a bell.

She missed them already.

"Miss, do you need me to call someone for you?" Cara seemed even more worried.

Valentine shook her head. "No. I... I'll go now."

Valentine pushed away from the table edge and past the concerned onlookers. Why was she here? Had the gods made a mistake? A chill chased down her spine as Valentine stepped outside of the Hoity Toity and into the rain.

What about John and Emma? Were they alive?

Valentine ducked under the awning of a nearby cafe. *It's really coming down.* A cold breeze washed over her, further chilling her. Pain pulsed through her wrists, and she peered down. The familiar music lines still encircled her; the notes shimmered black and gold. Her hands crept up to her skull and found short, shorn locks underneath trembling fingertips. Her hair was still gone. Valentine stared out into the evening. She *knew* she was alive. Blood rushed through her veins; she felt warm for the time since the night she had died. Her heartbeat rattled in her ears. But if she was alive, why did she still bear the marks of the penance?

"You need a coat."

She knew that voice.

Valentine turned to find Dale Wright next to her, under the awning. The god wore a tailored trench coat over a blush satin gown, with her curls pinned to her head and her ruby lips fashioned in a half smile. A slender ivory cigarette holder extended from her lips. Wisps of smoke drifted up from the glowing embers.

Valentine gasped. "Dale!"

The god inhaled. "Yes?"

"What am I doing here? Are John and Emma alive?" A belated thought occurred to her. "Is Six here?"

"Mortals are so excitable." Dale exhaled, the smoke drifting into the rain. "The Mother Road is not here. He has returned to his highways and tourist sites."

Valentine felt a pang in her chest. "Oh."

"Right now, John and Emma are on their way to grandma's house for a birthday celebration. Emma's," Dale confided.

Valentine's shoulders sagged in relief. "Thank god," she muttered.

"Yes, thank *us*." Dale chuckled.

"Yes." Valentine studied Dale. "I'm alive, right? I'm not dreaming in some afterlife?"

Dale chuckled. "You *are* alive. You're not crazy."

"So I was successful?" Valentine had to be sure. "You get my music and John and Emma get to live?"

"You did," Dale said.

Valentine slumped against the building behind. *I did it.*

"I did tweak something, though."

Ice congealed the relief in Valentine's body. "What do you mean?"

"You're not getting the record deal with Defiance Studios. You've given that up and the fame you thought you needed. But you still have your music."

Hope flared like a match being struck in darkness. "I don't understand." *Could it be true?*

"Let me ask you a question: Why did you choose to give up your music for them? Was it guilt?" Dale studied Valentine through cigarette smoke.

Valentine stared at the ground for a moment. The rain had begun to flood the gutters, to seep onto the sidewalks. Finally, she spoke. "They shouldn't die for my mistake. I couldn't rob the world of them. With the penance, I...I had a life, of sorts. Or, at least, an adventure. They deserved the same." Valentine shook her head, frustrated with herself. She couldn't find the right words. "I couldn't profit from their deaths. And even with the penance, after all of those tasks, if I had chosen my life at the costs of John and Emma's, I would have."

"That's why the three of us gave you your life back."

"Wait. Paul Bunyan agreed to this?" Doubt threaded Valentine's voice.

Dale laughed. "Even Paulie. It had to be unanimous."

"I still don't understand."

"Valentine Cash, this world is hard on a lot of people in a lot of different ways. When the gods find a mortal who can place the well-being of others above their own gain and comfort? Well, isn't the world better for having that person in it, alive and well and doing what they do best? Doesn't the world need more of that?"

A short silence fell between them.

Dale finished her cigarette, then waved away the ivory cigarette holder into thin air.

Her voice was thick with emotion when she spoke. "Thank you, Dale. So much."

Dale accepted the gratitude with a nod. "You have a new chance to live your life. I think you understand how rare this opportunity is. Do not waste it, you hear?"

"No, ma'am." A pause. "How are Six? And Church?"

"The Mother Road is well. I put in a good word him and he's getting a nostalgia festival, with his diehard fans." Dale smiled. "And the Church Grim is happy to be home, with his pack."

"So what do I do now?"

Dale gave a crack of laughter. "You live. Make mistakes, chase your dreams, don't harm others. You build a life that makes you happy."

A car horn pulled Valentine's gaze away for a second: An angry driver, upset at being cut off.

When Valentine looked back, Dale was gone.

Valentine sighed, then stared out into the evening. Tourists and locals filled the sidewalks as they dashed through the rain towards their destinations. Laughter and gripes filled the air, alternately cursing and embracing the sudden adverse weather. She supposed she should go home. But Valentine didn't want to be alone, not right now. Her phone buzzed in her hand, and her heart skipped a beat. Was it her parents?

When she looked down, she saw Loretta's number. *Even better. She's true family.*

Valentine swiped across the screen with trembling fingers.

"Hello?"

"Hey, kid. How are you?"

ACKNOWLEDGEMENTS

My deepest gratitude goes to the fantastic cover artist, Vivien Reis; my wonderful editor; and my beta readers. You transformed this project into something special and I'm thrilled I was able to work with you. Thank you for sharing the gift of your skill and talent with me.

My friends and family have long championed me. They knew, even when I doubted, that I would publish my novels some day. Their unwavering belief, support, humor, and kindness has helped me in innumerable ways, especially when I went through the hardest years of my life. I wish everyone in this world were as lucky in their community as I am in mine.

Lastly, a heartfelt thank you goes out to Rachel. You've read everything I've sent your way, even the earliest, shittiest drafts, and your incredible insight, superb GIF reactions to our meme exchanges, and stalwart support have been a blessing. Thank you for everything.

About the Author

Rebecca Rook designs tabletop games, manages a little free library dedicated to sequential art and comics, writes young adult fiction, and lives in the Pacific Northwest with two wonderful dogs. A 2021-2022 Hugo House Fellow in Seattle, WA, she also attended the 2021 Tin House YA Fiction Workshop in Portland, OR. Prior to this, she completed the wonderful Yearlong Workshop for Young Adult and Middle Grade Fiction at Hugo House. She writes young adult fiction in the fantasy, thriller, and horror genres.

Learn more here: https://byrebeccarook.com/

Sign up for her email newsletter, The Rookery, to stay up to date with new releases, giveaways, and more!

ALSO BY REBECCA ROOK

False Haven (Available February 2024)
A Strange Affinity (Available March 2024)
City of Graves (Available May 2024)

DISCUSSION PROMPTS FOR BOOK CLUBS

1. What was your favorite element of *The Penance of Valentine Cash*? And your least favorite element?

2. Which character was your favorite? And who did you least like?

3. *The Penance of Valentine Cash* comes with a playlist. Which songs most resonated with you? Which songs would you add or remove?

4. Did you find the author's writing style easy to read or hard to read? How long did it take you to get into the book?

5. Did the author use any literary devices, techniques, or styles to enhance their writing, and to what effect? Discuss the author's use of symbols, metaphors, or imagery to convey the story.

6. How did the author use the setting, characters, and atmosphere of the book to enhance the fantastical nature of the story?

7. The author explored themes such as redemption, faith in oneself, connection to others, and perseverance. Which themes resonated with you? Was the author effective in using these concepts to tell this story?

8. Were you satisfied with the outcome of the novel? Why or why not?

Coming Soon: False Haven

False Haven by Rebecca Rook.

Available February 13, 2024!

Get ready for a young adult horror novel where _Holes_ meets _The Haunting of Hill House_.

Seventeen-year-old Vivienne Barston's life has fallen apart.

With her mother recently dead, her father disappears into his grief – leaving Viv to deal with her sadness and anger alone. Viv turns to destructive behaviors like petty vandalism, but after a disturbing stint in a juvenile detention center frightens her, Viv agrees to a court mandated service opportunity designed to expunge her record. The deal: work for six weeks with a trail conservation crew in the rural woods of southern Oregon, and she'll be free with a clean slate.

She knows it's her last chance to fix her life.

When Viv arrives at the small town of Hard Luck, Oregon, she meets her motley crewmates, all with troubles of their own. The unusual group travels to Grafton Stake, a remote and derelict former asylum with a haunted history–and now Viv must face the ghosts of the past while fighting for her future.

False Haven is a young adult horror novel for fans of _Anna Dressed in Blood_ by Kendare Blake, _Asylum_ by Madeleine Roux, and _Fiendish_ by Brenna Yovanoff.

EXCERPT: FALSE HAVEN

False Haven by Rebecca Rook.

Chapter One

The Greyhound breathed cold, sterile air on the near comatose passengers. Vivienne folded further into her seat, her forehead resting against the window despite the chill. She traced a single drop of rain across the fogged pane with a fingertip. Her backpack rested in the seat beside her, a sentinel against the few others that remained on the tall and narrow bus. After a moment, the raindrop flicked away, and Viv dropped her hand. She resettled her black hood atop her head.

The bus had shed more and more passengers as the vehicle wended its way south along I-5, until only Viv and three others remained. The bus driver, a weary and capable Latino woman in her fifties, switched on the PA system.

"Hard Luck, Oregon, in five minutes."

The PA switched off with a sizzle.

That was her stop. Viv forced herself away from the bus wall, and gathered her phone, earbuds, and wallet into a tidy pile before tossing them into her pack. She watched the trees and the underbrush along the road thin, becoming less dense, less green, as signs of human habitation took over. Billboards stood stark against a dark gray sky and promised great grub at Honey's Diner or a cozy stay at the Hard Luck Motel. As the Greyhound sliced through the outskirts of town, a worn wooden sign welcomed newcomers to Hard Luck, Oregon, Established in 1898. The bus slowed, coming to a stop in front of the foretold Honey's Diner.

The PA switched on again. "We have arrived in Hard Luck, Oregon. If this is your stop, please gather all of your belongings before leaving the bus. Greyhound is not responsible for lost or stolen items."

Viv joined the short line to get off the bus. Outside, the rain-laden air was damp against her skin. She smelled exhaust and cold. Viv pulled her hoodie tighter around her body. She watched a mother and a daughter with matching dark rims around their eyes wrestle four enormous suitcases off the bus, struggling to move them onto the nearby sidewalks. Viv eyed the pai r. *They look exhausted.*

Once they stepped away, Vivienne ducked into the carriage hold and grabbed her large, navy hiker's backpack. She waved off the bus driver's attempt at assistance and shrugged the pack onto her shoulders, holding the smaller backpack in her hands.

Viv felt her phone vibrate and glanced at the screen.

A text from her uncle: *At Honey's Diner. I grabbed a booth.*

Viv looked up at the restaurant in front of her. Well, she wouldn't have far to walk.

The diner was busy. A line of people trailed out the door and into the parking lot, which housed trucks, Suburbans, and motorcycles. Viv stepped inside, dodging the line and the irate looks cast her way. She searched for her uncle, inhaling the scents of deep-fried foods and coffee.

He sat in a booth by a window, chatting with a man in a booth nearby. They sported similar outfits: jeans and work boots, with plaid flannel over a worn T-shirt and a baseball cap over thinning hair that had seen thicker days. Viv trudged through the aisles, dodging a harried waitress with a stained apron and comfortable but ugly sneakers. Stopping in front of her uncle's table, she waited for a pause in the good-natured conversation. After a moment, the stranger in the next booth cast her a sideways, skeptical glance.

Viv knew what he saw: A rail thin teenager with long brown hair and black eyes, in a black hoodie and blacker jeans, decent work boots (a gift from her uncle), weighed down by an incongruous hiker's backpack so full it strained at the seams. Silent and dark, she stood out like an inkblot in the colorful noise that echoed through the diner.

She waited.

Without looking at Viv, Rick spoke. "Tell Honey I'll have the number two with a side of minestrone soup."

"I don't know who Honey is, Uncle Rick," Viv replied.

Her uncle stilled with recognition. His eyes twinkled as he stood up to hug Viv. She returned the hug with a tight embrace of her own. Never a tall man, Rick seemed even shorter than she remembered. His auburn hair, a family trait on her mother's side, had faded in his middle age but his enthusiastic manner of conversation, punctuated by wild hand gestures and boisterous laughter, remained the same. Viv remembered how his often bawdy sense of humor had offended her father. Her mother had enjoyed his silliness, though. Viv remembered the pranks Rick pulled in the hospital to cheer her mother up during treatment: rude noises made by balloons and machines, snakes that sprung from a can... Her mother would chuckle until she started to cough. Then her father would frown at Viv and Rick until they fell quiet.

I haven't seen Rick since the funeral, Viv realized.

Rick stepped back. "Good to see you, kiddo. Sit down, sit down."

Viv tucked the hiker's backpack into the booth, then slid herself onto the bench seat opposite of her uncle. The tabletop was sticky with soap residue. *I hope it's soap.* The harried waitress with the ugly shoes came to collect their orders – a Rueben sandwich and a burger – before Rick leaned across the table.

"How was the ride down?"

Viv shrugged. "It was quiet, for the Greyhound."

"No trouble at all?"

Viv shook her head. "No. Cold, smelly." She shrugged again. "It could have been worse."

"Did your father see you off?"

"He dropped me off at the station."

Rick frowned, then shook his head. "Well, how is he?"

Viv rolled her eyes. "Like you care."

Uncle Rick chuckled. "We're not besties but we both love you."

"You can admit it: He's kind of an asshole."

"Hey." Uncle Rick's voice sharpened with disapproval. "Be respectful. He's still your father."

Viv stared down at the tabletop, her teeth grinding together. Her dentist had wanted her to wear a nightguard. Viv hadn't cared enough to tell her father. That was the least of her problems.

"Vivienne." Her uncle gentled his tone. "I'm sorry to be short with you. You both lost your mother and I feel for him. It's not easy."

Viv looked up. "You mean, it's not easy to lose your wife and to gain a loser for a kid."

He shook his head. "That's not what I meant. At all. I'm just saying the man means well."

"I got a reuben and a burger here." The waitress and the sandwiches had arrived.

Grateful for a distraction, Viv dug into her burger. They ate in silence. Viv was pleasantly shocked by how good the food was. *Or maybe I'm just hungry.* She hadn't expected much from Hard Luck, Oregon.

As the food dwindled away, the tension returned. Viv fiddled with a french fry.

Rick broke the silence. "You ready for this, kiddo?"

Viv looked at him. Worry wrapped across his face and his thick auburn brows pleated in concern. His beard had so much silver that he had a roan rather than rust coloring.

He deserves the honest answer. "Probably not."

He let loose a gravelly chuckle. "That's comforting."

Viv gave a half-smile. "How did you even find this program, anyways?"

Her uncle sipped from his coffee mug before answering. "Working for the Bureau of Land Management, I encounter a lot of third-party contractors and nonprofits tied to land conservation and stewardship." A pause for another sip of coffee. "Your program is loosely based on the Civilian Conservation Corps from the 1930s, part of the whole New Deal environmental initiatives. But it's different because it focuses on helping kids get back on track, expunge their records, and the like." He focused on Viv, his tone hard. "From what your father shared with me, this program is your only chance. Don't waste it."

Viv dropped her French fry onto the plate as a tremor shook her hand. She leaned back against the booth seat, grateful for its solidity. She thought about her nights in the juvenile center in Portland, only weeks ago. After the first night on the thin, hard mattress, she simply didn't sleep. She couldn't relax. She didn't trust any of the others in the ward. Viv had napped during the day but even that was hit or miss. The concrete walls, tile floors, and metal bars across the windows had wrapped around her like an unwanted quilt. The very air had tasted of astringent cleaners, body odor, and somehow, anger. Then there were the other girls. One of them, a large girl with unnaturally yellowed hair and teeth, had pinned Viv to the wall and breathed foul imprecations into her ear while choking her with a single hand. The ward guard had been slow to intervene, irritated by the extra fuss rather than concerned for Vivienne.

Viv had almost sobbed with gratitude when her father had picked her up a week later.

He hadn't noticed anything unusual. But then, he never did these days. *Not since the funeral.*

Viv refocused on her uncle. "I only have to get through these six weeks, right? Then I get to go home?" She cleared her throat. "I don't go back to the detention center?"

She saw sadness seep into her uncle's gaze, like he could see inside her head. "This program is literally a get out of jail free card. You just got to do the work, okay?"

Viv nodded.

Her uncle cleared his throat. "You want something else to eat?" he asked with forced cheerfulness. "You've got to put some meat on those bones if you're gonna do trail work."

Viv shook her head.

Her uncle checked his phone. "When do you check in with Helen Whiteaker?"

"4:00 p.m."

"We should get going then."

***

Uncle Rick carried her hiker's backpack as they walked to the Bureau of Land Management office and commented on the limited points of interest in the small town. Many of the buildings along Main Street were decorated in the Wild West tradition, with false balconies on the second floor and signs inscribed with Ye Olde West typeset. They strolled down the old-fashioned walkway, covered in wooden beams fixed together in a snug fit. A large, wooden silhouette of a miner with a pan of gold rose above the main drag of shops and stores, and the town's main street doubled as the freeway that wove through it. The overall result was a calculated attempt to cash in on the nostalgia for the town's historic appeal. Aside from the tourism angle, the town seemed to have one of each establishment: One diner, one general store, one hardware store, one gas station.

Viv shivered. The day had grown chilly.

"Wait." Rick's sudden command interrupted her thoughts. "Your sponsor. They know you're here?"

Viv looked up at Rick. "She knows. We text and talk when we need to."

Rick looked doubtful. "And that will work for you?"

Viv shrugged. "It will have to, won't it?"

Rick lapsed into silence, worry and skepticism veined across his face. Viv studied him with a sideways glance, and her heart sank within her chest. *He doesn't trust me,* she thought. *Not anymore.*

Fog had settled on the mountains surrounding the town, cloaking the green with gray. Just past the post office, Viv saw the Bureau of Land Management office. Reminiscent of a log cabin, the office was obviously built to retain the rustic Old West aesthetic, with a low roof and log walls. Only the small metal overhang that projected over the glass double doors modernized the office. The American and State of Oregon flags flew at the top mast, rising from a manicured lawn.

They paused before the double doors.

Her uncle scrutinized her. "If you need anything, you call me."

Viv nodded. "Sure."

Uncle Rick dropped her backpack, then wrapped Viv in another hug. He smelled of Reuben sandwiches, coffee, and soap, and his beard was soft against her forehead. Viv leaned into him, grateful for the warmth. He felt like home.

"You're gonna be fine." His voice was gruff as he released her. *He sounds like he's trying to convince himself.*

Viv didn't respond.

Time would tell, wouldn't it?

False Haven by Rebecca Rook.
Available February 13, 2024, in e-book and paperback!